Arthur Imperator (Forg Book 2)

Paul Bannister

© Paul Bannister, 2013

Paul Bannister has asserted his rights under the Copyright, Design and Patents Act, 1988, to be identified as the author of this work.

First published 2013 by Endeavour Press Ltd.

Table of Contents

I Bear	7
II Deva	9
III Garrisons	13
IV Cavalry	17
V Sentenced	21
VI Execution	25
VII View	27
VIII Council	31
IX Raiders	36
X Yr Wyddfa	41
XI Frisia	46
XII Grimr	50
XIII Equus	55
XIV Taken	61
XV Channel	67
XVI Bolted	70
XVII Rescue	74

XVIII Obsidian	79
XIX Magi	84
XX Corvus	88
XXI Candless	91
XXII Piddock	96
XXIII Aqua	102
XXIV Hemlock	107
XXV Parthian	110
XXVI Muirch	115
XXVII Chart	118
XXVIII Javelin	123
XXIX Eidyn	128
XXX Skegga	135
XXXI Hibernia	137
XXXII Concrete	140
XXXIII Frozen	146
XXXIV Prepare	152
XXXV Thames	157
XXXVI Severn	162
XXXVII Caria	166
XXXIII Invasion	171

XXXIX Hilltop	177
XL Convert	182
XLI Siege	186
XLII Raid	192
XLIII Heart	199
XLIV Defected	202
XLV March	207
XLVI Humber	210
XLVII Firedrake	214
Historical and other notes:	218
Arthur and Carausius: legend and links	221
Map of Arthur's Britain	223

I Bear

Men call me Emperor, but I have had many names. I began as Mauseus Carausius, and my family called me Caros. When I grew to my warrior manhood, men called me Arth, which in British means The Bear.

After I became imperator of Britain and northern Gaul, it was politic that I took family names which linked me to past Caesars, so I followed custom and my full and formal name became Marcus Aurelius Mauseus Valerius Carausius, the dutiful, fortunate and unconquered Augustus.

After I sank the Roman fleet and turned back their invasion, consolidating my hold on Britain, it was meet that I assumed the throne as Imperator Britannicus, Emperor of Britain, so I shed my Roman identity to become a part of my people. Thus, I chose the name I had earned: Bear, called Arto-rig for 'bear-king' or Arthur as the common people have it, and that is where I am today, the unconquered monarch Arthur Britannicus.

Logic says I shall remain unvanquished as ruler of Britain, so long as I have my wooden walls to deny our coasts to the enemy. For of all my names and titles, the one that matters most is Lord of the Narrow Sea. While I hold the grey-green waters that surround this island, and especially while I control the strait which separates us from Gaul, Britain will not again be trampled under the nailed *caligae* of grasping Rome.

That is my vow to my murdered father, and I am capable of keeping it. My history shows it. I was taken from my homeland as a child, but I returned as a soldier, hardened to suffering, almost indifferent even to the fate of my own lost brothers. But that lack of compassion and the aid of the gods and a symbol they sent to me, had let me unite the tribes of this small, mist-covered northern land against the rapacious masters who treated them so badly.

The Romans did try to take back their *colonia* but I had the fleet which once was theirs, and my expert mariners easily defeated Rome's raw crews, and repulsed its attempted invasions. Now, the Caesars are fighting for their own existence against the hordes from beyond the

Rhine and Danube, so our small island in the north is no longer so important to them, and at least for now, they are leaving us alone.

Britain still has enemies, and still has divisions among its tribes, but there is hope that we can rebuff the hostiles, that we can heal the rifts among ourselves and that I will bring a long peace and security to this pleasant, green island. This, as Arthur, Imperator Britannicus, is my task.

II Deva

The vast Roman-built fortress at Deva Victrix, called Chester, is sited on a rocky bluff, and is near-impregnable behind its coronet of thick, red sandstone walls. The stronghold is big, spreading over an area that would contain a fair-sized farm, and commands the river bridge over the Dee and the wide harbour downstream. Looking west from the high vantage of the walls, looking far beyond the curls of woodsmoke from the cooking fires of the barracks, you can view the blur of the Welsh peaks where the soothsayer Myrddin creates his magic and where my lover Guinevia Avenae is planning to travel to see him, her mentor. It is a journey she must make soon, before the winter snows, and it is a journey that fills me with foreboding, for no reason I can understand.

I will miss her fragrant presence in my life and in my bed and I smile as I think of her snuffling sleepily and contentedly against my neck. I will miss her insights and advice, for she is an adept of powerful gods and can provide glimpses of the future as well as perform useful, practical magic. She once called in a cloaking sea fog that destroyed a Roman flotilla; she used her sorcery to save my life when I was helpless at the mercy of a treacherous Pict, and most magically, she is the mother of our son, who one day will be emperor in my place.

She and a nurse will care for Milo on that journey, and she will leave her beloved garden of herbs and flowers to the care of her bees. Guinevia will take the harsh road to the mountains of the Cornovi tribe to consult the great sorcerer, and will be gone for several months, because she wishes to strengthen her powers in that place of mists and magic where the gods commune with man. There, I promised myself, one day I will be wrapped for the final time in my military cloak, and lie in my long sleep overlooking my kingdom.

I know that land and love it. As a soldier, I have marched the rocky wilds around the great snow-topped mountain called Yr Wyddfa and crossed the steep passes that lead to the shining sea strait and the island where the Druids were butchered by Suetonius' legionaries. As a seaman, I sailed close-hauled the coastal cliffs of that bloodied island, when I voyaged completely around the whole of Britain to survey invasion points, anchorages and sites for signal towers, to prepare for battles to come. Today, although the Augustus Maximian poses no imminent threat to me since I defeated his Caesar of the west, and hold the man in chains, there are others against whom I must guard.

The Saxons and Franks are a major menace on our east and south shores, the Danes and Jutes press us in the east and north, and the Celts and Scoti raid from their own island home in the west. If that were not enough, the Picts who live behind the northern wall of Hadrian are as treacherous as ever and have broken their most solemn treaties, crossing at will to raid and loot our border lands. Their memories must be short, as they seem to have forgotten the punitive force I sent to ravage them just a few years ago. It is time to mount another expedition, to slaughter the rebels, burn their homes and to fill the slave pens once more.

The frontier problems held my thoughts as I paced the parapet between watch towers and a couple of stiffly attentive soldiers anxious at my presence.

Below me, the scene down to the River Dee waterfront was a bustle of slaves and merchants, sailors and chandlers all handling and stacking cargoes. A Phoenician trader had just sailed in, come from very far, a dangerous journey through the Gates of Hercules and along the coasts of Spain and Gaul before braving the open ocean and crossing to Britain.

The trader's dark-complected crew was gazing as curiously at the onlookers as they in turn were gawping at them and their unusual caps and clothing, when a file of bronze-helmeted legionaries from the 20th Valerian moved with obvious purpose through the throng, their sergeant pushing aside the distracted who blocked their path. They seemed headed towards the amphitheatre, which is Britain's biggest, where up to 9,000 spectators can gather to roar on their favourites in the gladiatorial contests or bear-fighting events.

As I took in the soldiers, guessing that they were headed for some weapons training, I scanned them to assess their bearing, equipment and appearance. Then I saw that they had two wretched, chained prisoners among them. Certainly then, they were headed for the amphitheatre and a likely painful end for the captives. The chains sparked my memories.

As a boy, sea raiders had sacked my village on Britain's eastern shore and my father was murdered as I escaped. My mother and brothers were seized as slaves, I was taken to safety in the land of the Belgae, cared for by a river pilot and eventually became a soldier in the Roman Army.

The Romans were no seafarers, so my experience on the sea and great rivers of Europe marked me for the navy. In time, I took command of a seaport garrison and of a fleet ordered to drive pirates from the narrow sea between Gaul and Britain. The gods had favoured me and the pirates had unwillingly turned over their cargoes of loot, which I used to secure the loyalty of my several legions. I became lord of northern Gaul, and with the aid of my fleet, emperor of Britain.

My natural enemy Maximian had risen through the ranks to become the sacred Augustus, co-emperor with his Serbian countryman Diocletian. Each took half of the empire and each appointed a junior Caesar to help him to rule. When Maximian had attempted invasions of Britain to dethrone and execute me, my fleet had critically wounded his efforts until in one long day of blood and battle, a great alliance of British chieftains had defeated the forces he did manage to put ashore.

Back in Gaul and licking his wounds, Maximian turned away from Britain. He faces a rising tide of Alemanni and other tribes from beyond the Rhine river, and the Romans seem to have lost much of their interest in a swift recapture of their rebellious colony. Despite this lack of immediate threat, I am still spending much time and bullion to reinforce the island's south eastern coastal defences. There still could be a Roman invasion, and the fortifications also serve as bases for our fleet to turn back the flood of Saxons who are so eager to grab our land. There are lesser but still potent threats from Celt and Pictish raiders, as well as pressure from Jutes and Danes who continue raiding and settling Britain's eastern lands.

During the last invasion attempt by Maximian, his troops vengefully burned down my fine seaside palace at Fishbourne, an inconvenience as it had been a useful base from which to oversee and administer the reinforcement of the Saxon Shore. This stretch of southeastern British seacoast coveted by the Saxons is guarded by a chain of coastal fortresses, beacons and watch towers stretched along the southern coast of the island. That chain wraps its protective links around the foot of Britain and far up the eastern coast, too.

So, with the loss of Fishbourne, I needed to establish a new headquarters. Dover had been convenient as a departure point to my now-lost holdings in Gaul, but was unsuitable as a capital city as it was too far removed from the troublesome Picts in the north. The same was true of Londinium. Although Eboracum, base of the Sixth Legion, had served as the provincial capital and northern garrison of the emperor Septimius Severus and a host of governors, it was another couple of days' travel north of the Shore, so I opted to make Chester my kingdom's capital.

The old emperor Agricola had built the castrum there as Britain's largest garrison. It is bigger than Eboracum or the Second Augusta legion's headquarters at Caerleon, and Agricola had an eye to using it as his launch place for an invasion over the western sea to Hibernia. It has advantages over Fishbourne as this is a capacious, stone-walled stronghold with public buildings, baths, granaries, sewers, manufactories of ceramics and metal works of all kinds and temples to the major gods, but my chief consideration was its position. It is centrally located. The fortress is about equidistant from the eastern seaboard of Britain, the Wall of Hadrian and the Narrow Sea to Gaul.

A network of good, metalled Roman roads connect Chester across the high and windswept spine of Britain to Eboracum and the great road between the Wall in the north and Londinium in the south. Other military roads run north and south from the Welsh border fortress to the Wall and to Caerleon, and the vitally-important Watling Street goes directly from Chester diagonally across the island to St Albans, Londinium and Dover.

III Garrisons

With hard, straight roads, it is possible to make fast journeys. Famously, the emperor Titus once covered 500 miles in 24 hours to be at the bedside of his dying brother Drusus. Dispatch riders routinely cover 200 miles in ten hours, using relays of fresh horses. I had myself made a speedy circuit of Britain, using a three-horse *raeda* carriage to take me from south to north and back again when I needed to rally the chieftains against Maximian's invasion force. That swift journey had paid great rewards, but the real use of such roads is for troop movements. The straight and smooth highways allow rapid-response cavalry and even infantry to cover long distances in short time, and to meet an invader before he can establish a firm foothold. In good conditions, lookouts in watch towers can light their beacons to send smoke by day or fire signals by night ahead of any raiders so that our pony soldiers can hold them at the beaches, until infantry arrive and hurl them back into the sea.

These are tactics I learned from the Romans, who employed them on the Rhine frontier. They built a military road parallel to the river and stationed troops back from it, placed strategically so they could respond to any crossing. It is a tactic that calls for a few more forces, but lets them be used much more effectively than attempting to man the entire border with a single thin screen.

Chester has other advantages as well as its central position at a crossroads for the British plains and the Welsh mountains. It is a major trading centre. In its distant hinterlands are wide wheat-growing areas that have fed the legions for centuries; the Dee river on which it stands is navigable and can be used as a highway, and the commanding fortress overlooks a fine tidal harbour at the head of a 20-mile estuary to the Hibernian Sea and the trade routes to Gaul and Iberia.

Chester's legions were not positioned there for trade, though. The garrison commands a choke point, a bottleneck battleground through which invaders must come, and is well placed for troops to push into the mountains of Wales where the tribes of small dark men had felt themselves inviolable for centuries.

I mused about those mountains. Britain has three lots of highlands: the Pennines and north into Pictland, which is also called Pictavia; the southwest peninsula, and Wales. This last is bracketed inland by the estuaries of the Dee and the Severn, and whoever controls those two regions holds the keys to the kingdom, because military campaigns have to be carried out in lowlands, where armies can move. The Romans understood this and established their great camps at Chester and at Caerleon. Those two garrisons meant that the highlands where men could retreat in safety were separated from each other. The legions kept the rebels separated, and they could not provide aid to their fellows from one highland fastness or the other without challenging the legions of Caerleon or Chester.

With this principle in mind, I had also restored the great fort of the ancients at Cadbury, now called Caros' Camp, to further control the men of the southwest and to dominate the plains and rolling chalk downs of the south where I planned to breed my horses.

In the northeast, the old colonial capital of Eboracum similarly acted as a garrison against the hillmen of the Pennines and Pictland. The essential key to peace is to keep insurgents separated. The Picts are still an ongoing nuisance, but are essentially raiders, not invaders. The Welsh gave incomers their troubles, and their nation's steep terrain made fine protection for rebels who could escape before any major forces could trap them, but the Romans dealt with the problem by slicing a few military roads through their snowy mountains and dense forests. Then, when minor chieftains attempted to rally a national force behind them, the Romans isolated and captured the insurgents.

Four times the legions had held mock coronations for Welsh insurgents who would be kings, but they had not coronated them with a crown of gold, or grass in the old Roman way. Instead, a circlet of iron heated in a smithy's furnace until it glowed dull red had been clamped onto each rebel head, and the new, failed monarchs had died screaming as their scalps smoked and flared, their blood hissed on the hot iron and their brains cooked.

Those terrible deaths inspired others to quiet, and in time, peace became the norm; by the time the Romans had gone and I had arrived even the once-wild mountain men could be seen walking in our markets, gaping at the goods on display, and it was considered safe for a woman with a small escort to travel to the most remote corners of the wind-blasted, craggy region.

Which was what my Guinevia planned to do, and it was causing me an unease I could not explain. It should be a simple journey. In my mind's eye, I see her leaving with her servant and four legionaries, riding out through the elmwood gates of the castrum waving her scarf and smiling up at me as I watch from the parapet. An ominous feeling clutches at my vitals, but I can see no rational reason for it. I once told her of my fears and forebodings, and she had smiled gently. "I must go to see Myrddin, he has much to teach me still, and I foresee nothing to fear, but I shall cast for an augury again." I could not argue. She wanted to learn from her mentor more of his dark arts so that she could help me. Already, as an adept of the goddess Nicevenn, witch of the Wild Hunt, she can exercise magical powers before which I am just her waiting servant, not the scarred and bearded big soldier that others see.

But I have things to do, and I paused my parapet-pacing to gather my thoughts. I must have been staring for some moments at one of the nervous sentries, for I saw he had paled and was rigidly at attention. He must have thought I was studying him and trembled. I am no friend to most. I am a soldier, and I have seen my comrades die, which takes away your softness. Few think of me as friend, which is a pity as I am not hostile, just hardened. I stared at the sentry a moment longer, then told him: "Send the tribune Allectus to me," as I turned and limped into my administrative chamber, once again cursing the mouldering dead bones of the Saxon who chopped my foot. At least he died at my hand and in pain.

My work chamber is a big, airy room with the Roman luxury of a hypocaust pumping steam heat through underfloor pipes so that even in winter chills, which are still some months away, it is a comfortable place. I have a fireplace and proper chimney for winter fires, and even a window made with small panes of greenish Italian glass, replaced where they have been broken with thin slices of horn, so that even on cold winter days, I have some daylight entering. Today the shutters are open and admit a breeze, which stirs the wool hangings that cloak the stone-chill of the walls. The place boasts windows that overlook the harbour, a long, polished *mensa* on which to spread my working papers, petitions, lists and decrees, and a handful of stools and chairs for my guests. I keep a military cot in one corner so that I can wrap myself in my red officer's cloak and sleep if needed, while staying available at the heart of the garrison.

Allectus stepped in, sketching a salute with a forearm across his chest. A tall man, though not as tall as I, he has a snakelike head, and eyes that constantly flicker watchfully. Physically, we could not differ much more. I am a bear-like person with a pelt of body hair, he is wolfish, smooth and spare. He seems electric with energy, nervous and pale, always hungry-looking. He is a man with ink-stained fingers and seems constantly to be carrying a bundle of scrolls. For several years, he has been my treasurer and has overseen my mints, coiners and strongboxes, and although I have not doubted his fiscal honesty, there is about him an uneasy element that warns my instincts to be wary.

For all that, he has been my confidant and advisor. We together took the step of breaking away from Rome, knowing that a crucifix each and iron nails through the forearms to fasten us to it would be our reward if we failed, so we are partners in the business of creating and ruling an empire, even if I have that sense of unease about the man.

On this day, I wanted a financial picture from him, as I need to know what expenditures I could make. I have conceived a strategy to strengthen the defences of my nation. "The Saxons are an increasing menace, Allectus," I said, coming abruptly to the point. "They are swarming ashore in the south and east and although our coastal defences are enough to hold off the war bands, it's hard to turn back the boatloads of peaceful settlers who sneak in, abandon ship and move inland to farm and forage. They are not yet a threat to our security, but if some Saxon warlord opts to seize and hold some of our land, he could have a sympathetic population already in place to help him do just that."

"And," I added, "not all the settlers may intend to stay peaceful for long. The bold ones will soon enough realize they have increasing numbers, and they'll push our people out of the best lands. We need to act."

"That, Lord, would mean turning back the settlers," said Allectus. "It's one thing to identify an invading force and meet it in arms, but we can't build an impregnable wall along hundreds of miles of coastline."

IV Cavalry

I knew the situation, and considered a solution. Our wooden walls, the fleet that had protected us from the Romans' invasion attempts, could not be expected to intercept and turn back every boatload of farmers and herdsmen. Nor could we line the cliffs and beaches with soldiery to turn them back at spear point. What we could do was to build a mobile force that could be quickly moved in to flood an area if needed, either to turn back invaders or keep settlers under control and pacified.

"Give me money for horses," I told Allectus. "I want to start breeding horse herds from those on the downs near Aquae Sulis, where the ancient stone dances are sited. We can start with that stock, breed into it with heavy horses, and in a few years we'll have built a proper cavalry force we can deploy quickly, anywhere in our island."

My reasoning was that neither the Saxons who were landing on our southern and eastern shores nor the Celts and Hibernians who raided the west much used mounted troops. Their battle tactics are similar: surprise and bare-chested fighting madness to overwhelm their opponents in a short, sharp encounter. We need to meet their threats with a force capable of resisting the initial impetus, and to create a prolonged battle in which the lightly-armoured enemy simply cannot prevail.

We need power, but we also need mobility to face threats arriving from all directions. Horses provide the mobility to move troops fast and far. A chariot-borne force is one possibility, but I'd used chariots and wheeled warriors against the disciplined Romans, and found that those lightweight fighting platforms had some serious disadvantages.

First, the chariots are unreliable for long-distance travel. They might not arrive in time to be effective, or might not arrive at all if they were shaken apart on the roads. Next and most critically, the chariots can only operate properly in open grassland, and just a few dozen well-placed stakes or ditches can thwart their attacks. Horse soldiers, on the other hand, can travel long distances quickly and operate almost anywhere, and cavalry will always prevail against foot soldiers. In confrontations where the horses could be at a disadvantage, my pony warriors can simply dismount and fight on foot.

All I have to do is create a horse-borne army. It could be held centrally and could be deployed almost anywhere in the island in a few days. With the chain of fortifications I am building along the Saxon Shore allied to the naval patrols and lines of signal towers that cover much of the rest of Britain, a heavy cavalry force could be Britain's land-based shield.

"You'll need a lot of coin," said Allectus. "It isn't just the horses that cost money. Each cavalryman will need a mail shirt, lance, sword, scabbard, shield and helmet. He'll need to be fed and housed, he'll need at least three horses." He tapped his teeth thoughtfully. I asked him again about our treasury.

He told me much of what I already knew. The gold mine in southern Wales was producing well, the mints in Londinium and Colchester had created fat reserves of coin and we had a considerable amount captured from the Roman pay chests after their defeat at Dungeness just a few weeks before. "It would be good to have Rouen still," he said wistfully. That, I thought sourly, was whistling in the wind. Maximian had taken our Gallic possessions, including that mint and some considerable bullion before he sacked Bononia and drove us out of Gaul. One day, I thought grimly, he'll pay for it.

Allectus was talking again. "If we had to buy horse stock to start a breeding programme, we could manage with what coin and bullion we have. We'd need more as the thing went along. Maybe we could tax the Saxon settlers?" I nodded. Maybe, too, we could mount raids on Gaul and take bullion, slaves and horses. I'd robbed the pirates of the Narrow Sea in the past, maybe it was time to turn my fleet to some lawful piracy, but first, it was time to call in my officers and commence building a cavalry force, among other things.

Allectus checked the scroll he was carrying, and looked up. He told me that the donatives I had commanded had been struck. "The Colchester mint is busy producing some fine coinage, Lord," he said. "I should have samples here in the next day or so." I nodded. I had to go to Londinium to parade the Eagles and oversee some executions to impress upon the populace that Arthur Britannicus had met and conquered the might of Rome. The troops would cheer for their victory and the populace would join in, but there would be more enthusiasm when we handed out gold and silver pieces with my image and some suitable inscriptions: 'Rome conquered,' 'Restorer of Britain,' and, I liked this touch: 'Arthur and his Brothers,' above the likenesses of myself, Maximian and Diocletian.

The people knew we'd driven off the Romans, they had a vague idea that things might get better now they were rid of the absentee landlords, but to see their new emperor alongside the two masters of Rome, even if it was only on a coin, would validate my standing as rightful emperor. It would be good to have that validation, as I planned to have the losing general, the rogue general, as we would announce him, publicly executed.

Constantius Chlorus, Constantius the Pale, was that general. Not only was he married to the daughter of Maximian, Augustus Caesar of the West, but also he was the junior Caesar, too, third-highest official of the Roman Empire. In the weeks since we had butchered his invasion force on the shingle of Dungeness, and had chained Chlorus to the wall of his cell, I had daily been expecting a message from Maximian or his fellow Augustus, Diocletian offering ransom for the Caesar. None had come.

"They must think we'll just tamely send him home on his horse," I mused to Allectus. "They will not believe we'd execute him, as they would execute us. Well, we have nothing to lose and a lot to gain when he's dispatched. You have to behead a few, but only the right ones if you wish to make a statement. This will send a message to any possible British rebels and a shock wave through the Caesars' palaces, all of them, Milan, Nicomedia, Antioch and Rome. They'll be furious at the insult, but they'd cheerfully kill us anyway and a bold message might make them think again – if they lead an invasion that fails, they could be next. I'll announce that I'm executing Chlorus as a rebel against Rome."

Allectus nodded. "That's wise. You announce that Chlorus acted without permission of his Augustus, and they save face. They might even thank their new brother emperor for saving Rome's colonia. Of course, should they ever get the chance, we'll lose our heads, but that was long ago decided. I think they'll publicly castigate poor old Chlorus because they're too busy elsewhere. Just handling the Alemanni on the Rhine and Danube has them stretched. They won't want to divert forces for another invasion attempt that could end up on the sea bed like the last one."

A slave poured for us from a flagon of Rhenish wine. "Here's to a good parade, and better donatives," I said. "Polish your best helmet," I teased him, knowing he never wore armour. "We should be in Londinium in a week or so for Chlorus' final performance. You want to look warlike for that. By the way, brace yourself." He looked nervous. "It's eels for dinner."

V Sentenced

Davius Perseqius Ansonii was lolling in a wineshop, enthralling a handful of young soldiers with gory tales of his occupation. They pressed leather cups of rough red Gallic wine on him, and in return, he recounted the death struggles of the mad, the bad and the unlucky. For Davius was an official *carnifex*, crucifixioner to the emperor, and he'd nailed up, chopped up, sawed up, burned up, strangled or bled out hundreds of the doomed during his career.

He'd come close to adorning a crucifix himself a few months before, and he inwardly shuddered to consider that. Davius had been sent out from the port of Bononia, which was then held by Arthur, to execute a score of Bagaudae bandits captured further along the coast of northern Gaul. During his absence, the emperor Maximian's forces had unexpectedly struck and laid siege to the citadel.

The general Constantius had ringed the whole of Bononia with palisades, blocked the harbour entrance and trapped the garrison without hope of relief. Davius and his escorting troops had returned, cautiously come close, seen the impassable siegeworks and quietly slipped away again, knowing that they would join those selected for painful death once the Romans breached the walls.

The platoon moved steadily west, commandeered a fishing boat and crew at spear point and sailed across the Narrow Sea to Britain, a reunion with their legion, and safety.

This day, Davius was in a tavern in London, readying for the execution of a Caesar, and he was explaining some of the finer points of his craft to the open-mouthed soldiers. "Crucifixion hurts a lot," he said. "You flog the perp with a metal-tipped flagellum to bleed him, weaken him a bit, then you make him carry the crosspiece to the execution place. There, you already have an upright waiting. It has a squared end at the top, and there's a squared hole cut in the middle of the crosspiece, so they fit together nicely, like a big letter 'T.'

"You fasten the perp naked to the crosspiece. You can rope him to it, but it's better to use nine inch nails and you knock them in either through the forearms or just under the fleshy bit of the thumbs, angling them through the wrist. If you just nail straight through the palms, the perp's weight pulls the fingers off and you have to do it again. Keep the nails straight so you can re-use them, or sell them: people use them as charms if someone's died on those nails.

"When you have him snugged on the crosspiece, you haul him up and drop it onto the squared end of the upright. Then you nail his feet to the sides of the upright, nailing through the heels sideways. It's best to put the nail through a little block of wood first so the heel can't be jerked loose.

"If you want the perp to last longer, you can fasten a block of wood near his feet for him to take his weight. You can also make him sit on a spike, to make the blood and crap run. That brings the insects and adds to his punishment with a bit more humiliation. The whole point of crucifixion is to provide a long and painful death, to encourage the others not to do whatever the perp did. Do it right, and he can last two or three days, and the sight concentrates the minds of the onlookers wonderfully. Of course, if someone gives you a small incentive to be kind, you can break his legs so the weight goes on his arms and chest and he'll suffocate in an hour or so."

One of the young legionaries licked his lips and asked: "Will this be how you do the Roman general?"

Davius looked pointedly at his wine cup, which was hastily refilled. "No," he said, morosely. "Most Roman citizens don't usually get crucifixion, it's generally reserved for slaves, rebels, traitors. Romans get strangulation or a slit throat, but nobles get it even easier, and I expect that's what I'll be told to do to Constantius: lop off his head."

Decapitation was regarded as a relatively painless exit, he said. The eyes of the detached head sometimes moved and blinked for as long as a half minute, maybe indicating that the brain lived, but it was still a lot better than the other death throes he'd seen... the problems came if the executioner didn't get the first blow right and had to hack at the neck to sever it. In the early days, he said, carnifexes had used an axe, but it was now regarded as more honourable to use a sword, which was trickier. You had to hit hard and exactly to sever the spine, and not just anyone could do it, he said, puffing out his chest a little.

"One fellow, a big Saxon, fought his bindings, and I had to run around the scaffold after him, whacking away at his head and back with my sword until he collapsed and I could take off his nut," he grumbled. "Since then, I usually have an assistant to hold the perp by his hair to keep his neck still, and I also make sure they're blindfolded so they can't flinch away when they see I'm about to strike."

Davius was settling more comfortably in his corner of the tavern when a passing centurion spotted the group. "All right, you lot," he shouted, " 'aven't you got no work to do?"

One of the soldiers turned nervously and replied: "We're waiting for orders, sarge."

"Never mind that, fall in behind me, I've got something for you," said the officer.

Davius sighed. He'd have to buy his own wine now. Funny though, it was Constantius who would have ordered him executed in Bononia. In a day or so, it would be him who was executing Constantius... better go, he wanted to grind a really sharp edge to his sword.

At that moment, the defeated Caesar was having his shackles removed, preparatory to be taken out of his cell to meet his conqueror. His escort took him from the underground strong room in the old castrum of Londinium and walked him, shuffling stiffly, across the parade ground to the administration building where Allectus and I were conferring with several senior officers.

"Ah, Constantius," my greeting must have sounded almost cordial, as his head came up in surprise. "How are you being treated?" The Caesar - I spat inwardly at the title - shook his head, uncertain. "Look," I told him, my voice even to me sounding a tone of false bonhomie, "I won't keep you long, just wanted to go over a couple of things with you before, er, well, before. You know." Then I let loose. "I hear you gave my commander Lucius Cornelius a good flogging before you shamefully crucified him, and that all came after you'd given him assurances of safety if he saved his soldiers' lives.

"Is that true, Caesar? Is that true? And did you," I continued without waiting, "did you also execute five other of my officers of the Bononia garrison after they had agreed to lay down arms? Is that true, too?"

Constantius was no coward, but the natural pallor that gave him the nickname 'Chlorus,' or 'Pale' had been enhanced by his sunless incarceration and he stared back at me completely white-faced, then dropped his eyes. His voice was almost inaudible. "I did my duty, Lord." He looked like a dog about to be dropped in the pit with a bear.

I felt fighting anger rising in me. "You treacherously murdered those good men, and I'm going to have you punished. There will be no ransom for you, no return to your corrupt Augustus. You will be flogged like a criminal and then beheaded. I'm giving you a painful punishment, then swift death as a Roman even though you do not deserve it. You gave my officers a long and ugly death, but I am showing the world that what you get is just, not revenge. Now, know this: throughout your empire, you will be reviled as a traitor. I am telling the world that you acted against the orders of the Augustus and invaded Britain to make yourself emperor.

"The Augusti, both Maximian and his countryman Diocletian will publicly agree because they cannot be seen to ignore my liberation of Britain from them, but they are powerless to act. However, by declaring you a traitor, they will save their face, and hail me as their brother emperor who put down the treacherous Chlorus while they defended the empire from the Alemanni hordes in the east. Your family will be disgraced, your name expunged."

I considered how satisfying it would be to beat his white face to a pulp, but restrained the boiling urge. He should not appear to have been mistreated when he was executed. I turned away. "Just get him out of my sight." I heard the slight scuffle as his guards hauled him around and pushed him out, but I did not look. I'd see him dead, soon enough.

VI Execution

Two days later, the Caesar Constantius Chlorus was led out to a crude scaffold outside the camp that guarded the Thames bridge. It was usual for military executions to be held outside the entrenchments. A crowd of citizens had gathered for the spectacle, and ranks of armoured soldiery created a hollow square around the scaffold.

At one end of the platform was a whipping post where two provosts waited, each dangling a metal-tipped flagellum, the brutal multi-thonged whip used to flog slaves and rebels. At the other end of the platform was a wooden block that replaced the usual dug pit with block in it that was the normal site of a decapitation. I wanted the mob to have full view when they witnessed the death of a Caesar.

Chlorus' face was as white as his linen shirt as he stumbled up the scaffold steps, prompting raucous laughter and jeers from the crowd, laughter that intensified as his clothing was pulled clear and his blinding-white body revealed.

As the escort tied him to the stake, I climbed the scaffold steps and turned to the assembly.

"This man treacherously acted against me and against my brother emperors," I declared. "He broke his sacred oath of loyalty and attempted to steal Britain for himself. He is a common thief, and he will be punished for that before he pays the price for being a traitor. From respect for the customs of Rome, he will be beheaded, not crucified. My brother emperors and I are agreed. Now, flog the thief."

The flagella whistled as they struck in sequence, first one prefect striking, then the other. In moments, Chlorus was shrieking, his back and buttocks sheeted crimson as the iron tips stripped flesh from his ribs and spine, and spattered torn tissue and blood on the planking. After 40 strokes, the prefects stopped, panting heavily. Chlorus was slumped against his bindings, whimpering, semi-conscious.

The executioner Davius' assistant stepped forward with a wooden bucket of water and soused the man's ploughed back, the prefects cut him down and hauled him, feet dragging, across the scaffold. Chlorus was on his knees before the headsman's wooden block, moving his head from side to side as if to dispel the pain of his lacerated back. At a gesture from Davius, the assistant slipped a blindfold over the Caesar's eyes, being careful to tie it underneath his long hair. Davius stepped forward. In his right hand he held a Spanish gladius, the standard sword of the old republic. I noted with some interest the thing was an antique, longer than the standard Mainz armoury sword, not as broad, a bit heavier. I supposed that even though it was more unwieldy than the legions' usual equipment, it was excellent for this job.

I pulled myself back to the present. Chlorus had his neck on the block, probably pushed down by the executioner, and the assistant was holding the Roman's hair to keep him in place. Davius glanced at me, I nodded. He levelled the sword above Chlorus' neck, not quite touching it, then raised it high, one-handed and brought it down with a wet thump.

A red mouth-like gash open at once and welled blood. The blow had not been clean and Chlorus half-fell sideways, groaning. The assistant yanked the head back by the hair, across the block and Davius swung swiftly and hard again. He hit exactly into the gaping wound, severing the half-separated vertebrae, and the head tumbled free, spouting arterial blood from the jugular and carotids, splashing several feet of planking. The assistant looked down, open-mouthed. He was still holding the hair, and now Chlorus' whole head was dangling from his fist. He shook the head as he raised it, and the blindfold slipped. For two long seconds, I was looking straight into Chlorus' dying eyes, and they blinked.

I crossed the scaffold, and took hold of the hair in the assistant's hand, then turned to face the mob. I held the head above me, its blood running down my wrist and dripping onto my shoulder. "Hail Caesar!" I shouted, and a ragged chorus of ironic "Hails!" came back at me. I tossed the head to the executioner, who had bundled up the dead man's clothes for himself. "Above the gate with it, spiked," I said. Then I thought: "I must ask Davius where he got that old sword."

VII View

The parade had gone well, processing out from the camp and under the impaled head of Chlorus, whose eyeless, raven-pecked visage was decidedly darker now. We had followed a loop down the hill, past the baths, to the Temple of Mars where the priests had blessed our endeavours. Then, the donatives had been handed to the legions, the civilians had caught the scatters of small coin, the brass trumpets had sounded and the swaying files of bright-armoured soldiery under their nodding, plumed helmets had made a brave show. Finally, the troops had been dismissed to the pleasures of the whorehouses and taverns.

Guinevia had watched the parade and now joined me in my quarters, followed by my tribune Lycaon and my aide Androcles Lethius. The former was still recovering, as he'd been flogged and crucified when King Mosae's citadel fell, but several of his troopers had cut him down the same night and carried him out of Belgica and back to Bononia. From there, he'd been moved to Dover for medical treatment, sailing out only days before the Gallic fortress itself was surrounded and eventually surrendered.

"Lucky Lycaon," the men called him, and the terrible scars from his flogging testified to his incredible survival. Not a man could recall anyone else who'd been crucified and lived to tell the tale. About the only thing that had saved him from dying was that he'd been among the last of the condemned to be fastened up, and the executioner had used ropes because he'd exhausted his supply of nails. "I'd have died of blood loss, otherwise," Lycaon would tell anyone who'd listen.

"Brought back some memories, eh?" Androcles grinned at his fellow officer, gesturing back to where Chlorus' head stood above the arch.

"I felt every blow when he went under the flagellum," said Lycaon. "Being flogged isn't exactly a habit-forming thing to do."

I gestured to a slave to bring everyone wine, then led the two officers to a polished mensa on which an unusual map was unrolled. Unlike the normal itinerum, which listed way stations, towns and landmarks along the roman roads, but gave no hint as to what was off to either side of them, this map provided a picture of the southern shores of Britain as an eagle would view it.

The map had been drawn for me by my lover, the sorceress Guinevia, who had the ability to send out her mind across the world to view places without visiting them. She told me once of how she did it, meditating quietly with a silent scribe to record her spoken thoughts, then drawing what she saw, without attempting to interpret it.

"I can feel the wind rushing, see the grasses waving, even catch the scent of the salt air or the blossoms in the place I wish to view," she told me. "The gods give me the grace to see the place I want to see and I allow my mind to draw whatever is its vision."

In the past, Guinevia had been able to sketch dispositions of troops for me, and once to describe a vast river on whose bank my enemy Maximian was entrenched. My enchantress provided enough details of a bridge, cliffs and fortress for me to recognize part of a waterway I had often travelled as a young sailor who plied the Rhine, Meuse and other great rivers. Knowing where my enemy was camped had told me his intent, and had allowed me to deploy my forces to advantage.

The power of viewing something from a remote place so intrigued me, I'd asked Guinevia to reach out with her mind's eye and survey a whole coastline, to give me the view of a seagull hovering above Britain's Saxon Shore. When she had completed her task, I was able to compare her map to my own seaman's knowledge of the cliffs, bays and inlets that border the Narrow Sea, and I found her rendering astonishingly accurate.

If I could persuade her to map the coast of Gaul in similar fashion, then later to send out her spying mind to tell me where my enemies were along that coast, I would have a magician's powers harnessed to my military ones and could have a good ability to predict where and when my enemies might strike.

For now, I kept this wonderful secret to myself, and merely allowed my aides as we stood in a chamber in faraway Londinium, to look with astonishment at the unprecedented eagle view of the Saxon Shore.

"The *Litus Saxonicum*," murmured Androcles, a flamboyant dandy with a great sense of personal style and a most distinctive war helm, a Gaulish thing with green-bronze mallard wings on its sides. We teased him that his tunic always had to be immaculately clean and fragrant, his weapons and equipment kept polished to mirror-like perfection. How he did it, we never knew, but he was a hardened campaigner and experienced soldier, and nobody could say that he was just a parade ground toy soldier. "I have sailed this coastline and marched along it, too," he was saying. "This big island is off *Portus Adurni* where the tides come in twice as often as elsewhere, each day. I served in that fort. The locals call it Port Chester."

"Here," I said, jabbing at the map, "was my palace at Fishbourne, and here is the shingle of Dungeness where our antique chariots did the damage."

That was a day, I thought. Chlorus' men had come within an inch of turning our flank, and we would have been dead or slaves now, but for the help of the gods. And, maybe, as I kept hearing, thanks to the help of the dead. At a critical phase of the battle, we had thrown our charioteers into the fray on their pensioned-off vehicles. The surprise was total, the Romans wrecked. Mysteriously, our warriors had reported that among their frenzied horses and flying wheels, a spectre had urged them on. They said the shadowy figure of a long-haired woman, bare-breasted, helmeted and wielding a sword, had run wheel to wheel with them in her ghostly chariot, and that those who walked the killing ground to finish off the enemy wounded had found numbers of Romans dead on the shingle without a mark on their bodies.

I had questioned Guinevia about this, and she, adept of the witch goddess of the Wild Hunt, had shrugged. "I expect that the shade of Boadicea came to the aid of Britain," she remarked.

I'd stared at her. "The ancient queen of the Britons? Dead for two centuries?"

Guinevia raised her chin and looked at me steadily. "Nobody dies," she said flatly. "They might go to another place of existence, but their shades are with us. Why would the queen who slaughtered Romans not come back when her nation needed her?"

Behind her, I saw Lycaon and Androcles make the sign against the evil eye, and I secretly touched the well-polished iron of my belt buckle as protection, too. You must show respect when speaking of the dead lest their souls visit you as you sleep.

A new voice intruded on my thoughts, as my tribune Cragus Grabelius entered the chamber. "The ghost of Queen Boadicea would be a powerful ally, Lord," he said, slapping his forearm across his chest in the old salute.

I turned to him. "My friend, where have you come from?" I asked. "The last I saw you were knee deep in Roman bodies on the beach!" Cragus had led a flanking movement that pincered the invaders on the shingle at Dungeness, and was a longtime battle comrade.

"Better Roman bodies than dog fleas, Lord," he grinned. That made me laugh. He'd once halted a pack of war dogs launched at our shield line by setting loose a collection of mongrels that included some bitches in heat. The enemy dogs had settled for love, not war, and had mounted a different kind of penetration of our ranks.

"I didn't come alone, Lord," he said, gesturing. Behind him in the doorway was my British tribune, Quirinus, the officer I'd sent with fire ships to destroy Maximian's newly-built fleet. "We rode together from Colchester to Eboracum with dispatches for that garrison, and crossed from there." The news was interesting.

I nodded to Quirinus, who was a capable and intelligent officer. "Give me a report on the condition of the roads, bridges and bandit activity across the Pennines, and an assessment of how swiftly we can move a half-legion between Londinium and Eboracum, and again to march them across the spine of the country. Report on the availability of posting stations, *mansios*, smithies, food and equipment dumps, water sources for cavalry and anything that could affect our rapid response troops. Also, get me a condition report on the progress of the Car Dyke to Eboracum."

VIII Council

When finished, the north-south canal named for me would run from the hills north of Londinium to the fortress of Eboracum, and I had ordered it dug and fortified as a main supply line to carry leather, wool, corn and other heavy supplies to our frontier headquarters and garrison. My engineers had thousands of slaves working alongside our legionaries to create one of Britain's most modern and greatest engineering works, a ditch longer and more valuable than Hadrian's Entrenchment, and a great artery for our troop movements.

Hadrian had 12,000 Spaniards, Dacians, Gauls and Tungrians to man the ditch and wall he'd built as a control and customs barrier. I didn't have that luxury of numbers, but I was building an inland chain of forts along the canal to back up the coastal strongpoints. These two lines of defences were in contact by signal towers and would let us quickly deploy troops to respond to any invaders, while the canal traffic would move the vast quantities of supplies we needed under the protection of those forts with good speed and safety.

I looked around the chamber. These were men with whom I had shared much. Present were my three tribunes Lycaon, Quirinus and Cragus. The first - 'Lucky' Lycaon - was onetime commander of my holdings in Gaul and, like me, a survivor of the sack of King Mosae's citadel in Belgica. Bold Quirinus had sailed into the Roman anchorage and burned their invasion fleet. Cragus had personally led his men through chest-deep marsh on a flanking movement that had helped decide the bloody battle at Dungeness. Dandy Andy, my perfectly-presented aide, would have shuddered to have waded through those miles of mud, I grinned to myself, but he had done his bloody work in the shield wall, unflinching.

Allectus, my treasurer and close confidant who'd helped me seize an empire, was there, sleek-headed and smooth, a man to whom I had never quite warmed but with whom I shared an alliance that was as close as it was uneasy. Maybe, I told myself, it was just that he was a very private person, unlike my own bluff, outgoing self. Or, maybe, there was more. He seemed abstracted and I noticed that he twice moved purposefully to study the picture map that showed the land from its eagle's eye view. He caught my glance and raised an eyebrow. I shook my head. I had no intention of telling how Guinevia had seen the kingdom from that view. Something about his look, veiled and almost insolent, rang a tocsin bell in me.

I scanned the chamber again. A few of my closest officers were missing. My twin brothers had vanished after Mosae's defeat and the collapse of his Belgic fortress, and I supposed them dead or slaves. I had no time to grieve, and I had hardly known them, having been separated for 15 or so years. Besides, my life as a soldier had inured me to loss, and I had hardened my heart. Missing too were my longtime quartermaster Suetonius, whose knowledge of a coincidence had started me on this path to an empire, my aide Quintus, a good man and a good friend, and Papinius Statius, my baggage master and transport general whose efforts had brought us success across Gaul and in Britain. All had died under Roman blades on the shoreline of the Narrow Sea.

Then there was Guinevia, a slight, slender figure posed as usual discreetly at the corner of the chamber. I nodded to her, cleared my throat and launched into it. "We're all here, we've done this before, we'll likely do it again. The basics we have to consider are objective, intelligence, personnel, communications, supply and…" I paused. Like schoolboys, they all chorused: "Transport!" I grinned. "Well, there's a surprise, someone's awake." They grinned back at me, sunburnt, experienced young faces, men who'd stood by me on fields of battle, and who had walked from those killing places bespattered with hostiles' blood, and were willing, even eager to repeat the operation.

"The objective, gentlemen," I said like a schoolmaster, "is to turn back all these bastards who want to come here without our permission.

"Allectus, once again your overpaid spy ring will provide us with intelligence. I especially want to know about the Picts up there, trans vallum, and whatever you can discover about these Saxons. That, I accept is more difficult, but your merchants and traders should have something, and so should the shipbuilders around the Scheldt and Meuse and Rhine. We can't monitor every single clan or family that opts to set sail for our lands, but we can get tabs on the military movements." Allectus lowered his cropped head in agreement and murmured something inaudible.

I looked at Cragus and Quirinus, the Lycian from the home of the fire-breathing female Chimerae, the other, Quirinus, a Briton who had boldly sailed a fleet of fireships into the Romans' anchored fleet to destroy it. They were perched side by side on one end of the mensa, obviously relishing that we were preparing another series of campaigns. "You pair of fiery fellows," I nodded, "work your usual communications and personnel magic. Quirinus especially get on top of the construction and repair of the coastal fortifications and signal towers. I'll work with you on the Saxon Shore forts.

"Both of you focus on recruiting more auxiliaries, look to Gaul and even Wales, there should be warriors in both places we can take on as mercenaries. If you can, get some of those Syrian fellows, the Hamian archers who were posted up there south of the Wall. Cragus, you will liaise with me over building cavalry forces. That, gentlemen, will be a major thrust of our force in the next couple of years and you'll all be involved. I see us using horses from the southern downs and the plains south of Aquae Sulis, establishing breeding farms and studs for a considerable expansion of our cavalry as the Saxon and Frankish threats grow. We could also get some mountain ponies from the Welsh hills or from Cumbria, tough little horses that can go anywhere. We'll be needing to build some training facilities, too. Let's consider where best to place them.

"Next, we have supplies and transport. Well, we lost our good quartermaster Suetonius and our transport genius Papinius, both of them killed at Dungeness, so I'm putting my aide Androcles into post as supplies officer. We have some decent supply dumps and granaries in the hinterlands of the Saxon Shore, we'll need to develop more of them behind or along the Car Dyke and north east coast forts. Androcles, work with Allectus on inventory of things like grain sacks, barrels, amphorae and the like, especially on getting them to the ports where bulk supplies are unloaded. Make sure you have a supply of silver stoppers for the oil containers, to keep the contents from going bad. You'll be busy dealing with negotiators who bring oil, olives, things like that from Spain and Massilia, so be prepared for some uncomfortable travels, too, your soft life hanging around me is over. And, thinking ahead a little, make sure we have good groves of coppiced trees to provide us in the near future with spear shafts. Ash is best."

I glanced down at the tabulum on which I'd scratched my list in the wax. "Lycaon, I left you to last because you're lucky." The room laughed. They knew he'd drawn the short straw of managing transport. "The good news is that Papinius successfully moved us away from using oxen except for the heaviest equipment, because they're so slow. You'll be able to use the Car Dyke as a feeder high road for the heavy sort of stuff between Londinium and Eboracum, so that's a bonus, but you'll need more mules than ever to keep our frontier garrisons supplied. Send drovers and negotiators into Armorica and Belgica and Spain, see what you can buy in their markets and get onto the horse farms around Colchester and Aquae Sulis, to boost their stud programmes, we'll need plenty of remounts. Allectus will provide the coin. Get at least a couple of good Frisian stallions, too. You'll probably have to go there yourself to get them, they don't sell to just anyone, but you can pull some rank. Remind them who you are, and what I did against the Bagaudae." Lycaon nodded, he understood. The Frisians on the face of it were being told of the troubles I'd cleared up for them, but they also had the spectre of my wrath to consider. They'd cooperate, I thought grimly, or else I'd peel their faces from their heads.

The officers were looking at me, my expression must have given away some of my thoughts. "I want a mobile army," I told them again, "and if we employ more cavalry, they'll need swifter support from the transport boys. You did a splendid job in Gaul, maybe we can repeat it, use the smaller rivers here for swift movement of heavy goods. Someone talk to the shipwright Cenhud the Belge. He built a river fleet for us in Gaul, let's see what we can do along those lines here. I remember that we built demountable sheerlegs so we could load and unload big equipment for transport by river. That should speed our impedimenta transport needs. Investigate that. In summary, all of you, the rules are simple: fight, move, communicate."

I looked over at Guinevia, who had been scribbling on her wax tabulum and who would, I knew, have reports and inventories readied for me by midday tomorrow. She'd come to me as a scribe, but when I'd found out her background as a Pictish sorceress who had become a Druid, I'd found other uses for her. She'd used her magic to help sink a Roman fleet, she'd negotiated a peace with the Picts, she'd become my lover and she'd saved my life when I was a prisoner. Near her were my hounds Axis and Javelin, killers of a traitor who had been ready to execute me. The dogs alertly caught my glance where they lay by the door, ready for a command, but I gestured to them to stay. I worked with those dogs almost daily, and when we hunted together they responded to silent signals as well as to verbal commands. It was training that had cost a treacherous Pict his throat and his life. I did not know it then, but those silent signals would save me another time.

Guinevia looked up and smiled a small smile, and my throat tightened. Her magic was not confined to sorcery, and we had a boy child to prove it. My enchantress possessed powerful spells of many kinds…

IX Raiders

Being stranded for three weeks had ruined Iacco Grimr's already-short temper. The blond Suehan warrior from southern Scandza had sailed south from his home port where in summer the sun never sets, had safely skirted the lands of the Danes and Jutes and slipped unnoticed into the waters off Germania. To avoid the open sea, he had opted to sail inside a long line of barrier islands, and there he and his four longships had met disaster. They had anchored for the night, and had wakened in the darkest midnight hours to find themselves stuck fast on a plain of tidal mudflats, stranded by a rapidly-receding sea.

At first, Grimr was unflurried. The tide, he reasoned, would return and float them off. But a summer storm blew up, causing the green sea to race in like a hammer blow. The steep, thrashing waves scooped up the flimsy, clinker-built longships and tossed them around as if they were children's toys. Seven of Grimr's men drowned, but the rest of the 80-man century washed ashore mostly unhurt. They mustered themselves on one of the long, hook-shaped sandy ridges of low dunes which form an archipelago of islands among vast mudflats. As daylight showed through the lowering skies, the wind-scoured island where they crouched, chilled and wet, was revealed as a low-lying, miserable place.

The few residents lived in huts made from wind-dried mud bricks, huts constructed on platforms or atop the built-up highest spots of the islands, all of them barely above the reach of the maximum tides. The natives seemed like sailors at sea when the tide was in, or like mariners shipwrecked in a vast plain of mud when it was out. Worse, the desolate, wind-whipped sand dunes were treeless, offering not a scrap of timber for repairs to Grimr's ships. The food supplies were fish caught by the locals in nets and ropes braided from marsh grass or rushes and the only drinking water was rainwater collected in small tanks that stood outside the natives' sorry homes. Even the fuel that cooked their miserable diet was dried mud and seaweed, a poor source that reflected their hardscrabble existence.

Grimr had ordered his own hearth troops to repair two of the battered longships with materials salvaged from the other two, but the work had gone slowly and it had been only a week since he had dispatched one repaired ship south, with orders to capture a merchant ship and bring it back so the sea raiders could continue their voyage. "There's nothing here but mud," he growled to his lieutenant, Bjalf Fairhair. The residents of islands further along the chain had fled in their coracles, the two scrawny women of the island where the raiders had gathered had died under the incomers' brutal ministrations two weeks ago, and the few children were penned under guard to be sold as slaves while their fathers were sent to wade out and fish for their new masters' food. Once, just once in three weeks, the hungry raiders had eaten seal meat, and even that had tasted good, better than the score or so of seabirds they'd either shot with Grimr's crossbow or netted and eaten half-raw for shortage of cooking fuel. Work parties had gone out to scour the beaches for shellfish, but without success. The men were chilled, wet and hungry.

"Fish, feathers, water, and no ale," Grimr grumbled, but he had no intention of risking his one remaining longship on a journey to the mainland, damaged as the vessel was, in search of supplies. His best option was to wait until his other ship returned with whatever the crew had been able to capture. Then, he could rebuild his little fleet and sail for Britain, where he had heard there was loot and slaves to be taken, even land to be settled. Grimr narrowed his eyes against the battering gusts of wind and blown sand to scan the blue-grey loom of the horizon for the hundredth time. Not a sail in sight. He sighed, turned on his heel and strode to the scanty comfort of the beached longship to wait. Grimr's men were lighting a small fire near it with ruined spars from their wrecked vessels, and the flickering flames gave welcome comfort. He could see the crouched, half-lit crew as he moved towards them. Another chill, windswept night. By morning, perhaps the others would be back and they could leave this barren place.

Offshore, unnoticed in the thickening gloom, five dun sails were rising above the horizon. None of them belonged to Grimr's flotilla, and a lookout's sharp eyes on one of the incoming galleys picked up the fire's small glow against the darkness of the shore. Within minutes, all five vessels were alerted. Unheard in the blustering wind, unseen in the dusk, armed men were sailing steadily towards the telltale beacon, under cover of the shroud of darkness.

Hundreds of miles to the west, another sea raider had been scanning the horizon, too. Muirch 'Iron Sword' Corbitus – his tribal name came from '*corbita*,' Latin for a merchant ship, but there was nothing of the trader about Muirch – was planning mayhem. The black-haired Hibernian from the big island west of Britannia was eager to sail again on a voyage of plunder and rapine.

It was almost a year since he and his Scoti warriors had sailed out, around the western isles of the Picts and down the northeast coast of Britannia. They had sacked a monastery and several farmsteads and villages, loaded their oak-ribbed ships with loot, slaves and even a few cattle, then had turned their vessels' steep prows north for home, through the German Sea and into the Atlantic. Now, as the summer and its calms had just a few weeks to run, it was time to sail again before winter storms would keep them ashore.

Muirch looked carefully out to sea, no threats there, then turned his attention to the small shipyard where the carpenters and shipwrights were finishing their work. His two smooth-sided vessels, built the Gallic way, were shallow-keeled coasting ships that could take on any sea. Ribbed with foot-thick oak, sided in elm, they had their seams caulked with hemp and cattle hair, all sealed with pine tar.

The raider had made one alteration to his own ship, Brotherblade, reinforcing the bow with its iron-banded ram that could sink an enemy vessel. "Looks good," he grinned at the two carpenters who were chiselling the squared post where Iron Sword would slot the carved giant's head that would offer menace as they sailed.

"Looks like you," grunted one of the carpenters. "Big teeth, long hair, big nose."

Iron Sword nodded amiably. "Don't forget the huge ram, just like mine," he countered, "but I'll bet those British virgins would rather open to that wooden head than to your purple one."

The second carpenter spluttered. "Is it true that all those British women have huge tits?" he asked.

"Some of them," said the raider, "have four, two at the front, two at the back. They're good to dance with, and you always have something to grasp, wherever you're coming from." Both carpenters howled laughing.

Iron Sword might be a feared warrior, but among his men, he was relaxed and approachable.

They knew though, that when he pulled on his breastplate and slid the flat blade of his sword from the hanger chains at his left hip, he would be readying for the blood-boiling, fighting madness that had crashed him through shield walls and over the guarded gunwales of the ships he had so often boarded and burned. But, when the leather helmet with its nose guard was off, when the elmwood shield faced with waxed leather was discarded and the ash-pole spear set down, Iron Sword would drink barley beer with the best, tell tales to match the bards' and slyly drink an incautious husband under the table so he could make advances that were not always unwelcomed by a pretty young wife.

"They say you've left a whole tribe of Scoti bastards in Britain," said one of the carpenters, carefully shaving a curl of wood from the stem post. "They say there are more Scoti children where you've raided than there are British ones."

Muirch wiped his mouth with the back of his hand. "I'm not saying I always keep my sword in its scabbard," he agreed. "You can't let a blade go rusty, especially if it's a long one." The carpenters hooted again. "See this?" he said, tapping his right calf. "It's bigger than the other one because I have to swing this leg over all those women so often. Those god-bothering monks are no use to the local lovelies. They're skirted half-men who hide with their books and inks, they leave the flock-tending to us. Those British women look forward to our visits, and we try, we try. We are, after all, only here to oblige." He gave the carpenters a mock bow and sauntered across the beach to view the other boat, where a rigger was braiding a halyard to the leather sail.

Behind him, the village sat in a fold of green valley that emptied to a shingly beach on the shore of a wide lough. Hibernia was a green and damp place, a place of cool summers and wet winters. White-woolled sheep grazed, a few cattle lowed to be milked and an agreeable scent of peat smoke drifted on the breeze. Muirch sighed contentedly. With this to come home to, raiding and its pounding excitements was a perfect contrast. Now, he had a half-formed plan for his warrior ships' next excursion. Blood would be spilled, fires would be set and hopefully, he'd have slaves and loot to bring home. There would be a long winter to eat, drink, sleep with his woman and plan the next voyages. But first, he would be taking misery and death to Britain.

Muirch's satisfied contemplation was rudely broken. Down the hard pack of the strand walked a tall figure. He groaned. It was the woman Karay, a flame-headed, single-minded troublemaker who had standing in the community, a vicious swinging fist, a fear of nobody and a frequently-expressed ambition that not only the men should go raiding. "We," she said often in village councils, "are the important part of this community, but we have little part in the expeditions that sustain us. We can do better, and we should go with the men."

Muirch was a Celt, and the Celts accorded women high esteem. Those two facts were the bane of his life. He might sing, when deep in mead, of Cwylwch and great Hibernian heroes, but the women of the village, who were usually more sober, would out-sing his croaking male choir with their ballads of female heroes. They would remind him of the warrior queens, Boadicea, who butchered 70,000 Romans, and Sgathaich, who taught the great Cuchalainn to fight, of Aoifa and Niamh Golden Hair and all the other female Druids and warriors who had made the Celts feared.

Now he faced Karay on the sand, and behind her he recognized Jesla, a blonde Amazon with no fear of men, beasts or the sea. Just behind her, and his spirits sank more, was the slight figure of a third female troublemaker, Caria the Sybil, the village sorceress whose name was used by parents to frighten their children into obedience. Muirch glanced to see if she was carrying her usual totem, an old skull with a few vertebrae in it that she used to cast auguries. Yes, there it was.

He reluctantly turned back to red-haired Karay. She stared at Muirch from his own height, and he shrank away from her challenge. "You are going voyaging," she said directly. "And I and some of my women are coming with you." She paused. "Or we will burn your boats. Maybe we will just pound your heads to paste."

Muirch sighed and nodded. He'd been 'persuaded' by Karay before. It was like being knocked down and beaten senseless with a war axe.

X Yr Wyddfa

Myrddin Emrys, son of no father, sired by a spirit, Druid, sorcerer and reincarnation of generations of Celtic religious power brought to Britain from far Dalmatia, was struggling with his vegetable garden.

Although he had built his small home of good squarecut stone high on a blustery Welsh pass, the magician had sited it well. A spur of mountain protected it from the east and north winds, its aspect was southerly, and the garden, with its high wall, caught every bit of sun that the mist-shrouded land could offer. Myrddin could have lived in warmer climates, but he wanted to be close to the power of the great mountain Yr Wyddfa, to communicate better with his gods. "I could as well be living in a dark cave," he grumbled to himself as he tended the cabbage, onions and parsnips that lay in weed-free beds. Those crops were doing well, the cause of his irritation was that for the fourth, or was it now the fifth? year in succession he had been unable to persuade his grapevine to flourish.

He'd consulted his scrolls and he'd done all that the Romans could advise, but the vines simply would not bear fruit, and his plans to make a syrup of defrutum for sauces and as a condiment were again frustrated. "It will be nettle or damson wine and rowan syrup again this winter, too," he muttered. "I haven't the magic trick for these grapes. Some cambion I am!"

Tall, hawk-nosed, with long plaited dark hair and shaggy dark brows, Myrddin by repute was the offspring of an incubus and a king's daughter, but what demon and what king, nobody knew, although it was said he had been deliberately sired, to restore the ancient gods' hold on Britain. He walked in high places, was aloof with the mighty and carried with him an aura of overwhelming power that could crackle to life at a glance from his startling, crystal-blue eyes. When he wished, his swift and graceful athlete's movements could become the shuffle of an old and insignificant ancient, a useful act in a crowd that added to his reputation of being able to vanish and reappear at will.

Myrddin was young for a Druid and did not favour the shaven tonsure that was a uniform of the sect, but his influence as an adept of the sea god Manannan mac Lir and his acknowledged skill at looking into the future discouraged even elders among the Druids from mentioning the matter. When Myrddin came down the twisting mountain pass to the sea strait across which was Mona, home of the sacred groves of his religion, the Druids' ferryman had always been informed by dream of the sorcerer's arrival and would be respectfully waiting.

It was on Mona, called Ynys Mon by the Britons, that the Roman governor Suetonius had trapped and slaughtered hundreds of the sect that was the wellspring of resistance to Roman rule. The act had led to the Boadicean uprising in which the queen of the Iceni had put a Roman legion to the sword and had destroyed Londinium, St Albans and Colchester. The queen was later defeated, but took poison rather than be captured.

Suicide made her ghost restless, and Myrddin had used that vulnerability to call on her. At his demand, her shade had raced in its ghostly chariot alongside the forces of Arthur when the Britons again defeated the Romans, just weeks ago, on the shore at Dungeness. Myrddin took responsibility for calling on the dead queen's help, which he did both for Britain and for his own protégé, Guinevia, although he knew there could one day be a fierce price to pay for that help…

But for now, his concern was with his garden. Should he, he debated, give over that sunny wall he had dedicated to the grape vine to something else, maybe mulberries? Or to prosaic beans? He muttered again, and went outside the walled garden to talk to the two slaves who worked his pheasantry. Should he hang a few pheasants now, to mature for a future dinner? He studied the gardeners, both of them going grey. "How old are you?" he asked Pattia, a small, busy woman of the Parisi tribe, who had come to him as a captive after Arthur's raid on their Humberside settlement. She was nearing two score years of age, like her husband, she told him, smiling. She had, Myrddin knew, one or two children. It was uneconomic to keep older slaves and the sorcerer thought it might be time to give her freedom. Of course, under Roman law and by his own inclination, for no Roman magistrate would be coming near this Welsh wilderness, he thought ironically, the children would become freemen when their mother received her manumission. They'd probably keep working his garden anyway, he thought, they seemed content. Just so long as they didn't keep stealing too much of his asparagus... Yes, he'd free her and her husband.

His thoughts came back to the present. Guinevia was coming in the near future, and he supposed he had better make some arrangements for her stay. She could have that small, sunny chamber on the west side. Then, there would be meals. Oh, the pheasant, that was why all this had started. Maybe duck, or chicken might be better. Would Guinevia eat duck, he wondered vaguely? Anyway, it would be pleasant to have company for a while, and to ponder on things other than wars and oblivion, storms and treachery, the gods and magic. Pheasant would be an excellent choice, he thought. Yes, pheasant.

Company was exactly what Grimr and his stranded Suehan crew did not want, and the five galleys closing on their sandy island of dunes were an unwelcome sight. The stranger vessels were a powerful Danish or Jute raiding party, to judge by the gleam of weapons and the ridged, stitched leather helmets showing above the gunwales, and Grimr's swift estimate put their numbers at about three times his own halved force. He scanned the south horizon in hopes of seeing his own ship returning. Nothing. He had to decide and quickly.

If he were to fight, with his overmatched men weakened by hunger and unfortified by the hallucinogenic mushrooms that usually fuelled their fighting berserker madness, he'd lose. He would not surrender, not the prideful son of Grimr the Cruel, whose longboats had ravaged Germania's coasts for decades. But, he had no real defensive position to hold, the islands were low-lying drifts of treeless sand; he had no bullion to buy them off because he had only recently started his expedition. His value to them was as slaves, and as donors of their weapons and armour. So, Grimr reasoned, his only real defence was to make the enemy blanch at the bloody butcher's bill they would have to pay to capture him.

"Shields up," he ordered his crew, mindful that a shower of arrows could be coming. "Hold your position." Three of the galleys were closing fast, the other two were moving east, to land further up the beach and encircle the Suehans. He scabbarded his sword, dropped his shield, and walked forward to meet the incomers.

The first vessel crunched its keel on the sand and several Jutes, for that is who they were, slipped over the side to haul her bows higher ashore.

Only then did an imposing figure in a silver war helm drop down from the ship onto the sand. Grimr stood still, hands carefully kept away from his sword hilt, thumbs hooked in his belt.

The Jute straightened the sword that hung at his hip, glanced back to where two of his small fleet were riding the gentle surf, and strode up the beach to the waiting Grimr. "I am Alaric of the Cimbri tribe of the Jutes," he said. "Who are you, and why are you on our islands?"

Inwardly, Grimr heaved a sigh of relief. No open hostility. He could talk their way out of this one without bloodshed. He explained that he and his crews had heard the Danes and Jutes were to invade Britain, and were on their way to join them when they had been overcome by a storm. "I have sent two of my ships," he gestured, "that way to seek you."

Alaric's eyes flickered to the southwest, where Grimr had gestured. "That is not a direction in which to find us," he said suspiciously. "We were preparing to take this ship the other way," said Grimr smoothly. "We have no knowledge of your country."

Alaric took in the lined rank of the Suehans waiting patiently under the rain on the sloping beach. Disciplined, useful. He considered Grimr's claim of having two more ships' crews. He weighed the likely losses involved if he tried to take these men as well as their companions who were somewhere over the horizon, and he reached a swift decision. "You and a dozen of your men will come with us. I shall leave one crew and its ship here against the return of the rest of your men, and they will bring all of them to our settlement. You can join us on our voyage to Britain once you have sworn fealty to our king. Make your dispositions and join me in my ship within the hour."

Grimr acted fast. He told off the dozen who would accompany him as hostages, for that is what they would be until all had sworn their new oath of loyalty. He gave careful instructions to the crew who would wait for their companions, stressing that they had sent two ships not one in search of their new allies. If those idiots don't come back with a captured merchantman, there could be trouble, he thought, so, Odin help us. And he gave whispered instruction to his most trusted lieutenant to assess the chance of capturing the Jutes and their vessel once he and the hostages had departed. They might turn the tables, take the Jutes' ship, find Grimr and the hostages and release them. If that happened, well and good. If the rescue went wrong, at least Grimr would be in the feasting halls of

Valhalla sooner rather than later. And if no recapture and rescue came about, Grimr would look for his chance to slip away from his new lord when they reached Britain. It was in the gods' hands.

So, the Suehan hostages were subdued as they gathered their weapons and effects and trekked under the mocking scream of sea birds and fall of drizzling rain to be disposed between the Jutes' ships. They were captives, about to sail to meet whatever the Fates had in store for them. It was out of their control, for now.

XI Frisia

Loading the two Frisian stallions onto the galley had taken three hours. First, the work party had swum the horses out one by one, alongside two small boats, then had attempted to secure belly bands under them and haul them over the gunwales by sheer manpower. One thrashing horse had stove in the sheer strake, the topmost plank of the ship's side; the other had wrestled free of its restraints and swum away. By the time the exasperated Britons had rounded them both up and returned the beasts, shivering, snorting and belligerent, to the beach – doing so while the carpenters cursed and repaired their ship – nobody had any real hope the horses and the galley would ever come together.

It was the tribune Lycaon, sand-chafed, bedraggled and irritable, who had finally solved the problem. Arthur had not sent one of his most favoured officers to do this important task without thought, and resourceful Lycaon had risen to the challenge, as he had met every other test on this expedition to the land of the Belgae. He had already come ashore quietly on a shelving beach north of Bononia, away from any hostile Roman eyes, and avoiding the small ports of that coast in case word went to the authorities. Lycaon was mindful that the last time he had been in this region he had been captured, flogged and crucified. Only swift action by a handful of friends had saved his flickering life, and he had been shipped out of the country unconscious. This time, he vowed he would not be taken, and he had exercised every caution.

He'd hauled up ashore and concealed one galley and arranged a rendezvous with the other, marched a squad inland and located a horse dealer. That worthy's eyes had widened at the leather pouch of gold he was being offered. In two days, the dealer, the Briton and their escort were leading two fine, strong stallions back to the concealed galley, the other vessel was standing offshore, and Lycaon was facing the task of getting both horses on board and the galley afloat. Swimming them out had failed.

"Rollers, five rollers," he ordered, wanting smoothed logs laid on the beach. "Pull the bows of the damn galley up on them," he said, waving off an energetic centurion to organize ropes, men and tackle. With the vessel beached and steady, it was a relatively easy task to create a ramp and lead the blindfolded stallions to opposite ends of the ship where they would not be tempted to contest mastery. For Lycaon, as the galley was heaved back afloat and under the shelter of its escort warship, a tiresome task was ending only its first phase.

Now, he had to take the two stallions back, offload them - and he thought gloomily of that task - then move them to the plains around the ancient standing stones of southern Britain where wild horses grazed and he could capture a herd to be broken. There, he hoped, his subordinates would already be moving ahead with their duties and there could be a raw wood and stone new castrum raised for men and horses, both of which should start arriving soon.

Lycaon's minimal orders were to raise a horse herd that would be the core of a new British cavalry. He was grateful that his king trusted him not to detail all he should do, but the tribune had deduced that along the way to fulfilling his brief, he must find warriors for his horses, gather weapons, shields, fodder and equipment, create housing and horse pens, and find horse copers, halter trainers, herd managers and a breeder, he gloomed, who knew how to create better bloodstock. There was also this question of getting his men to use these new stirrups. Myrddin had told Arthur about the triangular things that meant his men could stand on a stable, firm platform however bumpy the ride was. It made a fine fighting footing, but the men needed educating away from the old knee-gripping technique they knew. And then, with his fine new steeds, he had to train the whole mass of horses and men into cohesive coordination to fight and win battles. Myrddin, thought Lycaon, could not have had to make more difficult magic, but first he would deliver these two steeds to Arthur.

Both horses were magnificent. I had rushed with unseemly haste from hearing petitions and delivering judgements on which peasant had stolen what small strip of pasture, or which youth had impregnated which daughter and who owed a bride price to whom. I had closed my meet abruptly to go outside and view the horses, pretending urgent business. The beasts were exactly what I had wanted, a pair of three year old Frisian stallions. I winced when I heard what Lycaon had paid the horse trader, but he had successfully slipped into Gaul, located and bought the horses, and spirited them out again, right under the Romans' noses in my occupied onetime citadel of Bononia. With these horses at stud, within three years I could have the beginnings of a cavalry force like none the world had ever seen. One of the horses especially was all I had ever imagined, and I vowed to become a cavalry king, on his back. Inwardly, I grinned. I had been a foot soldier, then a sailor and now I would be a horseman. Life gets better.

A barbarian had hacked off some of my foot and part of my face when I was campaigning across the Rhine in Germania. I had survived the injuries, killed the man and had learned to ignore my limping disability. After I healed, my duties changed. My knowledge of ships and war meant I had become an admiral, so had no longer needed to make long marches, and as an emperor, few expected me to walk any distance at all.

Of course, I had taken my place at the centre of the shield wall on the day we had crushed the Roman invasion of Britain, but that was hardly a role where fleetness of foot – half foot, I reminded myself darkly – was important. Now, with a suitable war-trained horse, I could be the warrior I was once, and more. My deficiency, concealed from my soldiers, would not undermine their confidence. Give me the horse, I told myself, and I will be the emperor and lord of war that none can resist. And now, that horse was standing before me inside the stone walls of our Dover fortress.

He was tall. I am a big man but his shoulders came up to my chest. He was black as charcoal, with a dense tail and mane and sturdy, feathered legs. He had an arched neck, broad chest, bright eyes, and sloping hindquarters; was wide in the hoof and possessed a powerful, muscled body. His companion, kept a discreet distance away to prevent them fighting, looked similar, but there was something in the eye of this stallion that drew me. I nodded to Lycaon, who looked drawn and tired.

"An excellent job, tribune," I said. "Put these fellows at stud, and work with them to make them into war horses, this one for me. I want a courageous and agile steed that will slash and bite, trample and turn to my commands in battle, and I want his seed to make a crop of foals.

"I shall call this fellow Corvus, or Raven, because, like winged battlefield scavengers, we shall make a feast of our dead enemies. That one will be Nonios, after Pluto's night-black horse. Fine stallions deserve fine names."

Lycaon saluted and turned to begin the next phase of his duties, to establish a military horse farm in southern Britain. I called him back. I had received reports of the new barracks alongside a huge Roman grain farm and was able to relay the news from my tribune Cragus. Lycaon, who would be sharing responsibility for recruiting men and training horses heard to his evident relief, that construction was going well, that Cragus had gathered a corps of two centuries of volunteer legionaries, some of whom claimed experience with horses, and that already more than 60 wild horses had been gathered and penned.

"It will take a month or so, sir," he told me, "to break the plains horses and some more time to train them for warfare, and we're likely still seeking a proper *archippus*, a horse master. Then, we'll have to drill and equip the men, too. Then there will be the brood mares...the next generation of horses... you can't really ride horses much before they are two or three years old, when the cartilage of their knees and back are closed. We'll have trained the older, wild horses much sooner, of course, but creating a heavy cavalry might take years..." his voice trailed off.

He looked anxious, as well he might. Creating a cavalry force was one of my priorities, and he knew it. I made no effort to reassure him. Without sympathy, I grated: "Just get it done."

I had plenty of other concerns and most of them were armed, murderous and coming my way.

XII Grimr

Maximian, Augustus of the West, was looking from his headquarters in Mainz at the bridge over the Rhine, and was frowning. In his hand he held a dispatch from Gaul that told him of the British officer and the purchase of two Frisian stallions. The emperor understood at once what it implied. Britannicus, as he now styled himself, planned to breed a heavy cavalry.

Maximian had hated Arthur from their second meeting, an instinctive dislike rooted in his desire for a particular woman, and since his junior Caesar and son in law Chlorus had been defeated and executed by the rebel, his loathing had turned into an obsessive hatred. Maximian had long since signed Arthur's death warrant, but his hatred ran deeper than a mere execution. He wanted the rebel upstart captured, tortured and dismembered. He wanted Arthur's head on a spear point over his palace gate. The army knew it, the Bononia garrison and the sketchy, rebuilt British Channel fleet knew it: any news of the hated Carausius/ Britannicus/ Arthur, or whatever he called himself this week was to be relayed promptly.

Now, the emperor mused, the British bastard was building a cavalry. That would be a real factor should he ever untangle himself from this soggy, foggy place of forests and barbarians. Well, it would take the bastard a few years before he had a real horse force, but it was a matter to be borne in mind. Maximian knew he could not mount any invasion of Britain in the coming year, he was simply too involved with the Alemanni, but in two years or so... he could put the bastard's head on the same spike his daughter's husband and his general, Chlorus, had adorned. Or, he could drag this Britannicus back to Milan or Rome and play with him there. Either would be sheer pleasure, and he'd crucify thousands of those British rebels, too. People might talk about how the Appian Way, after the Spartacus revolt, had been lined with 6,000 rebels nailed up in one day, but he'd give them a better spectacle with those insurgent Britons. He crumpled the dispatch and threw it on the floor. Two fucking forest horses, what was that? Hardly a cavalry force, not yet. He'd deal with it, and that bastard Briton, in due course. He might have Britannia, but even a blind pig can occasionally find an acorn…

While Maximian was staring absently at the flow of the upper Rhine, the sea raider Grimr was standing by its estuary, facing the Jute chieftain Web Brokenose. Grimr took in the man's appearance. Like a weasel, he thought. Web was narrow-shouldered and not tall. His face was pinched, his eyes suspicious under a shaggy fringe of straw-like hair. Even his voice, with its querulous high-pitched timbre was somehow offensive. How, Grimr thought, did this man become a chieftain? Web seemed to sense the question. "My father and grandfather before him led this clan," he said, "and we have held our lands against the likes of you for longer than you can imagine. We want no intruders, nor thieves here. What do you think you were doing on our islands?" Before Grimr could speak, Web jabbed at the big man's chest with his dagger. "I could have you killed," he said softly. "I could have you burned to death, crushed, or drowned under the keel of your own pirate ship."

The big Suehan shrugged and held out his hands placatingly. "You could do any of those things of course, king," he said. "We are in your power, but that is why we came here, to serve under you." Inwardly Grimr was gritting his teeth and trying not to say: "I should wring your scrawny neck, you chicken-faced blot," but overmatched as he was, and with just a dozen of his men present in the Jute's bustling settlement, he settled for the pragmatic approach. "We came because we heard you were planning an expedition to Britain, and we wanted to offer our swords to your service in return for what you consider fair reward." And that, he thought sourly, would probably be a fraction of what we're really worth, but the problem right now is to persuade this half-man not to enslave us, or worse.

"My crews," and Grimr put faint emphasis on the plural to underscore to the Jute the possible threat of reinforcements or rescue, "are fine warriors. Why would you not want them in your shield wall, or slaughtering your enemies? Of what use are we to you, lord king, if we are dead?"

"You were on my islands," Web repeated sullenly.

"An accident of weather," said Grimr firmly. "We were seeking your fortress." He looked around at the small port that sat near the confluence of the Rhine and Meuse rivers. Stone walls and thick timber palisades, stone quays, some jetties, a couple of warehouses and a small town. It was a sizeable, obviously important place and it was busy. About 20 vessels were tied up to the harbour walls or had been dragged up the beach. The quays and both shipyards were swarming with men readying longships and themselves for a long voyage. Web still looked suspicious, so Grimr threw his arms wide. "Lord king," he said as sincerely as he could manage, "how could a small party of men like ours even hope to confront your might?"

The flattery was swallowed uncritically, the Suehan saw, thinking 'May as well ladle it on, nothing to lose,' so he continued: "Just take us under your wing, lord, and we will be your faithful servants and soldiers."

Web cleared his throat importantly and handed down his decision in a ponderous manner. "I have considered your pleas," he said, "and you may swear fealty to me. You shall do it in front of all your men, when the rest arrive, so there is no mistake or possible misunderstanding. You will be my vassals. Displease me, and your head will adorn the prow of my ship. Meanwhile, prepare yourselves as best you can, and do as my officers order you. We are sailing for Britain in a matter of a week or so, as the weather and the gods permit. You may go." Grimr lowered his head humbly. He'd settle matters with this arrogant princeling at another time, but for now, he and his men were safe and were set for an expedition of blood and fire, as they'd wished. If he just happened to kill this pretentious clown who mistakenly thought he was a warlord, there would be no surprise in it to Odin.

In Chester, the sorceress Guinevia was readying herself for an expedition, and I was unhappy about it. My scribe, advisor, lover and mother of my child was planning to be away for several months while she studied with her mentor, the Druid Myrddin. Her journey would take her west into the mountains of Wales, to stay with the enchanter in his home under the shadow of the sacred mountain Yr Wyddfa while the pair worked on his scrolls and sky charts to untangle some mystery at which he would only hint.

In time, they might journey on, down the long passes to the coast, to take a ferry across the treacherous straits to the sacred island of Mona. It was there under the sacred oaks and mistletoe where the druids had soaked the ground with the blood of human sacrifices and eventually with their own, spilled by the swords of a Roman legion. Guinevia told me little of her mission, and knew less of Myrddin's intentions, but she was determined to acquire more of her mentor's secrets and to assume some of his powers, so she could help return Britain to the old gods. "We have the Christians confined for now," she told me, "but they have still weakened our nation. Their tattered priests with their bands of followers are still roaming the land and building their strength. Myrddin has a plan to redirect the energies of nature and to bring back the old gods who made Britain great." I nodded, not totally comprehending her words, but aware of the threats that beset my land and people.

It would be good to get the old gods looking over us again. It was they who had led me to locate, after its sleep of 200 years, the iconic Eagle standard. Finding it had proved the god's care for us and had helped me rally the cantankerous chieftains of Britain behind it to defeat our Roman overlords. For luck, I touched the great silver and amber brooch at my shoulder that is the symbol of my standing as a British jarl, then rubbed my fingers against the iron of my sword hilt to avert evil. Guinevia would be a strong ally if she could enhance her sorceress' powers…

The pack horses were laden, the escort of four legionaries were shuffling about tightening buckles and straps, Guinevia was fussing calmly over our small son Milo as he wriggled in his nurse's arms and I was swamped in a fog of gloom. This expedition to the wildest part of Wales was doomed, my instincts told me. Something bad was about to happen. I had told Guinevia of my fears, and she had cast an augury – positive – and sent out her inner eye to seek Myrddin – pottering happily in his garden, she reported. I could not dissuade her. I held her and smelled the crocus oil she had dabbed behind her ears, and I took in the faint scent of lavender from the flowers she placed in her clothes chest.

She took Milo from his nurse and handed him, squirming, to me. "I'll take good care of this fellow," she smiled up at me. I nodded, numbly. I had sent many men to their deaths, I had killed enough of them myself, but I had never had this sense of great doom, even when I truly thought I was about to die in some skirmish or other.

But the hour came and my hounds whined, sensing something. The gates were swung open, the escort formed around the pack mules and the two women in their raeda carriage. We bade farewell, may the gods speed and protect you, return soon, pay my respects to Myrddin and all the other words of parting, but I never could voice my fears, and the small procession clattered out of the gate, a small hand waved and I watched my best beloved leave on the road to hell.

XIII Equus

Lycaon halted his small group: a file of soldiers and three horsemen, two of them leading the black Frisian stallions they trotted on the last part of their journey from Dover. He scanned the long vista of the chalk downs where the horse camp Arthur had ordered was taking shape. His fellow tribune Cragus had chosen well, sitting the pens near a vast grain farm that had served the legions for two centuries. The place was well watered by a tributary of one of the four rivers that bounded the plain, and the vista of smooth, rolling grasslands seemed to his eyes a grassy sea, islanded with occasional clumps of trees where he could pick out specks that were work parties harvesting timber for the camp. Here and there were the long, low lines of the burial mounds of the ancient peoples who had constructed the plain's giant stone circles.

The Romans had slashed a road across the downs, aligning it spear-straight east to west like the sloping long barrows of the burial mounds, and it came close to one edge of the horse camp. The soldiers, who were disciplined and practised engineers of camps, bridges, signal towers and the like, had constructed it well. There were paddocks and stables, a barracks and an administration block, much of it to the established plan of a Roman marching camp: a quadrangle with a gate centred on each side, a timber-walled rampart and ditch around it all and a given, familiar layout for the various occupants. Because it would be a semi-permanent camp, some of the tent lines were missing and barracks blocks and a bath house had been erected. Equally, the cavalry lines that would normally be protected inside the castrum were outside in several paddocks. Lycaon noted with satisfaction that guard posts had been established around those well-fenced areas. No point capturing and breaking horses only for them to be stolen, he thought. You could rely on good old Cragus to consider everything. He turned and waved his group forward, and trotted across the turf to find his old friend.

The tribune Cragus Grabelius had served Arthur for years and was among his most experienced and trusted officers. He'd trained and readied the troops that turned back the Romans, had campaigned across

Pictland, clearing the tribes from between the walls of Hadrian and Antoninus, and forced the surrender of the rocky fortress of the Votadini that commanded the River Forth valley. He'd outwitted and outflanked the Picts by building a floating bridge over that river, and he'd surprised the Romans at Dungeness by taking a force through the flanking marshes and attacking them from the rear.

Now he faced the task of building a cavalry unlike any the world had seen. He had as raw material the wild horse herds that roamed the southern downlands of Britain, and he could draw on the legions for troops. He did the former, and ignored the latter.

"I wanted experienced horsemen," he explained later to Lycaon, "so I went north to Carlisle. For three centuries, the cohort Ala Petriana was stationed there, 24 troops of auxiliary cavalry, 800 men. It was the biggest cavalry force along the entire Wall, and many of them had been discharged to their farms and wives, so did not go to Germania five years ago when their legion was pulled out.

"I went with silver and five centurions who can recruit men, and I came back with about 90 experienced troopers, and the promise of more to follow when their crops are gathered. After Carlisle," he continued, "I went all the way across country to Colchester because one of my centurions told me how he'd always lost money on the horse races when he was stationed there. It is the only place in Britain with an arena for chariot racing, and of course that's where I found trained horses and men who are used to handling them.

"It was a goldmine. Some of the old soldiers were trainers who actually had an illicit business going, shipping horses for breeding to Gaul. It was a very easy matter to persuade them to use their skills in the service of the emperor, or perhaps they would prefer a trial and execution? I got a dozen trainers there, plus a few younger fellows. Yes, many of the recruits are not young, but they are trained soldiers and horsemen, and they'll serve our purpose. Some of them have already brought in half a hundred horses from the herds that run wild here and are busy gentling them right now. It could be that in just a few months, we'll have a cavalry force of some kind, and in three years we could have a very fine heavy cavalry, once we breed these Frisians and the other horses we'll be acquiring."

Cragus glanced around. The nearest sentry was 30 yards away, eyes forward, rigidly aware of his commanders' close presence. "There's one other thing: I sent a platoon down to Arthur's old palace at Fishbourne to see if there was anything to salvage after Maximian's men burned the place. They came back with some useful things, including a wagon load of amphorae which we thought was olive oil. Turns out, it's actually is some very good Rhenish wine. It's waiting in the barracks for us, and I think we should nobly do our official duty, and drink to the success of the cavalry."

In Chester, where I was looking morosely towards the mountains to which my Guinevia was travelling, the cavalry's success was not uppermost in my mind. I was standing at the edge of the dusty practice ground where the drillmasters were working with some new recruits from the south. They'd gone through exercises to harden them, swimming in the Dee, doing gymnastics under the city wall, they'd made long marches in full kit and they had been marched and counter marched on the parade ground until their feet were sore and their ears ached from the shouted commands.

At present, after slipping away like a truant schoolboy from giving judgements on court hearings, I was watching a couple of grizzled centurions overseeing combat training exercises. The men were attacking straw targets with wooden swords, and it recalled me to the day in Rome when the Emperor Carus had handed me my commission. Carus, called Persicus for his victories over the Persians, had also awarded a wooden sword, a *rudis*, to some brain-damaged gladiator as symbol that his days in the arena were ended honourably. I even recalled the warrior's name: Timminus, and his blank stare. The emperor had turned to me like an old comrade, calling me 'Bear,' and explained with a sympathetic nod as the man was led away: "They retire after six years or 30 bouts. Not many get that far, and the ones that do have usually got some head injury that prevents them becoming an instructor, which is what we'd prefer." Carus' uncondescending affability impressed me. The emperor treated me as a fellow soldier, and I vowed that one day, if I achieved high rank, I would do the same to my subordinates.

But not, I thought, to these young recruits, not yet. They were struggling to obey their instructors, and the two centurions' voices were getting shriller and louder with frustration. "You use that shield to fucking protect you!" one was shouting. "Fight like a boxer. Left foot forward, boot behind the base of the shield to steady it, right foot back, turned outwards to brace yourself. Stab, thrust hard, don't slash with your fucking sword! You punch them in the face or in the nuts with your shield, then stab them over the top with the sword point! You thrust, you don't slash, you're not reaping fucking hay! Puncture the bastards!"

The recruits were learning the battle-winning value of the shield wall. Overlap the edges of your shield with those of your fellows, keep the shield down to protect your shins, stab over the top of it. The press of the ranks behind you kept you upright even while your comrades in the rear were firing missiles, heavy darts, javelins and the like overhead and into the enemy mob. Meanwhile, the enemy's own forward pressure pushed their ranks up against our shields so we could jab into them. As they went down under the thrusts, our front line would move forward, stamping down with their studded boots, and marching over them, while the following second and third ranks would dispatch the wounded enemy as they lay crushed on the ground.

I turned away, and strode over the training field to where more experienced soldiers were practising battle formations. I nodded approval at the centurion who was prodding and shouting at his men to move smoothly from column to line, from line to shieldwall-penetrating wedges, then to spread into a chequerboard pattern so the rear ranks could move up when needed.

Our preferred technique was to approach the enemy in several columns, for manoeuvrability, and we usually advanced behind a screen of cavalry, light troops and the scouts. As we closed, we'd deploy into three wedged ranks, with each unit in a designated place and the whole forming up in a sort of chequered pattern to allow gaps through which the front ranks could retreat and the rear ranks advance.

The third, rear rank was always the veterans and they were usually only called upon if the battle got serious and the first two ranks of spearmen were tiring. We put the least experienced to the front to take the initial brunt while the second and third ranks dispatched volleys of spears and darts over their heads. Sometimes we'd use slingshot men who hurled lethal, egg-sized lumps of lead, sometimes, we'd send in cavalry, or we could even deploy some nasty artillery or archers, but the basic premise was to use the heavy shields, armour and training to move our men forward into lightly-protected enemies as a single grinding front.

Sometimes, that front took on the shape of a sawtooth wedge designed to pierce an enemy line, but always the chequered pattern allowed us constantly to funnel fresh troops forward, and the steady pressure usually broke the enemy, who typically were good for one or two wild charges fuelled by mead or hallucinogenic mushrooms. Our front ranks would fight until they tired, then funnel back. Fresh troops would move up to take their place while they rested, and then the original frontline soldiers would recycle back in. The third ranks would be held back. Often the officers would order them to kneel, to restrain their eagerness until the moment was right to release them to the kill.

Through all this, the enemy were usually fighting themselves to exhaustion, as they constantly faced fresh troops and unrelenting attacks. It was the way of the legions, had been for centuries, and it worked.

My plan was to continue the old tactics, but to introduce heavy cavalry and horse-mounted archers. With a swift striking force that could sting from a safe distance, and cavalry whose big horses could crash through an enemy line as their riders stood upright on those new stirrups, we could win battles easier and more cheaply, and could counter the growing inclination of our enemies to armour themselves in the Roman way. And, there was another way I planned to subdue the growing numbers facing us. I'd explained it to my tribunes: "We will get the least costly victories through attrition. That is, we can deplete our enemies not by attacking their forces but by simply seizing their resources. It is expensive for us to train, equip and maintain a single soldier, so it's prudent to use our troops in the safest way possible to reduce casualties. At the same time, we cause the maximum disadvantage to our opponents.

"Now," I said, warming to the lecture, "armies operate on supplies. If we seize or cut off those resources, two things happen: we have more, they have less. To achieve this, we can cut the supply line and attack the resources in transit, we can seize them in situ, or third, if the enemy is inside a fortification, we can besiege them and cut them off from their supplies. In all cases, they are much weakened by being separated from their reinforcements, from their food, fresh materials and equipment. We can grind them down even before we bring them to battle."

The tribunes nodded. They understood resource tactics, it was their job to ensure we were well supplied, but sometimes their eagerness to do battle was not the most intelligent option. I coughed as they murmured among themselves. "We should consider one other thing, gentlemen," I said. "We have to recognize that our enemies may use these same tactics against us, so we should secure our supply lines and dumps. We should keep our lines of supply as short as possible, and move our troops swiftly, not just by road, but also by river or sea to surprise our opponents. Using water transport is far more secure than taking a pack train through a forest or mountains where it is subject to ambush.

"Our strategy must always be to put as much strength to a given point as quickly as possible, to feed and supply it and to keep it unified." The group nodded agreement, and I felt a thirst coming on. "Time, gentlemen," I said, "to consider another supply necessity," and I gestured for a slave to bring in wine.

XIV Taken

Guinevia sensed danger, a prickle at the nape of her neck, a brightening of the light around her, a heightened awareness of the sounds of the forest where her carriage horses plodded nearly silent across the pine-straw-padded track way.

She was on the third day of her journey into northern Wales and was suddenly, uneasily, aware that her escort of four troopers had been halved. That morning, as they forded a moorland stream, all four soldiers had mustered to heave the carriage free of clinging mud. One of them had stepped on a loose rock and stumbled. At that exact moment, the carriage wheels had come free and lurched forward. One ran over the man's foot, breaking a couple of small bones. The man had fallen sideways, wrenching his knee so badly as he fell that the joint swelled up like an apple.

The sorceress had debated continuing the journey with the half-crippled man riding in the carriage, but she needed it for the child and his nurse. Already, with its passengers and the supplies she had loaded for Myrddin – preserves and herbs, sacks of good grain and seed vegetables – the horses had been struggling, and the worst of the journey was to come. Adding a big man to their load would not help matters. Instead, she had opted to send the fourth trooper back six or seven miles to a hamlet where he could hire a carriage to carry his injured companion to a refuge. The uninjured soldier could follow on by himself to catch the party before they reached the wildest peaks.

So the guard on the little group was smaller, and Guinevia suddenly felt in danger. She called the group to halt, scanning the forest around them for the threat she intuitively knew was there. It was about the worst thing she could have done. A whirr of arrows lanced out of the undergrowth. Two struck the first trooper in the thigh and ribs, a third smacked wetly into the other soldier's throat. Moments later, a handful of wolf-howling bandits burst from the greenery, the reins were dragged from Guinevia's hands and the two troopers were hacked to death as they lay on the ground. The ambush was as bloody as the dispatch of a pig by a butcher, and as shockingly swift and deadly.

Guinevia never did remember much of what happened later. She had a blurred recollection of being hurt, time and again, by men; a vision of pleading with a brigand not to kill her child and a recollection of stumbling through the forest, wrists tied to the tail of one of the carriage horses. Whatever had happened, and she did not want to recall it, would give her unknowable nightmares for years, despite whatever she did or whatever release she pleaded for with her gods. Her clearest memories began many hours after the brigands wrenched her down from the carriage, when she surfaced to consciousness in a cattle byre. The nurse was wiping her face, cleaning away crusted blood with a moistened scrap of her torn skirt, and Guinevia could hear cattle moving restlessly beyond the wall. "We are in a bad place, my lady," the girl, red-eyed from weeping, said, "we have been through terrible things but we are at least alive. I think they now mean to sell us as slaves. How can they do that? Can you stop them?"

The sorceress struggled to sit up as the girl supported her. Her head hurt, her limbs ached and her eyes and mouth were sticky. The croaking voice that emerged surprised her. "Where is my baby? Where is he?" The girl gripped her forearm. "They have him, one of their women has him. I think he's safe, for now. And I never told them who you are…"

Guinevia was so dazed and in shock she had no comprehension of what the girl said. She struggled to her feet, the byre seeming to sway around her, and stumbled against the rough door. Barred. She pounded on it and screamed. The girl tugged at her arm. "Don't, my lady, don't," she whispered. "Stay quiet. Don't remind them we're here. They are rough men. They have used us both, and cruelly. Just rest for now, just make yourself better." Grasping at the enchantress' sleeve, she tugged her gently back: "Look, have a sip of water."

Guinevia shook her head. "I must get my child," she muttered. "We can get out of here." At her urging, both women fumbled and felt their way around the walls and hoof-trodden muck of the floor until they found a rotted board. They pried at it until it gave, pulled out another and were outside, crouched low under crisp, cold starlight.

"That way," the sorceress said, trying to conjure a cloaking mist. Her vital energies were exhausted, and the gods did not hear, so the two captives moved, crouched low, across the stinking yard towards the rough slate building where they could hear the mutter of voices. As they got closer, the yellow rays of rushlight that shone through the wooden door became a quadrangle of illumination. They flattened to the mud, and froze. A man stepped out, fumbling at his trews. The two women lay, shadows on the ground, and caught his feral stink as he walked a few paces away from the threshold.

Guinevia had one arm outstretched where she had instantly stilled, and the man's nailed boot crunched across the top joint of her smallest finger. The bone snap was audible, but the man was pissing now and did not hear, and Guinevia stifled the cry that the jolt of agony had caused. The nurse was less courageous. As the urine spattered about her, she whimpered and half-rose. The startled man seized the girl by the nape, yelled alarm, and others stumbled out of the door. Both women were quickly manhandled back to the byre, where a disgruntled brigand was now posted in the cold, as guard.

The effort had drained Guinevia, and she allowed the nurse to lead her back to the straw pile where they had been lying. She slumped, sipped from the wooden bowl of water the girl put to her lips, and drifted into an exhausted doze, gently murmuring for her child. Moments passed, then the enchantress sat upright and declaimed in a surprisingly strong voice that caused the guard to growl a warning. "Nicevenn and Ogmia, do not desert me now," she said loudly. "Myrddin, send to Arthur."

Something seemed to shake me awake, and I looked to see a sleek, almost luminous white rat moving slowly across the corner of my sleeping chamber in Chester. My hand went for to the dagger under my pillow, but I consciously stayed the movement. I had seen this white rat before, at critical moments in my life. Now I was about to understand.

The Rat had been there when, as a boy, I ran from my father's killers. It had crossed my path as I ran through the trees. It was there on the day I opted to join the Roman Army, and I had remembered that other day in the trees. I'd seen it when I escaped death at the collapse of King Mosae's citadel wall, and it had been dropped into my path by a hawk, a tremendous augury of good fortune witnessed by the troops, as I rode into Eboracum to be acclaimed Imperator.

The creature seemed to fade away, and I felt the urgent need to sleep, although my mind was churning. Almost at once I went into a trance-like doze. An image of Guinevia was before me, and she was holding the Rat, offering it to me. A series of scenes flashed through my mind. Here was Myrddin, tall and dark and ominous, standing illumined against a dance of ancient stones. His eyes seemed to drill into my brain and I understood he had sent the Rat to my Guinevia as her powerful familiar.

A series of images rolled by. Here was the Rat that I had not noticed, at the times when it had been present but unseen. Here, it crouched in a corner as I was commissioned by the Emperor Carus, and here it was at the moment in Bononia when I heard of the scroll that led us to the lost Eagle. It was there in the Scots temple when Guinevia sacrificed a man, a gift to the gods that may have saved my life, as the next day I was captured and nearly executed. The images continued. The Rat was also an unseen witness on the day I opted to become Arthur, and tie myself closer to Britain; and it was there preening its whiskers on one of the cairns that marked the trap that destroyed the Romans at Dungeness.

It was coming clear. This could not be a natural creature that had been in Britain, Belgica and Rome, then in Gaul, and Pictland and Eboracum and Dungeness. It seemingly had been present at every point of great importance in my life. Now, for no reason I knew, another hinge of my history was turning and the Rat was here as its herald.

I sat up abruptly, fully awake. Guinevia. My enchantress was sending me her cry. Something wicked was happening, it was undoubted, as definite as if she had walked in herself to tell me. Across the chamber, the Rat was calmly viewing me, eyes glittering redly. Guinevia, or Myrddin had sent the messenger and I could not delay.

I was off the cot, stamping out into the courtyard, calling for Cragus, Allectus, the guard captain and horses. My big hounds Axis and Javelin, whose gaze had slid over the Rat without reaction, were at my heels whining. We had ground to cover and an enchantress to find. On a thought, I turned back, rummaged in Guinevia's clothes chest and pulled out one of her scarves. The scent might be needed.

It was the work of an hour to make the arrangements, brief Allectus and Androcles on emergency measures should the Saxons come, arrange a corps of couriers to race messages back and forth and to arm and equip a half-century, 40 pony soldiers, to ride with me. I selected a couple of grizzled *decurio* cavalry commanders to take charge of the horses and men and instructed them that we would be travelling light and fast, so to bring remounts and forage nets. It would be spears and swords only, no shields. What I planned would involve no defensive wall but an unexpected strike. I also commanded three scouts to go ahead at once. They would make better time than our whole troop, and would be less threatening when it came to questioning locals along the way. It could save us a day or more, critical time if my enchantress' life was endangered.

I had debated with Guinevia over her route to Myrddin's holding, and had urged her to take the easier, longer coastal road that ran west, then to turn south and climb the passes to his mountain eyrie, but she had stubbornly insisted on the shorter, direct route southwest from Chester that rose over the moors. Now, I thanked her obstinacy. At least I knew her path, would be able to follow her tracks.

We left at wolf light, shivering in the cold, but I was shivering more at what I might find, and I vowed agonizing death to any wrongdoers who may have harmed my lover or my small son. Sol began to rise at our backs as we cantered west, his rays burning off the mist and warming us, but they did not remove the chill I felt inside. I gripped the hilt of my war sword Exalter and rubbed its iron for luck. Axis and Javelin loped tirelessly alongside, tongues lolling. I thought grimly that I'd feed them the beating hearts of any brigands who may have bruised mine.

It was after two days hard riding before we came across useful knowledge of Guinevia. It came from a shepherd guarding his flock high on the moors. He had hidden behind a rock at the sight of our troop, but the dogs found him and the troopers brought him to me after a few moments' questioning. He talked after receiving both threats and a coin, and told of seeing armed men leading several pack horses and two women bound and tied to the tails of horses with riders. "Five men, lord," he told me. "Two mounted, with the women walking behind, three leading the pack animals." No, he had seen no soldiers, just mountain men with spears and bows. Two of the men, the ones on horseback, had worn helmets and had swords.

That told me much. Few men owned swords. Only soldiers, and well-equipped ones like our own, had them. Two horses, two swords, two helmets. Sounded like plunder. Where, I wondered had our four troopers gone? Had the mountain men been able to kill all four from ambush? It seemed unlikely, especially with only five mountain men to take them on, and the two swords said much. Guinevia's raeda had been drawn by two horses, and that too supported my guesswork. The shepherd could tell me little more than the direction the bandits and their prisoners had taken, and when. They were less than one day ahead of us. I split the column into three, to separate and search as we rode, and ordered a rendezvous at dusk.

Three hours after we left the shepherd, one of our advance scouts found me. He had spotted the bandits and had slipped away unseen. We changed direction and cantered on. We'd find them after dark, when they lit a fire. But we did not.

XV Channel

Grimr was disgusted. By the time the force he'd detached to find new ships had returned, Web had been joined by more Saxons, a sizeable contingent of well-armed battle Jutes and a Frisian king with a savage-looking war band of his own. At no time had the Suehan held a numerical advantage that would have given him a chance to seize control from Web and the others, and the gathered Saxons now comprised a considerable fleet. Their intention was to take and hold some of the mineral-rich land in the southeast of Britain and to use it as a beach head for further incursions and expansions.

Of itself, that seemed to Grimr a fine plan, but he was disgusted to find that he was no longer leader of anything and had been ordered to take a place at the oars of his own longship. About the only thing he could do that was positive was to persuade enough of his own men to join him on that ship, in hopes of breaking away from their new Jute and Saxon masters.

So the invasion fleet sailed down the coast of Gaul in brave style, before striking west for the mouth of the Thames and skirmishes with the Britons. Grimr noted morosely that Web had opted to command his own old ship, one where he now occupied a rower's humble bench. About all he had of his old chieftain's life, he thought, was his dagger, his crossbow and his memories.

The fleet was closing on the British coast when an autumn storm blew up out of the northeast and scattered the fragile longships. In an hour, the weather went from brisk to terrifying. Green waves shaped like pyramids towered over the vessels, the straits turned into a white-foamed millrace and the steerboards required the muscles of three men to hold them. Web, whitefaced with fear, chose to run before the wind, and turned down-strait. Dusk fell with only two other ships in sight, and Web ordered the exhausted oarsmen to rest, opting to continue under bare poles with the westbound tide.

Dawn broke with all three ships still miraculously in sight, and they pulled together for a council. Sailing back into the gale would be difficult, arriving days or weeks after the Danes had scorched the countryside would be especially dangerous for a small group such as theirs, when the Britons would have rallied. The Jutes opted to do some raiding of their own.

Grimr, eavesdropping on the shouted ship-to-ship debate, saw a chance, and joined in. He called out that there were gold mines in Siluria, north of the Severn Sea, and rich monasteries and churches, too. It tipped the balance, and the raiders kept on west, to round the land's end and head for the territory of the Welsh.

Meanwhile, in the north of that territory, the brigands still held Guinevia. They had spent the night at a farmstead, paying the suspicious owner with food from the captured packhorses, and had moved on westwards. A bandit who had stopped to relieve himself spotted the glint of weapons on the open country behind them, saw one of Arthur's columns and alerted his chief, a blue-chinned villain called Moel. He assessed the situation and rightly guessed they were being hunted, so turned his group aside and into uplands where forests would cloak their travel.

That night, the group camped in a shepherd's stone bothy and Moel called for Guinevia. "Your child is slowing us," he said in his sing-song accents. "I should kill him." In fact, he had no such intention. The child would bring a good price at the slave pens of Menai, where he also planned to sell Guinevia and the nurse. The sorceress, exhausted and battered, rallied. "I am a Druid!" she exclaimed. "I will curse you and yours to the end of days. I will bring worms and corruption to your eyes, molten fire to your vitals and the pains of Nicevann to your heart! Harm one fingernail of that boy and you will swim in boiling tar in the deepest pit of the Underworld. Do you comprehend what I am saying to you?"

Moel goggled at the bruised, bloodied woman standing before him who was displaying such power. A man's height above her head, a small cloud of white mist was forming, sure sign of magic being worked. His eyes were wide in fear and he was grasping for his dagger hilt when one of the other brigands began yelping and clutching at his hand. The man had stolen Guinevia's silver pentagram ring and was wearing it. As the sorceress called in her magic, the ring began to pulse and glow, and became as hot as a branding iron on the man's finger. A stench of burning flesh spread as he struggled the ring free and ran for the stream to dunk his scorched hand.

Guinevia limped across the bothy and slipped onto her finger the discarded ring, which still pulsed with light. "Where are we now?" she demanded.

"Not far, lady," said the awed Moel, "not far from Menai where the Romans had a camp."

"Tomorrow, I will ride there, unfettered," she commanded. "When we are safely there, I will give you silver for our lives. If you do not agree, I will consign you and your kin to unspeakable agony and terrible horrors." She turned away before he could speak. "You," she pointed at one of the brigands, "bring my child to me."

XVI Bolted

We had lost the men we hunted. I sent out patrols along all the likely lines they may have used, sent them plodding through the dark, seeking the telltale spark of a fire that would lead us to Guinevia and Milo. At dawn, the tired men scoured the sky for hints of smoke, eye-scanned the land for the gleam of metal or giveaway movement of men and horses, but found nothing. I rode my horse to foam-flecked exhaustion, and gave Axis and Javelin scent of Guinevia's scarf so they quartered the ground for miles, all without success.

We crossed the last spur of the sacred mountain Yr Wyddfa to arrive at Myrddin's stone house, a square, courtyarded place with high, sheltering walls that under other circumstances I would have been delighted to sight, as a haven and source of regal power. This day, with no tethered pack horses or men of my livery to be seen, it was obvious even from a distance that Guinevia was not there.

But Myrddin was. He stood imposing outside the threshold, grey-robed, bearded, and holding his lignum vitae staff of office. He nodded as I rode up. "I saw you were coming, and you know there is bad news." My mouth was dry. "But," he gestured a flick of his fingers, "matters are improving. Turn your horse down that pass and go to Menai. I shall see Guinevia here in a week or so." The wizard nodded again, showed his back to me and walked inside his home. I turned my horse's head and headed him down the pass, towards the sea and the holy island.

The three Jutish ships came up the strait in line astern. The sacred island of Mona was on their left side, the landmass of Wales on the right, the walls of Roman Segontium just ahead. Web viewed the fortifications intently. Guards were on the walls, which seemed in good repair. He did not have the force to take a place of this size and power, so there would be no raiding this day, but they would go ashore and view matters, maybe take a slave or two, or trade some of the Baltic amber he had brought.

The crews beached their longships and, on orders from town watchmen, left their weapons except for personal daggers under guard on the vessels. They walked into the town, paying a toll at the gate, where the guards eyed the strangers suspiciously and warned them against violence. One nodded to a rotting torso impaled above the gate. "That one thought he could come here and steal," the hard-faced soldier informed them. "He won't be trying that twice."

Web swallowed the implied insult. "Ale, mead, maybe slaves, that's all we want. We're just traders," he said.

The guard nodded. "Slave pens are over there."

Web chose to live up to his role, and walked that way. He was in time to see the brigand Moel ride in with his few men, an infant and two swaying, heavy-lidded women who shared the other horse.

"Want to buy a couple of women and a kid?" Moel called out. Web, curious, walked over.

"Are they all right?"

"Ah, just had a little something to calm them down, they were, you know, excited at coming here," the brigand shrugged.

Web looked at the drugged women. Both were attractive. Could bring a good price, and an infant could sell well, too. "How about some amber?" he said, taking a small leather pouch from his belt.

The deal was struck quickly, away from the auctioneer's eyes and the commission he would have wanted. Web desired to leave the town and its soldiery, Moel was eager to hand over Guinevia before she could start talking. A quarter hour later, most of the shore party had found the green bush over the door that signalled one of the town's several taverns and they were occupied inside. Web was back at his vessel, where Grimr had been left among the guards. He was escorting the near-comatose women and the child. "Get these on board, under wraps and silent," he said brusquely. "I don't want them talking to anyone before we leave." Grimr resented the tone, but held his tongue. He helped the half-conscious nurse off the horse and carried her to the gunwale. Another guard, one of Grimr's old crew, took the infant and Web carried Guinevia.

As he slid her across the ship's side, her dress fell open and he licked his lips as he saw one perfect breast. "Maybe there's time before I go for that beer," he said quietly, and clambered from the sand and over the gunwale, fumbling at his trews. As he did, he bumped against the infant

Milo, who had fouled his small clothes, was hungry and irritable from lack of sleep. The child began to wail loudly. Web reached out and cuffed the baby, hard, shocking it into breath-holding silence.

Grimr saw the act as he was reaching under his bench. The baby caught his breath and yelled again, louder. Web slapped him again. Grimr acted on pure instinct. He reached under the oarsman's bench and pulled out his crossbow. Web had dropped his trews and was raising the semi-conscious woman's shift.

The bolt went straight through Web's scrotum, pinning him to the bench. He howled in agony and jerked to free himself, causing him to whimper at the added pain, but the bolt was fast in the woodwork and he could not move it. He eased himself sideways, to be able to grasp the quarrel's shaft, still unsure what had happened.

Grimr automatically slotted another and with a practised movement cranked the crossbow cocked again. He hardly needed to sight it in, at that close range. The second quarrel took the Jute as he turned his head. It slammed through his left carotid and through the man's voicebox, cutting off his screams, then lodged in his right armpit, the point just emerging from the skin. Blood spurted in a thin jet, pulsing with the dying man's heart.

For the second time, Grimr reloaded. He glanced around. By chance, three of the four guards left with the ships were his own old crewmen. The fourth was scrambling over the side of the second ship, and Grimr knew he was on his way to bring Web's men.

The third bolt pinned the man to the top strake of the ship, going clear through his rib cage, lungs and spine. The man stood, held like a pinned butterfly. Grimr nodded to his crewman on the ship. That villain, a cheerful long-haired rogue with a back scarred from floggings, nodded back, pulled out a slender leaf-bladed knife, yanked the man's head back by the hair and casually slashed his throat from behind.

"Not a drop on me, boss," he called.

"Time we did some travelling," the big Suehan called back.

At a command, two of the crew trotted up to the town to quietly alert their old comrades while Grimr and the knife artist slashed the halyards and rigging and holed the hulls of two of the three Jutes' ships to cripple them and slow any pursuit. They relieved Web's body of a purse heavy with amber and silver, and dumped him into the outgoing tide, but left the impaled Jute where he was. He looked as if he was standing there dozing, except for the blood.

The two Suehans had loaded aboard the best weapons of the Jutes who were still drinking at the tavern, dropped the rest of the spears and shields into the water and were preparing their own ship for sea when their crewmates trickled back quietly from the taverns and down the beach. Together they heaved their vessel into the straits and made a largely-unnoticed exit.

Not a bad day altogether, Grimr thought. Disposed of a weasel, got my ship back, made a profit, got some new swords and met a couple of nice-looking women. Didn't that fellow once say something about having me killed? It must have been self-defence, then.

XVII Rescue

We rode into Segontium lathered and straggling, and the city guard snapped to attention without a challenge, as well they might, for I was their Imperator, with blood in my eye and menace in my bearing. If the misbegotten bastard who had taken Guinevia was in this city I would tear down the walls to find him. I reined in at the guardhouse and barked at the sloppy gateman to bring me the captain. Yes lord, he was fidgeting and eyeing my magnificent silver and amber jarl's badge and Exalter with equal unease. Yes lord, men with packhorses and two women had arrived earlier. Yes lord, they had a mewling infant. The women looked drugged.

I was off the horse and shaking him, an act that had his guard unhappily considering whether they should lower their spears, but wisely none acted. They were aware of my troopers who growled and drew down on them.

"Where are they now?" I demanded.

The buffoon shook his head. "They asked for the slave pens," his eyes rolling sideways in their direction.

"That way. With me," I was swinging astride my horse as I shouted.

We found the brigand Moel trying to hide in the crowd gathered on the beach, where the impaled Jute and broken ships had attracted half the town. The questions took only a few minutes. He denied taking Guinevia captive, denied misusing her, denied killing my men. I simply waved at the stolen packhorses tethered nearby. He'd found them wandering. Disgusted, I turned to where his men stood, sullen and afraid.

"What do you say?" I asked the nearest.

He nodded his head. "It was a robbery, lord. I never hurt the women." The others looked away as my gaze travelled over them. Guilty. I gave Moel the same chance he'd given my men from ambush: none.

"Kneel, you cowardly, lying bastard," I told him. Then I hacked off his head with Exalter. Three blows. It must have hurt.

With that sight to encourage them and concentrate their minds, the other brigands could not wait to tell what they knew, but the only knowledge I craved was where were Guinevia, my son and the nurse? From the eager babble it came clear. Some Suehans had bought the women and child, had taken a boat and had sailed north. The next question was where were the bodies of my soldiers? They described the ambush site poorly, and I thought grimly that the ravens would probably have to be our guides. The beach had emptied of onlookers by then, so we executed three of the other four kidnappers mercifully, each with a single upward thrust under the ribs, with the simple wrist-twist that guarantees the kill. We spared one to take us to the place where our soldiers had died, bound him and tied him on a horse. Then we moved on. There was no time to waste, I had to find a ship in which to sail after the fugitives. Had I known it, I need not have bothered. Grimr and his crew were coming ashore a mere handful of miles up the coast.

The Suehans had launched their ship, rowing past the floating body of Web, at which Grimr spat contemptuously, and had hardly cleared a line of sandbanks when it all began to go wrong. The outgoing tide was falling from the north, but the flow around the big offshore island made opposing currents in the strait, creating a clash of overfalls and whirlpools. The ship was barely under way into the stream, with many of the crew still fumbling to make room with the cargo and weapons, and only a few at the oars to give it steerage way. There were just two of the crew attempting to put up a sail and the steersman could not see clearly past the half-hoisted sheet.

It had to happen, and it did. The contra-flowing currents caught the ship and ran it broadside onto rocks hidden just below the surface of the falling tide. Holed at once below the waterline, the ship began filling as if someone had diverted a mountain torrent into it.

Grimr cursed, bullied his men to the oars and ordered the steersman to head for the beach before they all drowned. The mainland was less than a quarter mile away, and he turned in that direction. An alert sailor grabbed a couple of cloaks and leaned over the ship's side to fother them across the broken strakes, partly plugging the hole and successfully reducing the incoming torrent.

Other crew men frantically bailed with helmets, pots and anything to hand, and the current, which was flowing at the pace of a trotting horse, was kind and carried them inshore before they swamped. The Suehans gratefully waded the last 20 yards ashore, gasping and relieved, then began to drag their ship up onto the rippled sand after them.

And I saw them do it.

When we left the disabled ships of the Jutes, I had ridden to the town gates and questioned the frightened guard captain again. The nearest boats for pursuit, he said, would be that way, where some fishermen lived. North. I shouted for outriders, and set off, with my big hounds Axel and Javelin loping alongside as if we were going hunting, which we were.

After only a few miles, we rode up a bluff and had a fine view of the strait, right to the vast sandbanks that guard it from the open sea. There below us was the half-hoisted sail of a longship whose belly was alive with frantic men, and the vessel was sluggishly heading for shore. 'Mithras!" I muttered. "There will be justice and a red blade again, today." And we galloped our horses to deliver that fate.

Arthur's 40 horsemen were too much for the staggering Suehans. They'd been drinking, were half-drowned and they were now exhausted from their frantic efforts to row their sinking ship to safety. They had dragged the vessel partly up the sand, but few had retrieved their weapons from it, nor had they seen the Britons galloping in from the shelter of the dunes until they were almost on them. It would not even be a contest, Grimr thought bitterly as he spotted the oncoming cohort. He was busy carrying to shore the semi-conscious nurse he so shortly before had loaded onto his ship when the horsemen encircled his band.

"Down, bloody well kneel down!" he yelled at his confused crew. Twice, fucking twice, he thought. He'd be a captive again. He looked up into the sun as he put the nurse onto the sand. The big, bearded soldier with the heavily-scarred cheek, badge of office and a massive long sword in his fist was off his horse and moving at him, but the man ignored the Suehan to peer down at the girl.

"Where's the other one, and the child?" I said. My mood was such that if this pirate had blinked the wrong way he'd have empty shoulders. He looked up at me from the sand, dislike and disappointment shading across his face. He jerked his head at the half-foundered ship. "Still in there. We didn't get the 'Welcome Back' greetings yet." I was in the shallows, crippled foot or not, and over the side into the hull. Guinevia was there, unconscious but alive. I paused to take it in. She was laid comfortably on some packs, with a nested cloak alongside, and I could see Milo there, open-eyed, snug and contentedly quiet.

It was the work of minutes to lift them out and carry them to the windbreak of the dunes, to herd the Suehans under guard and to secure the area. When I was convinced by the nurse that the still-sleeping Guinevia was in no critical state, I walked over to our captives. Grimr stood up, causing a sentry to twitch his spear point in threat, but I waved the man away.

"You are the lord of these men." It was a statement, though it could have been a question, because the Suehan was not wearing any accoutrements of note. The fellow nodded. "You bought my wife from a slaver." Another statement. Another nod. "What did you plan?"

He shrugged. "She was a purchase. I may have sold her, I might have ransomed her, had I known about you."

Honest at least. "Who placed her in your boat? Who wrapped the child?"

Another shrug. "Not me," he said. "I carried the other one."

I thought for a moment. "You did not abuse them, someone cared for them."

He squared his shoulders. "We are not Gauls. We do not wage war on children. I may have sold them on, but I did not set out to steal them and we did not abuse them."

It made me chew my lip. He had done neither more nor less than I would have done.

I'd decapitated the brigand who stole my lover and child, and who had killed my men; this man had no part of that. And, he and his men could be useful.

"I shall buy her back from you for what you paid," I said, then corrected myself. "The three of them. And, I am reclaiming my goods from the pack horses. I will not take your lives if you swear allegiance to me. I will keep my word. I am Arthur Britannicus, I am imperator of Britain and you will join my force honourably if you swear to it. You will have to fight, but at least you will live. And, I shall reward you and your men with land and silver for your service."

The Suehan sighed. "My name is Iacco Grimr," he said heavily. "It seems I have a new lord, and I shall be your man." There on the beach, he knelt to put his hands between mine, to kiss the hilt of Exalter and to swear fealty. And there on the beach, I promised to have his ship rebuilt and to send him to sail it freely, but at my command. Then I took my troopers back to Segontium to capture the disarmed Jutish raiders who had been stranded. Some would join our ranks, the rest could be sold as slaves. Grimr and his men got very drunk that night.

XVIII Obsidian

Guinevia sat in Myrddin's courtyard in a patch of bright sunshine and paid little attention to the familiar white Rat dozing opposite in a shaded corner. In the several months since she had been brought here from the old fort at Segontium, her body had healed, and her wounded mind was recovering too, helped by the time she was able to spend with her small son. He at least had survived unharmed the nightmares of her kidnap and abuse, and as her sleeping hours grew less troubled, she increasingly felt peace and ease, and the flow of her powers returning.

She thought often of Arthur, who was back in Chester. He had brought her to Myrddin as the wizard had foreseen and left her with the baby's nurse and Myrddin's house slaves to be restored to health. Arthur, grim-faced and vengeful, buried what the ravens had left of his two murdered soldiers on a hilltop near the ambush site and hunted down Moel's kin, taking them to Chester to be sold as slaves. He gave the silver they brought to the families of the two dead troopers and told them of the land they now owned that had once belonged to the clan of Moel. The brigand who guided them escaped while the Britons were burying their dead, and Arthur had no time to spare to hunt him down. Another time, he sighed. Maybe the gods willed it.

In the past few days, Guinevia had felt a returning interest in her magic, and had begun working with the dark sorcerer to learn more, and to increase her powers as a Druid and pagan witch. Because of her distance from Arthur, she had put focus on sending out her mind's eye to distant places, in hopes of seeing her lover. Myrddin had encouraged her, and had tutored her in the technique.

"First, you must believe it is not wrong to succeed in this task," he told her. "It is a gift from the gods, and it can be used for good or evil, but that is a choice only you can make. It is best done with a helper, someone to record what you say, and it is also good to do this in a quiet, calm place without distraction."

Guinevia learned to relax and somehow will her mind towards the person or place she wanted to view. Then she spoke aloud what she saw, sometimes sketching in charcoal on a thin shaving of wood, or on a piece of vellum. She learned to say exactly what she saw: 'Large and green, leafy' and not to interpret it at that stage as 'tree' or 'bush.' She found that with practice, she could feel the wind, smell the grasses and view a site from the vantage of an eagle, from above, or even to come close enough to see the grain of the wood in a piece of furniture.

Distance was no boundary to her viewing, but although she heard natural sounds such as the soughing of the wind in the trees, she could not hear the words spoken by the people she sometimes saw. She was able to visit and view Arthur as he wrote on papers by rushlight, at his mensa in Chester. She saw the ruby ring on his finger, as richly red as a bubble of blood, and heard the crackle of the wood in the fire. Sometimes, as she viewed him, he would raise his head from his task and look intently around, seeking to see or hear something half-sensed. Once or twice, she saw his mouth move in speech, but she could not hear what he said.

As she practised, her remote viewing became easier and she found that sometimes, especially if she put her impressions down as sketched images, she could send her mind abroad without assistance in recording the fleeting pictures she saw. It became a daily routine, to send her inner eye to Chester to view Arthur; to float it north into the land of the Picts to see how her father was, in his chieftain's compound near the River Tay, or to send it across the Narrow Sea to look at the lost citadel of Bononia, where the Romans were again masters.

Myrddin was impressed by his pupil's ability to view afar, and produced some of the aids he used in his own work: a looking glass of highly-polished silver, made by Romans, a square of obsidian he said had come from a north country of ice and fire and spouting mountains, and a curious spiralling mirror whose back was coated in an amalgam of quicksilver.

He handed Guinevia the obsidian and asked her to look into it. She viewed some smoky half-images that seemed to move.

"It's hard to tell," she said.

The sorcerer nodded. "Use this, watch until you feel drawn into it, then look into the obsidian." The enchantress looked into the whirling black depths of the spiral mirror, and soon felt as if she were about to fall into a deep and wide cavern. Myrddin recognised the moment and pushed the obsidian slab before her. Her eyes slid into the glistening volcanic glass like a seal into water. Just as clearly as if she were present, she was viewing Arthur, pacing the parapet outside his chamber in Chester. She saw his cloak thrown back over his shoulder, clasped by his amber and silver jarl's badge of office. He was tugging at his jaw, obviously deep in thought as he came towards his invisible, uncanny watcher. He came closer and closer, then vanished as if he'd walked right through her ghost, and Guinevia seemed to zoom back to the sun-speckled room where Myrddin was watching her. "You saw him," he said flatly. "You have the gift." It was a gods' gift, he knew, that one day would save Britain.

She saw me, I found later, just after I had received word through Allectus' spies that a strong Saxon force had established itself on the downlands south of Londinium. My problem was that it was late in the year. By the time I had raised enough of an army to tackle them, we would be in winter snows and frozen mud. In any case, I really did not have the force I needed, not until my cavalry was mounted and trained. We had not long before defeated the Romans in a desperately close battle, and only with an extraordinary coalition of the tribes gathered against their hated, voracious, onetime masters' re-invasion.

At this time of year, the tribes were harvesting, and when that was done, they would be gathering the beasts for the seasonal slaughter and salting of those for which there was insufficient room in the byres, which could not be fed through the long winter. There was no national threat, those tribes would reason, and no sensible chieftain in the remote north or southwest would countenance sending his men to a faraway fight just to expel from the lands of the Cantii some fairly harmless settlers, as they would see them. Let the Cantii fight their own battles, would be the reaction, it's only a bit of land.

I sighed as I paced the parapet, the resting hounds raising their eyes from their paws each time I came near them. My choices were limited, and the best of them seemed to be to leave the Saxons alone for the winter while my cavalry was trained. Spring would be soon enough to take the horsemen to the killing fields, to face the fur-clad warriors with their fearful seax swords and double-bladed axes. I grieved for the new widows of the southeast and for the fresh-turned soil of the long graves there, where their menfolk rested, but I had to consider that even for war and battle, there is a season.

In Wales the weeks went by and Myrddin tutored his pupil Guinevia in the religious mysteries of the sacred oak and mistletoe, of potions to heal and poisons to kill, of the fungi that brought on prophetic dreams and of the solemn rites of human and animal sacrifice that made power flow through conduits like her silver pentagram ring.

"We are all immortal," he told her. "The gods view a sacrifice as receiving an honoured guest. It is not cruel, it is a respectful gift of a life to gods who will welcome the one you sacrifice. Important ceremonies require important gifts, and we often joyfully release our most favoured people, the sons and daughters of kings, to go early from this life to the feasting halls of the gods.

"In turn," the enchanter explained, "the gods send some of their power to us Druids, for we are the conduits between man and the afterlife. You need to create and open these channels to yourself," he continued. "I will not always be here, and there is a great deal of work to do. As an adept, and my acolyte, you must be as powerful as possible, to help accomplish what we have to do."

Myrddin was speaking as the living incarnation of generations of Celtic power that stretched to Britain from faraway Dalmatia. His was the voice of Britain's oldest deities, the gods of mountains, forests and rivers, and especially of the sea god Manannan mac Lir, who was Myrddin's personal great deity. The sorcerer explained himself calmly, almost casually: "I am the son of no father. The old gods sent a demon to sire me on a king's daughter so they could restore their hold on Britain. That was broken by these Christ-followers, which is a pity, because we would allow their new god to join our old ones, but they insist there can only be one deity. It's why Rome has persecuted them for not recognizing their Augustus and it will only get worse."

Guinevia nodded. She knew the Christ people were traitors because they said theirs was the only god, and refused to acknowledge the Augustus emperor as one, so furious Rome had killed their stubborn selves in thousands. She had heard of crucifixions, of men being thrown to beasts, of drownings, mutilations and burnings, but could not understand any of it. But there was a distraction.

Myrddin told her: "An important man is coming, and will be here soon." How he knew was beyond the knowledge of ordinary men, but he looked into the volcanic glass each day, and he saw the future, or the present that was still to come.

XIX Magi

Just a few days later, an unusual group processed up the misty pass, dark-complected men, hawk-nosed and black-eyed, shivering despite their layers of fur and wool.

"They are," Myrddin said smug as always when his predictions came true, "men of Assyria, men from the birthplace of mankind." And so they were, except for two of the party who had come even further than the legendary land between the Tigris and Euphrates rivers. They were bronze-black men from the eastern shores of a great land south of Carthage, in Afri, called Ophir, or Saphir, a land of precious stones, much gold and a prized, scented wood called algum. Those two brought ivory and cedar wood as gifts, had tales of cats bigger than horses and of river horses that lived under water and could swallow a man. In their own land, they were great sorcerers, Myrddin knew, and they had come – a great compliment – to this small and misty northern island to confer with him.

Guinevia was also honoured by them, as women held high rank in learning in the libraries of Aegyptus, and Myrddin had also made plain that she was his acolyte and prized pupil. In turn, as she healed, she learned some of their magic, and heard of the wonders they had seen, from the mountain-shaped gardens of Nineveh, which they said hung in the sky like clouds and were the great work of their king Sennacherib.

"To see it, you must sail beyond the sunset," they told her, a concept that made her marvel. There are, she asked timidly, lands beyond the sunset? The magi understood. We have come from a fine city called Ephesus, they told her gently, a place dedicated to the fertility goddess Artemis, and it is so famed that the harbour is always crowded with a hundred or more ships from all over, pilgrims who come to seek the goddess' blessing. Travel, they explained was less dangerous, easier even, in the relative calms of what the Romans arrogantly called Our Sea, but which others called the Midland Sea. One day, you will travel on its calm waters and warm zephyrs and see the fine temples and palaces.

The wise men spoke, too, of mystical things and practical things, of spells and potions and charms, of medicine and of long watercourses to bring rivers to cities, and a bronze screw that could raise that water hundreds of arm-spans high. They told of Sennacherib's enormous palace, its steps studded with precious stones, its statues of alabaster and its roofs covered in gold leaf. They explained how, centuries before dung-stinking Rome had brought water to itself, the shining limestone city of Nineveh had channelled crystal-clear waters in aqueducts to every street. But the gods had not been kind. In one short day, they had shaken the city to rubble, collapsing great buildings, killing people, causing fires and plague. Now that fabled city of hanging gardens, gold and alabaster was ruined.

It was, the magi said, their duty to find how to placate their gods, to collect the knowledge they needed to restore their civilization. So these scholars had travelled long, hard months to find the wise men who could help. In turn, they shared knowledge the Assyrians had learned of star patterns and readings, of times when the sun would be eaten by the moon, of tides and weather, omens and prophecies. They brought a bewildering mass of knowledge, some of it gleaned from ancient lore, some of it from far travels. They had met men who travelled the Silk Routes, which were a variety of travellers' roads from the farthest lands of the East, even beyond the wood and rammed-earth wall that forms the boundary of the land of the imperial Qin dynasty. These travellers had exchanged knowledge and goods, so they had learned of a demon-defeating technique the Qinese called 'exploding bamboo,' or 'baozhu'.

The orientals who shared their secrets said their priests had known of this for several hundred years. By making a mix of kitchen ingredients and packing it into a bamboo tube, the package made a combustible fire dragon that could later be ignited to scare off ghosts and evil spirits in a shower of sparks and explosions. Myrddin was especially intrigued by this, and the wise men worked with him to detail those ingredients, salt petre, charcoal and sulphur, and their correct quantities so he could create some of the mix. The magician had an idea to build a flying chair with what he realized could be a new propellant, and vanished for days into his workroom. He took his experimenting outside soon after an incident when his bushy eyebrows were scorched off, and began a week of open air trials that sorely tested the calm of his flock of sheep.

Guinevia had little interest in the smoking, fizzing, exploding fire drakes Myrddin created, but she talked at length with the visitors. She earned their respect as an adept practitioner of the art of divination by examining the entrails of a sacrifice, and the men from Nineveh and Assur told how their priests had created mazes to represent the entrails of animals. These were useful in divining medical problems, or to determine crop planting times, and their ancient library held texts of divination from centuries before, but their sacrifices were always of animals. Guinevia, a practitioner of hepatoscopy, or the art of reading entrails, was able to tell them how she had sacrificed human men and how their auguries differed from the animal ones of the Mesopotamians.

She told of the gross mule trader she had once had disembowelled and how the shape and position of his liver had matched exactly those of a hog, but his colon's odd colour had warned of the near-death of her emperor, a precise omen she had never seen in an animal sacrifice.

"The gods must have appreciated us sending a human to them," she concluded, "and they spared my lord."

The exchanges were valuable, and Guinevia soaked it up, but she retired nightly with her brain reeling. Dazed or not, she learned and retained and absorbed and quantified as the winter came on and Myrddin's now-crowded house became a college of sorcerers. Happily for Guinevia, she had small Milo for comfort. He helped her both to heal from her ordeal and to fix in her mind what she had learned each day. In the evenings, when the braid-bearded men of the east put their foreheads close and talked with Myrddin, she would slip away to her small son and tell him what the day had brought. Her fierce determination to learn, to absorb this astonishing knowledge of a secretive priesthood drove out the painful memories, and recounting the day's doings to small Milo clarified them in her agile mind. As the months passed, she had an astounding education put in front of her, and she retained it.

Not too long before, Guinevia had been a bruised and bloodied captive. Now, her powers were increased dramatically. She had become a potent sorceress who casually used small magics, and owned channels through which she could access some very powerful and elemental forces for good, or evil, too, should she choose that road. She had paid the high price of learning with the agony required of a full divine, and had been tempered in her own mental fires. Now, the time was coming for her to make the journey back to the fortress of her emperor to practise her dark arts. Whether she would use them for good or for ill, to take revenge on men like those who had tormented her was still in question. A thought flickered across her mind. One of those brutes who had abused her and threatened the life of her child was still alive. He had escaped when his village was sacked and his kin were sent into slavery. But he still lived, unpunished. In the once-clear mind of the sorceress from beyond the Wall of Hadrian, where memories are long and inherited feuds run deep, a dark stream now ran. And somewhere, a malicious demon stirred inside her.

XX Corvus

Behind them on the hillside was an ancient tribal symbol, the giant white figure of a horse, made centuries before from trenches cut and filled with crushed chalk. It was a fine sight but the tribunes Cragus and Lycaon had no eyes for it. In front of them on the rolling grassland was a corral, raw new wood gleaming in the sunshine, containing a horse herd of about 100 animals. They were grazing, standing quiet. All, that is, except two young stallions that were stamping and snorting, posturing and baring their teeth at each other as they began a contest for leadership.

"Best separate them two, sirs," said a cavalry decurion, an auxiliary of the northern Brigantes tribe. He was a grizzled old soldier who had been recruited by the Romans, served his time, retired when his legion left for Gaul and had recently been unwillingly swept up from his comfortable, illegal life as a horse trader.

"Er, yes, sergeant," Lycaon said, wondering how on earth he was to dominate a great brute of horseflesh equipped with teeth and hooves and with its mind on sex and fighting. The decurion looked morosely at the two tribunes.

"Ah'll do it, sirs," he sighed in a gust of stale wine breath.

"Would you, please?" drawled Cragus, unconvincingly pretending he himself was on the verge of stepping up to the task. The decurion gave him a disbelieving look from a face as hard as a hoof.

"Aye, happen I might," he said, taking a length of rope from the rail and stepping into the corral. The two tribunes watched in awe when the soldier walked up to the two pawing stallions. "Piss off, you," he snarled at one horse, flicking a hand at the stallion he judged was losing the blustering match. The animal backed away, but its opponent was not going so quietly.

As the decurion strode up to it, the horse reared, pawing the air with its hoofs. The soldier acted as if this was an everyday event, which for him it might well have been, stepped up between the horse's flailing legs and reached upwards with his right hand. As the surprised stallion began to come down, he seized its muzzle in a particular way and to the officers' astonishment brought the beast directly and easily to its knees.

The soldier stood above the humbled stallion, still gripping its muzzle somehow, and spoke to it. Then, after a long minute, he released the horse. It staggered to its feet and stood, head down, quivering. The decurion casually looped the rope around its neck and led it quietly to the rail, where he tied it. "Let t'bugger think on it for a few minutes," he said cryptically.

Cragus, all pretence of equine expertise abandoned, looked slack-jawed at the soldier. "How the devil did you…?" he said, his voice tailing off.

"Ah," said the decurion, "tha puts thy fingers up t'nostrils as they come down. Makes their eyes water a bit, then you tell 'em that if they boogers you about onny more there's lots where that come from. They allus listen." He turned back to the tethered horse and released the loop of rope. "Right, cock," he said, smacking the horse on the rump, "off tha goes, and behave."

Cragus looked at the soldier carefully. No disrespect, just casual competence. "Stop by my adjutant when you're done," he said, "and tell him to give you a skin of the Rhenish wine from my store. Tell him to make it the good stuff, you've done well."

For the first time since he'd been drafted from his cushy billet and his woman in Colchester, the decurion grinned. "Aye, sir, thanks," he said. "Ah will."

Lycaon nodded to his fellow tribune. "With operators like that, we'll have a cavalry faster than Arthur thinks," he said. "Now, did you say you had more than one wineskin in that wretched hovel of yours?" The pair sat and wrangled happily over their Rhenish, discussing progress and plans for their horse breeding and training program.

So far, matters were going well enough. Cragus' recruitment efforts had paid off, with 180 or so horse guards recruited who were experienced in equine husbandry, and a steady trickle of recruits was still arriving from south of the Wall, where once the Romans had maintained a cavalry force of about 800 men. Many of those horse soldiers were Sarmatians or their descendants, some of the 5,500 hostages taken from their homeland and stationed in Britain a century before. They lived, as they always had, in carriages not in houses, even after they were given land grants, and seemed to spend all their waking hours on horseback.

"Those fellows," said Lycaon, who'd recruited a contingent from Ribchester where horse farms were noted as immune to the depredations of wolves, "those fellows ready their horses for long journeys by withholding their fodder the day before they go, and only allowing them a little water. Even Pliny knew of it. He said they could ride 150 miles non-stop with such preparation."

The two Friesian stallions Corvus and Nonios that Lycaon had spirited out of Gaul were at stud, carefully separated in pens at opposite ends of the paddock and the tribunes thought that a number of mares were already pregnant. Meanwhile, the task of taming and training the wild horses was well under way and already 50 or more cavalrymen were mounted and working with their steeds, wheeling, forming and reforming in squadrons. Several dozen cavalrymen were working with foot soldiers, having the infantrymen hang on alongside their stirrups, taking great bounds and leaps as the horsemen cantered towards the 'enemy' lines. The tactic was a successful one to deliver a surprise attack, fast, for the arrival of infantry right behind the shattering shock of a cavalry charge was almost guaranteed to break an enemy line.

The tribunes nodded approval. "By spring, we'll have a viable cavalry force," said Lycaon contentedly. The duo strolled out of Cragus' quarters to view a decurion who was demonstrating the correct way to knot up a horse tail to prevent it being grabbed by an enemy in combat. "You also braid the mane, to stop all that loose hair getting in your way if you're a horse archer, or if you're swinging a sword or pointing a lance," he declared.

Cragus saw that the horse on which the decurion was demonstrating had a bloody handprint painted onto the shoulder. He nudged his companion to draw his attention to it.

"It's a Celt thing," said Lycaon. "It's to bring fortune in battle. The story is that a bloodied, dying Celtic hero gave his horse a last, farewell pat and left his handprint on there. He was such a hero, the groom never cleaned the blood away and soon all the warriors imitated the decoration." Lycaon turned away. "We'd better get a report together for Arthur," he said. "Herd management, halter training, remounts, horse archer equipment, forage bags, he wants to know the status of everything. Bring those lists of yours, would you?"

XXI Candless

The bishop stood on the rampart that was once the northernmost boundary of the Roman Empire, and looked south into Britain. He had climbed to the top of a watchtower on the 74-mile stone wall built at the orders of Publius Aelius Hadrianus, but even though the tower was many times a man's height above the berm and deep defensive ditch of the Entrenchment, he could see only mist and cloud. On a fine day, unlike this one in the month of Mars, he knew he would have been able to view miles into the rolling countryside where shepherds watched for wolves and eagles, and for raiders like himself.

This bishop was no ordinary cleric. He looked the part: he wore a surplice and wide leather belt. He assumed the tonsure and, on a gold chain around his neck, wore the tau-rho looped cross of a follower of Christ, but he also hung a well-used gladius sword on his hip, and kept a punching knife discreetly out of sight under his cloak. Beneath his tunic, on his shoulder was the tribal tattoo that marked him as a Painted One, a Pict, and his startling blue eyes and fair hair attested to a long-ago Scand ancestor.

Bishop Candless was born in Dunbar, beside the sea forth where the Votadini buckled the belt at Pictland's waist. He had fought the British when they took the steep-sided clifftop fortress that controlled the valley of the Forth. He had seen his king, Alpin, killed by a lucky bolt from a ballista there and he had finally been forced to flee the legions when they had outflanked and surprised the Damnoni with a makeshift floating bridge across an 'unpassable' sea inlet.

Candless was not a bishop in those days, he was a maddened howling warrior with bare chest and whirring blade, but the invaders had rolled up the tribes, sent coffles of slaves to the southern markets and burned the settlements of the Painted Ones.

Candless had gone on the run. While making his way near the crumbled timber-and-turf relics of the Antonine Wall, high tide mark of the empire, he had come across a cleric on a mule and had elected to relieve him of the responsibilities of both office and wealth. Rather than be spotted as an escapee of the last rout, he had assumed the cleric's robe, money purse and animal and had in turn been received well as a holy man. With scant Latin, an engaging manner and a newly-shaved head, he began a successful career as a mendicant, seeking food, shelter and frequent comfort in return for his prayers. He modestly let it be known that the faithful believers, and only they, could sometimes see the blessed nimbus that surrounded his saintly pate, and a few declared that indeed it was visible.

"Somf," he would say to his congregants, "et pax," using a mix of invention and pig Latin on blessings they all received humbly and offering indulgences to some of the female congregants that they especially enjoyed.

Now he was looking for his next opportunity, but was foiled by the mist. The bishop grunted in disappointment. Nothing to see. He climbed laboriously back down from the milecastle's tower and strolled to where three men waited with horses.

"Customs post. Long time since they were here to collect taxes, eh?" one of the men said, nodding to where the outline of a fortification marked the ground. "They were good at taking. They even took all this – timbers, stones, the lot." Standard practice, thought Candless, who was no military fool. When they moved on, the Romans removed everything for use elsewhere and sealed the ground with a layer of clay and turf. They left nothing for the enemy. He didn't bother to tell his brigands, just grunted at the comment. He had other things on his mind.

I too had plenty on my mind. One of the regular couriers from Segontium had travelled by Myrddin's house to gather news of the sorcerer and of Guinevia, and I heard that she was planning to be back in Chester soon. My problem was that I was in Londinium overseeing improvements to the Saxon Shore fortifications and chivvying the chieftains of the Catuvellauni and Tribantes clans. I wanted them to support the overmatched Cantii to push back the Saxons who were establishing themselves in that tribe's territory on the Downs. The invaders had already seized a couple of small hamlets and two valuable iron ore quarries, and their roaming bands of marauders were a threat to travellers to Dover and Chichester. So far, they had not menaced any major settlements, but that was just a question of time. I needed that tribal cooperation, and I needed to muster my troops soon, especially to have my cavalry at training.

It was early spring, the weather would be right in a few weeks, and once the barley and wheat crops were planted I could call territorial forces away from their gardens and grain fields to supplement my soldiers. The balancing act was a delicate one. Just as we waited for fair weather to release our farmer-soldiers, so too did the Saxons wait, for then they would be reinforced by the ships that brought warriors with their land-hungry settlers. The farmers wanted a place to grow their crops and their families, so they hired soldiers to help them establish a foothold, and the warriors came for the rape and loot. For the Britons, the result was the same. They lost their lives or their land, and in many cases their freedom vanished in unhappy circumstances, too. Fair-skinned females and children brought a premium in the slave markets of the south.

Also on my mind was the growing threat from north of the Wall. I'd sent an expeditionary force up there a few years ago. They'd taken the great fortress on the rock above the Forth more by good fortune than anything, but a smart move had outflanked the next force of Picts and then it was just a question of marching down the old line of Roman garrisons and mopping up the rebels. Evidently time had worked its usual healing on memory and the Picts had forgotten their punishment, for reports were coming to me of raids across the old Wall, of citizens taken into slavery, homes and crops burned and flocks driven off.

A courier stamped into my quarters, dust-covered, sweat-stinking and streaked with horse spume. He saluted the old way, fist to heart, and handed over a soft leather pouch that had been sewn closed, then sealed with wax. I looked him over. He was young and he looked very tired.

"Where have you come from?" I asked as I picked up a small knife and sliced the stitching.

"From Chester, lord," he said, still at attention.

"Relax, fellow," I said, "that's a long ride."

"Two days, lord, I was told to make speed," he said proudly. I looked up sharply. "Watling Street, lord," he said in explanation. "The mansios and staging posts are very good."

The dispatch rider referred to the hostelries and stables at regular intervals along the road that bisected Britain. A government rider with authority could change horses every dozen miles, constantly riding a fresh mount, to bring important news at incredible speed. This dispatch had to be vital. It was.

I recognized at once my steadfast Guinevia's clear hand and school-grammar-correct Latin. The message was brief. In one of her seer's meditations, she had sent her mind to view her father at his compound on the River Tay, near Bertha. This town was the ultimate limit of the Roman empire, the place where the Picts had forced Rome's legions to a halt. Since then all kings of the Picts had been crowned there, seated on a sacred stone of authority, and the place had become a symbolic centre of resistance to their southern neighbours. It was also a running sore for me.

The Picts had broken every treaty we'd made, they'd made their promises, taken the concessions and then continued to raid and plunder south of the Wall, taking hundreds of Britons into slavery, driving off the herds and burning crops, settlements and farms. I'd overlooked their non-payment of agreed tributes but they had taken the gesture as weakness and had become insolent, and now, a threat.

What Guinevia saw had caused her heart to crack. Her father was in discussion with four other Pictish chieftains, all of whom she knew, for she had once acted as my ambassador and had gathered their solemn oaths of peace while we fought the Roman invasion. Now she was viewing them plotting, but worse was to come. The man with whom they were dealing was my own treasurer and tribune, the wolfish Allectus, disguised in the habit of a Christian monk.

As she observed from her faraway chamber, she saw the traitor hand over my legate's fustis, the baton of office I had received from the Emperor Persicus himself. It was a stolen token that he would be ruler once I was deposed. She saw the chart Allectus laid before the five chiefs. On it, they sketched the divisions they would make of the lands they would take while I was engaged with the Saxons in the south. Lastly, she saw them each make a cut in the palms of their hands, then clasp them in brotherhood. A blood oath, a mingling of life forces, and all of it against me. I crumpled the scroll with its report of treachery and threw it into the fire. Allectus had shaken hands on his own death warrant, but how was I to serve it? I had to return to Chester and take up the reins before I became an executioner's victim. What they planned, I did not know. I could guess they would join forces to confront me. If I acted quickly, I could meet them separately, with the reduced forces I had available in the north. They might be sufficient, or they might not, but I did not dare to draw other forces to meet them. I could not ignore the huge threat of the Saxons, which was growing by the week.

It was a deadly game of chess, and I would send my mounted knights to hold the Saxons while I took my foot soldier pawns north, to crush the Picts. And, I swore to myself, I'd have the head of that treacherous cleric Allectus. He would be a bishop removed from the chequerboard, thanks to my queen and her magic. I had no inkling of what that vision had cost her.

XXII Piddock

Matters moved as swiftly as the couriers I sent out from Londinium. I summoned Guinevia urgently back to Chester, where I was going to be very soon, for I needed the information she could gather from her psychic spying. I ordered the cavalry tribunes to move their forces from the training grounds near Aquae Sulis to Londinium. They should be readied for action on the southern downlands which favoured their movements and which were where the Saxons were gathering. The Narrow Sea fleet that was based in Portus Chester, where it could take advantage of double tides each day, I ordered moved to Dover to intercept and sink incoming Saxons before they set foot on Britain.

I gambled on the security of the west country, and moved most of the garrison at Caerleon north to Chester, where they would re-equip and continue north to the western end of the Wall. There, they would join the strong force which I had already dispatched from Chester. Meanwhile, apart from a small garrison to hold the fortress, the troops at Eboracum were to cross the Wall at its eastern end, scout the dispositions of the rebel Picts and form a pincer with the combined legions from Chester and Caerleon.

The movements would strip our western garrisons nearly bare, but we could put horses and ships against the Saxons in the southeast, and catch the Picts in the north between a crushing hammer and immovable anvil. The rest was in the hands of the gods. I just hoped they were listening, I thought morosely as I hastened back to Chester. Events seemed to show that they were not.

It was a long and bloody summer of fire and sword. The British fleet took a bad battering, but it turned back a wave of ironclad Saxons, and many brave men struggled and drowned in their armour as the longships sank in the straits. The Suehan sea raider Grimr, who was now serving Arthur, distinguished himself time and again. By chance, it was his ship that caught and engaged the galley of the Jute Alaric, the man who had found Grimr stranded on a Frisian island. Alaric wanted revenge for the death of his commander Web and led his raiders in a mead-maddened charge over the gunwale, killing the Suehan captain Bjalf in the first moments of the battle, but Grimr's men had prevailed and vengefully took no captives that day. Alaric died hardest, drowned slowly on the end of a rope towed behind their ship, but his was not the last death that day.

When the invaders' flotilla turned back, Grimr followed them at a distance and after dark, sent a fireship into their fleet. It destroyed four ships, took a score of lives and blunted the Saxons' willingness to sail against us again at any time in the near future.

On the downlands, the cavalry tribunes Lycaon and Cragus had some success, too. They shattered a Saxon shield wall with their charging line of horses and their tactic of racing infantry to the attack as they clung to the cavalry steeds, but the relatively raw equestrian force had not inflicted the heavy casualties needed to inflict a decisive loss on the Saxons. Equally, the British infantry was a force too small to take on the greater numbers of invaders. The weeks of skirmishes ended without conclusion, but the fleet's victories meant at least that the Saxon threat did not grow, and each land encounter left the cavalry more experienced and confident.

In the north, the pincer movement failed. The nimble Picts escaped Arthur's trap, retreating quickly into the heather before they could be surrounded, and although Arthur's troops took a number of captive Votadini, the tribes dispersed to fight another day. Worse, Allectus had learned through his spy network of Guinevia's viewing of his treachery, and suspected her father the chieftain of betrayal.

In vengeance Allectus executed him by boiling him alive. The seer had seen and felt her father's agonizing death, and it had driven her to near-madness. She had survived the kidnap of herself, her nurse and her son. She had witnessed the deaths of her guards, and survived that. However, the serpent of vengeance that had been dormant had stirred when she learned that one of the kidnappers who had abused her was still alive. Her bruised mind that had once rejected the idea of vengeance was changed when she saw the images of her father, her own beloved father, dying in agony in a boiling cauldron.

The men who plotted against her lover Arthur had condemned him as a traitor and had given him an unbearable death. Guinevia could not take this latest horror. She did not know if her father had betrayed Arthur, but she knew his fellow chieftains had certainly betrayed him. She knew too, that treachery was rampant. Arthur had been betrayed by Allectus his treasurer, and she herself had been stolen and abused brutally. The game was cruel, so she could be cruel also. She would, she decided, use her new power to exact punishment.

The once-gentle Druid became fearsome in her quest for vengeance, and turned to the old druidical ways of sacrifice. She slaughtered a Pictish slave as offering to her witch goddess Nicevenn and swore to give that leader of the Wild Hunt the heart of Allectus in return for his death. A coldness had permeated her once-generous spirit, and the only time Guinevia seemed to be her old self was when she cradled her child, crooning and murmuring, but Arthur was dismayed to overhear just what blood-freezing promises she was making to the toddler, and wondered for his lover's sanity.

Elsewhere in Britain, the Hibernian raider Muirch Iron Sword, who had persuaded his crew to allow three women warriors into their raiding party, had joined forces with the brigand bishop Candless and his troop after confronting them at the sack of a coastal abbey.

Candless had arrived from the landward side, drawn by the smoke plume of burning farm buildings. He walked into the yard where Muirch had the abbot stretched across a hurdle. The Gael was beating the churchman's bare backside with the scabbard of his sword to encourage him to reveal where the community's silver was buried.

"Ye'll have to do better than that. We clerics have leather arses and knees from all our pew-polishing and kneeling," Candless called out.

Muirch interrupted the beating, which he was quite enjoying, having during his boyhood endured a few priest-administered thrashings himself.

"Who are you?" he asked, genuinely astonished that anyone would walk in on a group of raiders. It was even more surprising that the bold intruder was dressed in the habit and cross of a Christian monk, although he noted the fellow did have a useful-looking sword at his hip.

For his part, Candless, while confident that he and his handful of scar-knuckled brawlers could handle any sailors, was equally astonished to see women among the marauders.

The belted bishop ignored Muirch's challenge. "Who," he said, "are these harpies?" His instinct to dismiss the two tall Celts and the diminutive haruspex was a mistake he never repeated. Flame-haired Karay and blonde Jesla both bridled. They easily overtopped Candless as they closed on him, but his eye was taken by the slight figure of Caria the Sybil. She advanced, hissing as she high-stepped towards him, and levelled two fingers directly at his eyes.

"Guard your tongue, monk!" She uttered the warning in a monotone as if reciting a lesson. "Render respect to those who have powers you cannot imagine." Candless stroked his beard as if pondering the problem, then spat derisively on the ground.

"Aye, I'll do that," he said, "as soon as a woman is my master, and when dragons fly out of my arse."

The words were hardly spoken when Karay bludgeoned him on the temple with her swung elbow. The blow dropped him like a sack of grain.

"Pay attention to what she's saying," she said in calm, reasonable tones. "She's helping you." From his position, stunned, supine and with two menacing Amazons looming over him, the bishop saw the force of their argument.

He sighed and nodded. "You have a point there," he mumbled.

That night, as the sea raiders and the bishop's brigands sat around the fire in the abbey's refectory, Muirch and Candless discussed their next move. The two groups had agreed to join forces. The bishop and his men had knowledge of the border country south of the Wall, the raiders had the numbers and the longship that would allow them swifter escapes and greater surprise. Candless nodded at the three women, who were talking together.

"Why bring a witch?" he asked Muirch.

"She can terrify a village into submission all by herself, with magic," said the Hibernian.

"Superstition!" scoffed the bishop, rubbing the iron of his sword hilt as a precaution.

"No," said Muirch, "she really does magic. She even foretells the future. Wait." He walked over and spoke respectfully to the three women and Candless saw the sybil Caria nod, although reluctantly. Moments later, she rose and left the hall, and the matter seemed closed.

An hour later, the incident had escaped Candless' mind and he was concerned with fumbling at the shift of a red-eyed girl who was the recent widow of one of the monks. A booming noise echoed from the refectory ceiling and interrupted his concentration. He looked around to see the sea raiders looking apprehensive, although he noticed that the two Celt women seemed relaxed and were exchanging knowing glances. A movement in the dark doorway caught his eye, and the girl on his lap screamed. A ghostly, glowing figure moved into the room, and a ripple of movement among the men showed they were gripping weapons and touching iron against evil.

Candless squinted through the gloom beyond the firelight and distinguished the slight shape of the seer Caria. Her lips glowed like white fire, streaks of the same eerie luminescence circled her eyes and striped her face and hands. She did not speak, but pointed her fingers, forked and glowing in the semi-dark outside the firelight, right at Candless. The bishop shifted uneasily and she bared glistening bright teeth that shone like moonlight. Then, to his astonishment, she exhaled a cloud of ghostly white flame at him. It hung in the air for seconds before the eerie glow faded to nothing.

Candless shrank away and a mutter of curses and imprecations to one-eyed Odin showed that all in the room were reacting to fear of the unknown. The sybil stayed silent. Without speaking a word, she spun on her heel, arm still outstretched to encompass the crowd. It was a threat or blessing, they did not know which, before she flickered soundlessly through the doorway and disappeared into the darkness outside.

"Did you see that?" the bishop, awed, asked Muirch.

"Aye, seen it before, too," he nodded. "She has some power, that one. She can raise ghosts, she can hear their echoes as they adhere to places, and she's able to turn herself into a part ghost, too. It makes me shrivel, and I did not dare refuse her or the other witches who wanted to come."

Across the room, the two Celt women had their heads together, arms around each other's shoulders, near-helpless with suppressed laughter.

"She's done it again," Jesla spluttered. "A mouthful of crushed clams and you can glow in the dark! Have some piddocks, my dear."

The women laughed. "Even that old Roman Pliny wrote about them and angelwings. They're good to eat and they go luminous like sea foam when you squash them. These stupid, stupid men!"

Karay snorted: "Did you see that she'd smeared her face with the stuff, too? I hope she washes it off before anyone works out the trick."

Jesla laughed again. "That won't happen. The next time I meet an intelligent man will be the first time I ever met one," she said.

XXIII Aqua

For me, the summer had been spent on horseback, shuttling between the Pict campaign and the Saxon one at opposite ends of the kingdom. It was weary work, cantering for hours on end, but the fine roads made it possible to cover long distances in remarkable time. I'd never come close to matching the 500 miles in 24 hours that the emperor Titus once covered to be with his dying brother, but I could ride from Chester to Londinium in less than three days, thanks to relays of horses, good roads and fine summer weather.

And I needed to be in several places, and often. There was much work to do to reinforce the fleet, and as the autumn days drew shorter, bringing misty mornings and chill nights, I gradually drained away the forces opposite the Saxon encampments, relieving them from patrols and skirmishing to return to their holdings, plant their winter crops and ready their beasts for the coming cold.

My campaign tent was pitched on the heights above the Roman camp that guards the crossing of the Medway River, and the sight of the waterway made me consider how close we were to finishing building the Car Dyke. That channel was coming along well, with hundreds of slaves worked on the excavation. It is a waterway that stretches from north of Londinium through Granta to Eboracum, and it would be a vital transport link for the next campaign against the Picts. In the longer term it will help to drain the fenlands and give us valuable crop growing areas, too. Another use is a military one, for it runs alongside the north road and creates a minor defensive line against invaders. I did not then realize just how vital it would become.

Next, my thoughts turned across the Narrow Sea. Our spy network was severely reduced since the traitor Allectus' defection, for he had been my spymaster. An old ally, the Frankish ruler Gennobaudes, who'd been forced to become a subject king of the Emperor Maximian had been useful, and his couriers brought secret dispatches of the Roman's activities. The news was not good. Rome's legions were making progress subduing the Alemanni over the Rhine, and had also inflicted severe punishment on the Visigoth horse tribes beyond the Danube. Gennobaudes warned that Maximian was already planning to recapture his old colony of Britain, and that a threat from a combined force of Danes and Jutes was also brewing. The spring, he warned, would be a dangerous time for me.

I sent Gennobaudes gifts of gold and three couple of hunting dogs with my request to be kept informed of Maximian's shipbuilding efforts, knowing that the emperor would use the shipyards of the Rhine and Meuse where Gennobaudes held sway. I thought I might have success repeating the fireship attack that had crippled a previous Roman fleet there. It would be a question of good timing, to catch as many near-complete vessels as I could, and information would be vital.

Other things were on my mind, too, and one was the sad state of my woman Guinevia. I had seen her only infrequently as I staged through my headquarters in Chester, and her health was poor. She was having nightmares after her kidnap, was a semi-recluse and rarely left a chamber she had created that was lined with mirrors and divining tools, including a deep and dark water tank in whose depths she would seek visions. She claimed she communed with the dead, and had mental converse with Myrddin, her wizard mentor who lived leagues distant. She was slipping away into an occult realm and seemed to be only partly of this world. I thought that maybe a new home would bring her back, and ordered my major domo to create a suitable place for her. He decided to engage as designer the mosaic artist Claria Primanata, with whom Guinevia had bonded in the past, and I sent a silent prayer to the gods to bring back my lover's mind.

Then I had to move to military matters again. I had to find what Allectus was planning, I needed to deal with the increasing raids by the Hibernians, who had sacked a handful of settlements and church holdings south of the Wall. There was, too, unrest among the Christians in the southwest, plus pirates in the Narrow Sea who were preying on our traders, unprotected since the fleet was occupied with the Saxons.

Added to all that, the Cornish Dumnonians were forging an alliance with other Gaels from Hibernia to break the fragile truce I had formed with some of the British tribes. I sighed so gustily that my hounds raised their heads from their paws to see what I was doing. Tomorrow, I'd take horse to Granta, checking on progress of the dyke, then cross the limestone region of central Britain where all this had started, when I had found the lost Eagle in its cavern. I called for an aide to give instructions and arrange an escort for the journey and wondered if I had lost the good fortune the Eagle had brought me. As I eased my weary limbs I did not notice the white Rat crouched in the lee of the tent. That would have brought me comfort. Another long stretch in the saddle, I thought, but maybe the last for a while. I was wrong.

Lycaon had remained with a portion of the cavalry to monitor the Saxons as they began establishing their winter camp northwest of Dover. All seemed quiet, the skirmishing had ended, the season for fighting was over. Cragus had left him, taking the greater part of the horse squadrons back to the training camp in the grasslands south of Aquae Sulis. The grazing there was good and the men could rest and repair in preparation for the depths of winter and the expected spring campaign. Nobody fought in the snow and ice, and the commanders opted to release almost all of the troops to go home and plant the winter wheat, slaughter and salt the beasts they could not keep stabled and tend their holdings. Our decision brought disaster.

I was in Chester when I got the news. Under cover of night, the Saxons had daringly brought a fleet of longships down the Narrow Sea, slipping past our depleted flotilla. A strong force of their warriors had landed and advanced undetected to within a mile of Lycaon's cavalry lines where he watched the Saxon winter quarters. The two sets of invaders had coordinated attacks and our pony soldiers had been caught in a pincer like the one I had recently failed to execute against the Picts. Only a few dozen Britons had escaped, our horses were in the hands of the invaders, Lycaon was a badly-wounded prisoner and the butcher's bill of our dead was lengthy.

Worse, I knew, was that the combined Saxon forces would not be content to huddle in huts on the southeast hills for the winter. They would make the march on Londinium, snow or no snow, take the city and winter in proper buildings, safe behind city walls.

I had to rouse my legions, drag every last cavalryman back from his hearth and home and get them to the Thames. And even then, with my men tired from days of marching, with my cavalry a shadow of itself, there was no guarantee we would be strong enough to defeat the Saxons.

Mentally, I reviewed the chessboard of my forces. A strong contingent was at Eboracum, returned there from the Pict campaign. The problem was one of time. The Saxons were a day's march from Londinium, the troops in Eboracum would take five days to march there, and would arrive exhausted. Then I remembered a successful tactic I'd used in Gaul. I'd deploy soldiers by water.

I'd put as many as I could on barges towed by horses and mules, and race them down the Car Dyke waterway, which was virtually completed. With couriers going ahead to organize relays of beasts, we could move the troops almost nonstop for several days, and have them arrive close to Londinium relatively fresh. My aide Androcles sent those orders at once.

Couriers also sped to Londinium to order as many men as possible to the Medway crossing. I gambled that the Saxons would try to cross the Thames east of London. If we could hold them, delay them at the Medway, we could save the city, but only if the troops from Eboracum arrived in time.

The gods were kind, at last. Eboracum has a good trade on its River Ouse, and we found both watercraft to take us south and beasts to pull the vessels. We stripped the ships down to their shells, loaded our troops and sent them riding a bow wave of water down the length of Britain. The bargees were skilled. They knew that once the horses got up to a canter, the water washing back from the sides of the dyke created a rolling wave on which they could surf their craft, and the troops could be moved effortlessly at far more than their marching pace.

Better still, they only needed to halt every eight or ten miles to change horses, through daylight, night dark, daylight and dark again. It was a magical journey, and I exulted. I had put myself in the lead barge, and to stand in its bows under a three-quarter moon, hearing the thud of the horses as they galloped, watching the white wash of the canal surf, and feeling the rush of wind on my face was exhilarating. I knew we would surprise the enemy with our fantastic speed. We disembarked the men at the end of the Car Dyke, a half day's march north of Londinium, reasonably fresh, without them having had to march a step. It was the most rapid deployment of troops Britain had ever seen, and it was only possible because of the new waterway, and the great road alongside it which let us bring fresh horses and mules to meet us and then race the convoy south.

It would have been a close-run race that we might have lost, but a naval squadron under the Suehan Grimr had spotted the beached longships of the invaders and had burned them, then intelligently sent scouts ashore while he prowled along the coast to find the force which had moved inland. Our sailors could not match the Saxons' numbers, but they did burn their lightly-guarded winter quarters. The smoke from ships and barracks brought a halt to the raiders' advance when some hurried back to protect their loot. Others halted, refusing to go on in case their comrades looted their own treasures, and the whole army ground to a standstill. The delay gave our Londinium troops time enough to hurry to the Medway and establish themselves in the old Roman fort there. By the time the Saxons returned, our troops were ready for them to hold the river crossing. It bought the vital time we needed until our northern troops arrived in Londinium to reinforce the city's defences. Only then did our Medway garrison make a fast retreat to the city, and we slammed the gates shut in the Saxon's faces.

So it was an angry, frustrated group of Saxon war lords who found themselves literally out in the cold. Enough Britons were inside Londinium's city walls to hold them off, more were arriving by the day, and the Saxons' winter quarters and their ships were burned. We did not even have to fight. The invading horde turned aside to find food and shelter, taking with them several score of unfortunates who had not raced for safety quickly enough. We watched the Saxons trudge away to the east and finally, with a sigh of relief, I knew that the winter campaign would not have to happen. The blood, pain and smoke would come with the spring. For now, we could regroup. Once again, I straddled a horse and turned its head to the north.

XXIV Hemlock

Guinevia was almost insane. Myrddin knew it, but had ignored it, instead plunging into his mission to placate and recall the gods of Britain. He was occupied working with his sorcerer's tools of vision-inducing mushrooms, mirrors of all kinds in which he might view glimpses of a road to power, a hypnotic device of dangling chimes and a heaped pile of stinking sheepskins inked with formulae, spells and charms. He had seen Guinevia's reaction to her vision of her father's death and had known that her mind was snapping, but had shrugged it off.

Every Druid had to suffer to be a conduit for the gods, he knew. This was part of the price she must pay. When she faced the debt for which her witch goddess Nicevenn would demand payment, she'd know real suffering, he thought grimly. An adept's powers did not come cheaply...

So he was almost indifferent when his student announced that Arthur needed her, and she must return to Chester. The nurse had gathered up their possessions, prepared the child for the journey and hired guards. Guinevia had been spending most of her time gazing into the obsidian block, seeking images as if she too was on a mission. Which, had Myrddin known it, she was. The seer was looking into the past, and viewing her own capture and trauma at the hands of the brigands. She was seeking the face of the one survivor who had led Arthur to his village. And she found it. For the first time in weeks, she smiled. The journey suddenly became urgent, and the small group had left the next day, moved by Guinevia's pressing need to begin. All, except Myrddin, were heartened by her enthusiasm, thinking it was eagerness to see Arthur. Myrddin guessed at the truth.

Guinevia insisted on returning to Chester by the inland route on which she had been ambushed and kidnapped, saying she wished to visit the graves of the two murdered soldiers. The truth was, she wanted to travel close to the abductors' village. She had psychically seen the lone surviving brigand living near it, existing in a stone bothy despite the winter, and she had a plan for him.

The escort soldiers found the brigand sleeping under several old sheepskins and dragged him out shivering and half naked. Guinevia smiled at him. "Do you remember me?" she said, "Do you recall taking me when I was protecting my baby? Do you remember my pleas for mercy?"

The man shook his head. "No lady, I did not do anything."

Guinevia smiled again. "Oh, but you did," she murmured. "Tie him to that," she ordered, waving to a nearby conifer. She fished in her saddlebag, and gestured to the nurse to move herself and the toddler Milo away a short distance. "He should not watch this," she said casually.

The brigand was fastened. "Hold back his head," she commanded, and a guard yanked the man painfully by his lank hair. "Open his mouth, keep it open." It took a couple of broken teeth before the wretch was secured, head tilted up, a stick of wood jammed between his jaws and lashed behind his neck. Guinevia held up two small flagons of Roman glass, stoppered with silver. "This one," she explained, "comes from a purple-belled flower, a pretty thing called 'Witch's Gloves,' or in your case 'Dead Man's Bells.' It will make your heart beat faster and you will see haloes around the objects you view, but it will not kill you quickly. You will have great pains in your gut, you will perhaps vomit and foul yourself. You will suffer."

She held up the other flask of delicate green glass. "This is an element found in volcanoes, a poison from gold, and I have added essences from almonds and apple seeds to its pretty crystals. It will stop your heart in moments, and you will pray to receive it, to take away the agony of the first of your fatal drinks."

She passed the second flask to a nervous soldier, who held it gingerly. "Time for you to try on a witch's glove," she said quietly, as she poured the hemlock solution down the captive's throat. He choked and gagged, but the mixture went down. Guinevia watched with satisfaction. "Let me help you breathe better," she said, slipping a small knife into his nostril and slicing outwards. The man screamed at the pain, then screamed again as she slit the other nostril. "Just so you can experience the feelings of pain and helplessness," she said amiably. "It's an education for you. We've all had to undergo it." The man writhed, sobbing through his fastened jaws.

The seer stepped back to watch. Blood from his mutilated nose ran down the victim's chin and chest, and his abdomen heaved with cramps. He groaned and struggled against his bonds but was held fast, and gradually his efforts weakened. Suddenly, Guinevia seemed to tire of the spectacle. Briskly, she took the second flask, the arsenic solution, from the guard. "Time for you to go," she said conversationally to the dying man, and held the flask over his upturned face to tip its contents down his throat. In just moments, his face and hands went blue, his tongue seemed to balloon past the wooden stick that held his jaws open, and his destroyed nose bubbled fresh blood. The man gave out great shuddering gasps and slowly buckled into limp lifelessness.

"Leave him there for the crows," the seer commanded. "They can eat him. The next one is the one whose heart I will take." She moved to where the nurse played with Milo, picked him up, buried her face in the child's soft neck and sobbed great, aching sobs.

"They took so very much," she whispered. "So much that I might never recover it." Then she shook herself into composure. The guards, visibly frightened of their mistress, were gathered together in a loose knot. She handed the boy back to his nurse and paced to the rocky ground in front of the bothy. She ignored the suspended body and her guards and raised her face to the low, grey clouds. "Nicevenn, I have sent one of them to you. I will also send you a heart."

Her eyes were closed, so she did not see it, but the awed guards did. The pentagram ring on her finger pulsed with a glowing light, once, twice, five times, then faded out. The witch of the Wild Hunt had responded to her adept. Evil was present, and with it came power. Now Guinevia would take that power to Arthur.

XXV Parthian

Seasons and years slid by as smoothly as the great rivers of my youth, and my grip on Britain was slipping away just as fast. The Saxons were growing in numbers and in the spread of territory they had over-run. They now held swathes of the hinterland behind Dover, which once was my headquarters for the fleet, but was now an isolated fortress sustained only from the sea.

I had been forced to move the fleet away to the safety of Portus Chester, where my Saxon Shore fortifications were strong, but which I reinforced still more with constructions from the great heaps of squared stone, kiln-fired brick and the CLBR-stamped red tiles that showed they were abandoned Roman property, carrying as they did the 'Classis Britannica Romana' indent. They were there because like us, the Romans had made Portus their main naval base. They recognised that an effect of the sheltering island of Vectis on the surge of the Atlantic through the Narrow Sea gave the benefit of double tides each day, highly useful for ships entering and leaving.

Additionally, this naval centre was readily defensible, and our fleet was growing again, so I clung to the place, hoping for matters to improve. Although we kept the coast of the straits patrolled and clear, there was near-free passage further east for the Saxons to sail from Germania to the estuary of the Thames or anywhere along the eastern seaboard, and it meant that inland, all was not well with Britain.

I felt gloomy as I surveyed the fortress at the harbour's head. A deep ditch and moat surrounded a square enclosure of flint and limestone, with walls twice the thickness of the height of a man and nearly four times as tall as one. The fort had bastions along each wall, and projecting corner turrets to allow archery or catapult fire down their lengths. Should enemies cross the moat, the gateways would not easily be stormed, indented as they were to trap attackers in high, three-sided stone boxes. The place was a stronghold, but I had been forced to retreat into it. This was not the way to drive out invaders.

My withdrawal from Dover had come despite successes in battles with the incomers, but it was like struggling to hold back the sea with a single wooden bucket. In the three years since we had scrambled south to save Londinium and force the Saxons to wither in the cold for the winter, it had been one grinding campaign after another. We had lost land, men and horses, and the enemy had even tortured and murdered my captured tribune Lycaon, hanging him over a fire and roasting him to death, an act which made me swear vengeance on his killers.

Worse, the hatred that burned my soul was also in once-gentle Guinevia's, since she had vowed to take the heart out of Allectus for his part in the cruel death of her own father. Privately, I considered that she might have to wait behind me for that privilege, as the man who had once been my treasurer had treacherously bid for my throne and raised the Picts against me. They were a thorn in my side, and a growing threat in the north. I had to find allies against them and their coalition with the Gael and Hibernian raiders who plagued our northern shores.

One bright spot in my defence plans was in the development of our cavalry. The tribune Cragus had raised a force of pony soldiers and even an elite squadron of dragoons mounted on heavy horses. That herd was sired by two Frisian stallions spirited out of Belgica four years before, and I would use one of the stallions as my own warhorse. The threat of sea raiders had forced us to move Cragus' horse corrals and training camps north, away from the plains of the great stone dances of Avebury and Stonehenge, and close to the old Roman city of Aquae Sulis, but the coming spring campaigns should see us for the first time with an effective heavy cavalry to hurl against the Saxons.

I had been studying their battle tactics, observing them in our many skirmishes, and had seen the pattern of their fighting. They did not use archers, and they were ineffective cavalrymen who relied on captured horses, as they did not bring many steeds with them across the sea.

Their strength was their infantry, and they were personally led in battle by their kings, each of whom was surrounded by his hearth warriors and nobles, who were oath-bound to him. The kings led by their own example of courage, which was a weakness if we could kill those figureheads and dishearten their followers. They were not a disciplined army. Their best warriors were trained in individual combat, and for set-piece battles they did adopt the shield wall of the Romans, preferably with the tactical protection of a river or other geographical feature as a defence, but generally they relied on a surprise attack at dawn. That usually was fuelled by mead or forest mushrooms to inspire the men to bare-chested fighting madness, and then they would throw their shields over their backs and fight two-handed and drunk.

The majority of their army was a militia called a 'fyrd,' comprised of men who worked the land, reinforced by some Jute or Dane mercenaries. Their equipment generally was not of a professional standard: a basic helmet of horn and leather, cone-shaped to deflect blows, a small round shield of about two handspans' width, the seax long knife from which they took their name, barbed javelins, and their main weapon, a long thrusting spear with slender leaf-shaped blade.

Only the wealthy house warriors had swords, and they also used the two-handed 'broad axe,' the skeggox that was very effective in battle but required much training of its user, so was a relatively rare thing to see facing us. I thought ruefully that there was one skeggox I'd rather not have seen, the one wielded by a big Saxon years before that had taken half of my foot and a big slice out of my face. That man had died on the blade of my gladius sword, but I had limped ever since…

My thoughts snapped back to the problem. The Saxons' obvious weakness was against archers and cavalry, and Cragus had been given his orders, and had earned his salt. He had trained squadrons of horse archers to race in, turn and deliver volleys of arrows from short range, mostly the bodkin-tipped arrows that would pierce even a coat of mail, and he had worked hard on our secret weapon, for the tribune had also been training my elite knights of the Chevron.

The red wool chevron had begun as an award from me to those soldiers who had been with me at the recovery of the lost Eagle of the Ninth Spanish Legion, an icon that showed the gods' support for me when I took the title of Britain's Imperator. The red cloak of the long-dead Roman who had wrapped it around the hidden Eagle was made into insignia to be worn proudly by the companions who found it with me. Most of that small cadre of soldiers were now dead, but I had appointed other warriors to the elite and they had trained as heavy cavalrymen. Mounted on our valuable big horses, armoured and equipped to the highest standards, they should be capable of crashing through any shield wall to break it for our foot soldiers, and to deal death and destruction themselves from the backs of their chargers.

I would lead them personally, on my war horse Corvus, who was named for the raven that was his colour. I considered the horse soldiers' equipment the best any professional could own. Not for them the heavy mail coat of the legions. Instead each knight wore around his upper body expensive segmented armour that was much lighter than mail. Its hoops of iron overlapped like a lobster's shell, and all was held together by internal leather straps, laced tightly. Above the torso armour, the rider's shoulders were sheltered under hinged iron plates and the whole carapace was worn over a padded leather jerkin. This was liberally greased with lanolin taken from fresh fleeces, which let the armour move freely over it. In the spots where the iron was more exposed, a coating of bees' wax both lubricated and protected it from the constant British rain.

The body armour was augmented by a Roman cavalry helmet with a protective face mask, cheekpieces and nape shield. The knights carried lances as long as the height of two men, a longsword at the hip, a small shield strapped to the left forearm and a short bow made of horn and wood, fastened together with cattle sinews and hoof glue.

The dragoons used a wood and leather saddle with four horns and they controlled their horses with their knees and reins, but could stand in the newly-issued stirrups to fight. Cragus trained the lighter cavalry, the horse archers, in the Parthian shot. They would race in, turning their mounts by knee pressure on the horse's ribs, then fire facing backwards, left arm extended over the horse's rump, arrow drawn back with the right over the braided mane. The horse archers would gallop in, turn, fire their volleys and circle back to their lines.

As they did, another squadron of archers would gallop at the enemy and repeat the punishing volleys, always keeping out of range of the javelins and axes the Saxons might throw. Under such sustained pressure, the undisciplined Saxons would often break ranks and charge, and then we had the advantage. That was the time when we could use our heavy cavalry, and our disciplined shield wall, and then our lesser numbers would not matter so much. But my real hope for success lay with those big horses, those long lances and heavy swords....

The cavalry were trained to do much and in a very short time we would test them against the Saxons. It would be crucial. If they failed that test, we might well lose Britain to the invaders. I shook off the gloom. Blue sails were approaching from the east. My fleet patrols might have news, and I hurried down the rampart steps to head for the harbour.

XXVI Muirch

Muirch the Gael was lying prone in wet grass, peering down into the valley where a column of armed men had halted. They seemed to be receiving instructions from a leader and the sea raider was cursing to himself. He had beached his longship and split his force into three, with orders to move inland and plunder what farms or settlements they could. Now, armed men who were likely hunting him had cut off his route to his ship. He was outnumbered and in difficulty and he swore, this time aloud.

"Don't do that," said a voice at his elbow. He scowled. It was one of the women who had insisted on coming along - Karay, the tall red-haired one with all the opinions and the willingness to flatten any man who displeased her. Muirch remembered the bishop's downfall but grudgingly acknowledged that the females had been more useful than any of his men. They'd patched up several raiders who had been injured, and Karay had displayed a remarkable knowledge of herbal cures. She'd used poppy seed and henbane to ease one raider's wounds; had made an infusion from dried Illyrican iris to stem Muirch's own terrible headaches and when one youth had suffered badly from seasickness, had cured it with a broth she made with ginger root and thyme.

The blonde Jesla had been especially good at finding where villagers had hidden their possessions and stores and, after more physical persuasions had failed, she and the sorceress Caria had used invented spells to scare an obstinate abbot into revealing where the abbey coin was hidden.

"Keep quiet, they may not know we're here," the woman said. Muirch glanced around. His handful of men were all crouched, back from the skyline, obedient to the instructions of the female, Jesla, who wore her hair with a ribbon of tight, flat curls around the face. It was a style much prized by the Romans, who liked a low frontal hairline. Muirch wondered how she kept it that way, then stopped his musing. "They know we're here, they didn't come out fully armed to catch rabbits," he growled.

Karay looked levelly at him. "So, your plan would be?" she asked.

The Gael grunted. He had no idea.

To get back to the ship, they'd have to cross open ground in full view of the column. They couldn't outrun them, they were too few to fight them. Muirch scratched his crotch in puzzlement. He was not accustomed to thinking and planning. It was usually his technique to find a village, storm in, burn the place and carry off whatever he could find before he had to fight. Karay slid backwards, and crouching, moved to talk with Jesla. Then she came back and flopped on the grass beside the raider. She smiled at him, and tore at the neck of her tunic. "I have to look like an abused captive," she said. "I'm going down to meet them," she said. "Jesla is organising the men."

Muirch looked on, open-mouthed, as his men began running, doubled over to avoid being seen above the skyline. Some went right, the others went left, and they separated themselves by several hundred yards. Jesla joined Muirch just as Karay patted his shoulder and stood up. Then the red haired Celt began running down the hillside towards the stalled column.

"Stand up and start shouting, wave your arms, turn and look behind you and start signalling," Jesla instructed the bewildered raider. She took her place next to him and began shouting to an invisible someone behind her. Quietly, she explained to Muirch: "Karay's gone down there to say she's escaped from a huge war band and they sent a few of their men to bring her back." Muirch looked along the crestline where his men were now showing themselves and shouting back and forth. Karay was at the valley floor and was speaking urgently to the leader of the column, pointing back up at Muirch. In moments, the soldier called his column to order. Quickly, they formed up and began to move away, Karay going with them.

"She'll slip away after dark. She knows where the ship is," Jesla said confidently. "Now, call your boys back, form up and march down the hill towards those people."

Muirch started. "They'd butcher us!" he protested.

"They'd think you were trying to delay them so the huge war band behind can catch them. If you go after them, they'll march away even faster," she explained. "Tonight, we'll camp in an open place, where our fires can be seen, and we will have a dozen or more big blazes. That will keep the soldiers away until Karay can join us. And when she does, we can gather up the others and sail away." She turned to beckon the raiders together.

"I'll never get to go voyaging again without these women," Muirch thought unhappily.

XXVII Chart

Once again, I swung onto horseback, the familiar twin saddle horns both before and behind me, and for the next, uncounted time I set out on the long journey back to Chester. My riders and I went steadily, clattering along the metalled Roman road to Gloucester, and crossing the ghostly, ancient Fosse Way that was once the rampart-and-ditch frontier of Britannia. We forded the brown Severn river and trotted on through the lush valley of the Wye. Escorted by my armed, grim troop, I passed unhindered across the territories of the Atrebates, Dobunni, Silures and Cornovii. It was a journey of hasty changes of horse, snatched food and swilled wine, of dozing jolting in the saddle as we rode over sheep-nibbled turf ridges and through ancient forests. Finally we arrived, sore and stinking of horse sweat, rank leather and foul mud. We were hungry and dizzy from lack of sleep but grateful to see at last the familiar red sandstone fortress above the harbour. There, I knew, Guinevia waited, her mind cracking from the nightmares she had undergone, her steely soul holding on only because of the powers given to her by her goddess.

I have never taken her into my arms so gladly, never looked into her tormented eyes so hungrily. I carried her to our sleeping chamber and she curled in my arms like a kitten and slept, and slept. Her healing had begun, but she still carried a dark vow in her heart, and I guessed what it was. I had made the same grisly promise to myself, and one day Allectus would be disembowelled because of it.

When the morning sun's fingers crept over the stone sill of my window and the nurse brought in our burbling four year old son Milo to play with us, the dark thoughts were dissipated for a time and I held hope of healing for my sorceress. I had to give her time, and life was improving, but as always there were the dispatches. I had a kingdom to manage, and it was unravelling.

First came news of the Saxons, who were collecting ominously powerful new strength. There were reports from beyond the Wall of a Pictish gathering, reports on which I focused, as Allectus could well be behind them. Raiders had burned settlements and an abbey in the northwest, far on our side of the Wall. There was significant news from spies of a revolt by Christians who had been dispossessed of their lands for treason against the old emperor, and not least was a rumour that the Augustus Maximian had now subdued the Alemanni beyond the Rhine. Released from that urgent business, he was supposedly turning his thoughts and his energies to recover the lost colonia of Britain. It was a huge threat.

Guinevia came into the chamber and leaned on the mensa where I was working. "I wish I could line these enemies up one by one," I grumbled. "It's a mess keeping them straight in my head, I feel like a juggler with too many objects spinning at once."

She yawned and rubbed her eyes. "I could chart them for you, easily enough," she said casually.

Something jangled in my brain. "Chart them?"

"Yes," she said, smoothing a strand of hair from her forehead. "I can just put them down on a piece of papyrus, make a map of them and tell you what each is doing."

Maybe my lower jaw made a noise as it hit my chest, or maybe I imagined that. "Tell me what they are doing?" I echoed her.

"I can view them, watch them without ever leaving this room," she said simply. "And I can give you an eagle's view of the kingdom."

What she told me and showed me in the next turn of the sandglass gave me hope that with the aid of her knowledge, we could take Britain back for ever. First, she sketched what Myrddin had once shown her: a view from the sky of the islands of Britain. Guinevia had trained as a scribe, and she had the powers of an adept of a mighty witch goddess. Instead of offering the usual Roman itinerum's list of places along a road, she could draw on her mental view of the land to produce a chart that showed the positions of settlements, roads, rivers and mountains, all displayed as if looked at from above, from under the wings of a hawk or an eagle. But that was not all.

From Myrddin and a group of Mesopotamian magi, she had gained the power to send her mind out to far places where she could see what was happening. She could see the people, hear the wind, feel the warmth of a faraway sun, all as it happened. She could not hear what those people were saying, but she could see them clearly in their most secret conclaves, at their very actions. As well as this tremendous ability to view events far in the distance, she had developed a way to reliably peer into the future. This she explained to me as I tried to grasp its staggering implications.

"When I found that I could send my mind out to view in a remote place what was happening, I wondered if I could also see what would be happening in the future. So I devised a small experiment. I told my maid to choose two objects without telling me what they were. One would represent 'Yes,' one would represent 'No.' The question I posed was simple. Would her lover's fishing boat come back within two days? When the time was up, she would show me the thing that meant 'Yes' if he had come back. If he had not, she would show me the 'No' object.

"I would not know before the two days were up what either object was, but after two days, I would be shown one of them. Once my maid had decided on the objects I would be shown in the future, I went into my chamber and sent out my mind, and I saw a shield.

"Two days later, as planned, she showed me the object that was relevant to events. Because he had not yet returned, she showed me the 'No' object. It was a shield, just as I had seen, and it closed the circle: I had foreseen what I would be shown, and it was correct."

Guinevia had made the tests more elaborate, but they still did not fail her. By choosing objects that were not similar, she could easier identify the symbol that would reflect a future result. It was critical that she should be shown the correct object after the event had happened, but if that were done, she could predict events. She could tell me if I would be successful in battle, she could tell me if Maximian would invade, she could predict the future. But that was not all.

By sending out her mind, she could also tell me what was happening at this moment. It was how she had seen Allectus plotting with the Picts, how she had witnessed her father being boiled to death by my traitorous lieutenant. Thanks to her Druidical learning and the painful price of her suffering, I had a psychic spy who could tell me of my enemies' actions as they performed them, even if they were scores of miles away, even if they were safe inside their own strongholds. It was a weapon more powerful than any sword like Exalter, more potent than any fleet or army. It was a secret armament that could save Britain.

So I planned to start with the Picts. They'd been a thorn in my flesh for a while, raiding across the Wall, burning settlements and taking Britons as slaves. They had broken the agreements we'd made, had not sent the tribute they'd promised. I'd tried to slap them down, but our last expedition had failed. When we tried to pincer their army they had slipped through our steel noose. This time, with Guinevia's vision to guide me, I could trap the troublesome bastards and bring them to heel.

I had put aside the endless reports concerning supplies and rosters and was pondering this pleasant thought when a commotion at the gate below my window attracted my attention. Guards were bringing in an unusual coffle of shackled prisoners. They were led by a tall Celtic woman whose fiery hair hung in a single braid down to her waist. Behind her was chained another woman, equally tall, whose fair hair was surprisingly worn in the style of a fashionable Roman matron, low across the forehead and tightly curled. A big shaggy-haired brute shambled behind the two women, well shackled and with a battered and bruised face that spoke of resistance to his capture. Behind him trailed a dozen more brigands wearing an array of tattered finery, much of it clerical and likely plundered. One, in full monk's cowled habit, had an empty scabbard at his belt and looked around furiously, his face red with anger above his blond beard. The coffle was brought up at the rear by a pair of villainous brigands chained to and pulling along a small handcart that was sheeted and roped, and probably contained plunder. I called down to the guard to halt while I went to examine them.

"Got this lot near Carnforth, trying to sneak back to their ship, but it had already gone – we'd chased it off, lord," said the centurion. "They tried to fool us with a fake hostage and pretended there were more of them so we didn't get too close too soon. It paid off at first, but the Scotch one, that bishop over there, the one with too much to say, led the others right into us just before dawn. I think he was trying to reconnect with the others, and got it wrong."

The women were eager to talk, the bishop and his men admitted nothing and claimed to have been spreading the gospel of the Jesus prophet, and the surly, black-haired brute simply spat at me. Their stories were simple and gelled with what I'd heard. One group had been separated from the rest of their longship's crew and when they had returned to where they'd left their vessel, it had already sailed without them. After some muttering in Gaelic to get their stories straight, the others said they had never seen the first group before, but it was obvious enough to me that they had been raiding together as a joint force.

"They fooled us for a while, lord," admitted the guard captain. "Made us think there were more of them than we could cope with. This one," he gestured at the redhead, "pretended to have been their hostage, but she's as savage as any of them and worse than most."

The Celt smiled sweetly at me. "Can we have our cooking pots, please?" she said, nodding to the wrapped plunder. "We only came here to trade."

The guard sighed and shook his head. "She's giving me an ear ache again. They burned five or six farms, sacked an abbey and gave the abbot a good spanking. He won't be sitting down between prayers for a while. Oh yes, most of the abbey goods are on the cart."

I nodded. "Bang the captives up, we'll deal with them later. Take anything useful on the cart to the quartermaster, get the coin and silver to my aide Androcles. I'll send thanks to the abbot for his generous donation. It's good to see the Christians wanting to help keep Britain free."

The furious-looking monk overheard what I said and spoke up loudly. "I am Bishop Iacomus Candless," he said. "I represent Mother Church and it is sacrilege to take what is rightfully hers. Set me and my men free, and return our goods to us." He paused, then added: "At once." I probably flexed an eyebrow at this chained, muddied wretch with the imperious manner, but I responded softly.

"I am Arthur, Imperator Caesar Britannicus, Marcus Aurelius Mauseus Carausius, the dutiful, fortunate and unconquered Augustus," I said slowly. "You will be pleased to be my guest, and your accommodations, dear Bishop Candless, are waiting for you, so please do not delay us in our hospitality." I turned to the centurion. "Do have care about the good bishop's quarters," I said.

The soldier grinned. "Yes, lord," he said. "I will give it my full attention." As the prisoners moved away, I saw the bishop take a kick up his hindquarters from the centurion's nailed caliga. Not a good time for churchmen's bottoms, I thought, if that abbot, too, was standing to pray these days.

XXVIII Javelin

That day, the hunting had been good. The beagle pack had worked with the big hounds and had scented, tracked and brought to bay a scarred old tusker of a wild boar. He had made his defiant stand in a thicket of brambles, but the canny dogs had wormed in after him and he burst out with Axis grimly hanging onto one ear, Javelin on the other, a shaggy yellow Agassian hound called Aurum ripping at his gut and a couple of game little beagles biting furiously at his hooves. The infuriated pig turned to shake one dog from his ear, and Aurum was ripping into his belly. When he turned his attention to Aurum, Axis had his great fangs tearing into the pig's throat. I stepped forward with my heavy ash-hafted boar spear to stick the beast, but my mutilated foot slowed me, and one of my house carls was quicker.

His blade was into the boar's wide chest as the beast lunged forward, its impetus driving the iron deeper. The man tried to lift the pig like a hay bale on a fork, but the weight was too much and he skidded to one knee. I skipped sideways as nimbly as I could and drove for the beast's ribs but another houseman was again quicker and his blade hit the pig in the throat, stopping it before it could reach the grounded man. Finally, I put my blade in under the ribs, into the beast's fighting heart, saying a prayer to Mithras as I did. The thrust was all that was needed. The furious beast was dying, slumping sideways. The dogs, bloodied from shoulder to paws, were mauling at the expiring boar and we let them have their reward for a few moments before calling them off.

My blood-spattered house carls, panting and grinning, slapped each other and me on the back and we laughed like boys and boasted noisily about what a feast we'd have that night. And we did. We ate and caroused in the domed Roman hall in Chester that had been a council chamber, a splendid edifice unlike any other. Ingenious engineers had created it by rotating several arches to support a roof made from concrete that was lighter than any stone. It intrigued me, and I called on a military bridge builder to explain how it could be.

The fellow said the Romans had invented a liquid rock from a mix of rubble, lime, volcanic ash and sand. They mixed it with water and poured it into wooden moulds. To make the dome, the old Romans had constructed scaffolding and moulds, packed the mix into it then poured in water. Because concrete is much lighter than stone, it could be supported on the stone walls and pillars below, where stone would have been too heavy. Its ability to be shaped also was an advantage, allowing concrete to be made into the dome shape that creates such spacious, airy chambers.

What the engineer told me next made my military mind buzz. This concrete would set underwater, and when seawater came into contact with the mix it triggered a hot chemical reaction that set the whole mixture quickly. I wondered about an application to make bridge piers that might allow us to cross unfordable rivers without the enemy's knowledge. It was an idea that could be extremely useful one day…

I came back to the present when Guinevia tugged at my sleeve. "The floor is warm," she hissed. "I think the building is on fire!" I smiled. My widely-read Druid had never been in the hall before and knew nothing of the hypocaust that provided piped heating under our feet and through the wall tiles. I explained it, and though she looked at me doubtfully, I later noticed with pleasure that she had slipped off her sandals and was warming her feet on the flagged floor. When I teased her, she blushed. "My father's hall was regarded as very fine," she said. "It had a wood-planked floor over a wide pit that was filled with straw to keep it insulated in the winter, but it was chilly. The walls were just wood reinforced with wattles and mud. There was a fire in the middle, but it was cold around the edges of the hall, and it was always smoky because the smoke's only way out was through a vent in the roof."

It was a splendid evening, Guinevia seemed to be recovering and, though pale, was smiling and gracious and listened attentively to the musicians who accompanied several bards in a musical story-telling contest. I had no ear for the music provided by a couple of reed flutes and a lyre, though I enjoy the sound of drums and trumpets, but the bards' stories were wisely-chosen epics of battle and hunting, of monsters slain and sea voyages taken. I enjoyed them, though I noticed Guinevia sometimes yawning surreptitiously.

It was a rare evening of relaxation. The wild boar meat was good, we had hare and pheasant, root vegetables, fruit, soft cheese, mead and some thin red wine from Gaul. I was a tired and satisfied Imperator that night, when I unpinned my silver and amber badge of British office and slipped onto our sleeping pallet beside my returned queen.

However, before I could sleep there began one of the worst hours of my life. Guinevia's maid, who acted as nurse to little Milo, rushed into the room, screaming and hysterical. In her arms was my son, limp and covered in blood. The nurse was shouting: "The dogs! The dogs attacked him!"

I was on my feet, grabbing for my scabbarded sword Exalter where it hung, racing for the door, throwing aside the sheath and belt and bursting into the child's chamber. Both my hounds were in there. Axis was in the far corner, in the shadows, panting hard. Javelin was lying near the door, his broad chest sheeted in blood, his jaws open, gasping, and dripping gore. He looked up at me and thumped his tail feebly, but did not rise to his feet. I looked at his golden brown eyes, and he gazed up at me, remaining still, and unusually not rising. The blood was puddled around his great paws and I said: "You treacherous killer! Why? Why did you attack my son?" He was looking at me with what flashed through my mind was reproach, but I was committed to the swing. "Why did you?" I said. They were the last words he ever heard, and I hacked down hard at my hound's neck.

May the gods forgive me, but at least he died painlessly, silently. Axis, curiously motionless in his dark corner, growled and I turned to kill him, my other hound, then Guinevia was at me, grasping my arm, tugging at me. "Milo is unhurt! He's not injured!" she was screaming. Behind her I heard the thuds and clatter as guards came running. I turned, stupid with rage and fear at what she might say. "What?" was all I could say.

"Milo is fine. It is not his blood." I still did not comprehend. A movement from Axis caught my attention, and he groaned and slid to the floor. A guard was entering with an oil lamp and in its light I saw that my big dog was lying on his side now, blood puddling under him, too.

I stepped forward and caught a gleam in the shadows to my left. Teeth. I moved towards it, the lamplight moved and I saw a large, humped shadow in its own pool of blood. "Lights!" I shouted, and two or three lamps were raised as the room began to fill with people. I moved towards the gleam of teeth, Exalter readied to strike. Then I saw what I had done.

The motionless, shadowy hump was a dead wolf, its throat torn out. I swivelled to see Axis. He raised his head and thumped his tail weakly against the floor. The flesh of his ribs was torn open, I could see the white gleam of bone. I went to my knees beside him, hearing a scrape and thump as a guard ran a spear into the dead wolf's carcass. Axis licked my hand and seemed to sigh. The odd angle at which his forepaw rested showed me that it was broken. His pelt was hideously torn open, he was bleeding profusely.

"Get a medic here!" I shouted and glared around me. "Get a medic, now!" I tried to raise my big hound, but he groaned, so I eased him back down. Guinevia, weeping, was kneeling beside me.

"The dogs saved Milo," she said simply. I moaned aloud and left her petting my black hound's lacerated head. I stumbled as I picked up Javelin's body from the floor, his noble head lolling, near-separated by my killing sword. For the first time since I was a boy, I wept hot tears.

My faithful dog had given his life to save my child from a predator wolf, and I had rewarded him with death. The medic rushed into the room, scared-looking and tousled from sleep. "Save that dog," I sad harshly, pointing to Axis. "If he dies, it's your back that will be torn open." Then, tear-stained and humiliated, I stamped out of the room to compose myself.

Later, we found scratches on Milo's neck, marks we believed were inflicted when the wolf had seized him in his cot. From the punishing wounds on my hounds, we saw how they must have taken on the gray killer and fought him to the death. Axis had escaped with the lesser wounds, but they were still terrible. His ribs and head were lacerated, his forepaw broken, but even lamed, he must have fought on, his gallant heart refusing to give in.

Javelin had the worst of it. His throat was torn, his pelt shredded and a rear leg was crushed by the wolf's huge jaws, but he too must have fought courageously to allow his litter mate Axis to inflict the killing throat wound that had finished off the wolf.

"How did we not hear the fight?" Guinevia asked. I shook my head. It could have happened while we were still in the hall, feasting, it could have been a silent, desperate battle as our dogs offered their lives in exchange for the child they guarded. It was something we would never know, and I still grieve for the faithful dog I killed in error.

We buried Javelin just below the crest of a hill where he had played so happily as a puppy. I ordered a headstone for him, to record his tale of devotion and courage and I made sacrifice to the gods to treat him well in the hall of Valhalla. I especially asked that they give him the crusted ends of beef he loved, and to let him sleep warm by the fireside on winter's nights.

Two nights later, I walked alone up that hill, wept unashamedly, and placed a bone, with well-cooked beef attached, on my hound's grave. "Go into your long sleep, my friend," I said, and my heart tore as it never had for any human.

Axis recovered well from his wounds, although the marks of the terrible lacerations he had sustained could be seen through his glossy fur, and his broken forepaw, which the medic had set well, slowed his speed so I would joke with him that we were a pair of cripples together. He would look up at me with his wise brown eyes when I fondled his ears or chest and I swear he forgave me. I shall have to wait until I end my life and cross the bridge of swords to see if Javelin will lick my hands in forgiveness. Somehow, I think he will.

XXIX Eidyn

Years before, I had served in the Roman Army, so it was natural that I ordered my own troops in the disciplines and methods of the men who were now my enemies. We trained as the legions did, we marched, made camp and fought in their time-proven victorious ways. We used their equipment and armour, practised their hygiene and dietary methods. Like the Mules of Marius, the emperor who reformed the army of Rome, my soldiers carried full packs and tools that totalled the weight of a small man, yet they could cover 40 miles' march in a single day and were still able to dig and establish a defensible camp each night.

So it was a familiar experience when I rode out of Eboracum at the head of a legion, headed north to put down the Picts. We tramped along the paved military highway of Dere Street in disciplined columns, obedient to the cadence of the centurions who counted the number of paces we made each day. We passed through the garrison towns of Caractonium and Corla and arrived once more at the stone frontier that was the Rampart of the Augustus Hadrian.

This gated wall that was once the northern extent of the vast Roman Empire was built by the Spaniard Publius Aelius Hadrianus, cousin and godson of the Emperor Trajan, more as a customs barrier than as a defence line. The Wall of square-cut stone ran from sea to sea, was three times the height of a man, and was fronted by a vee-shaped deep ditch that made it all but impassable to invaders, even if they had been able to overcome the garrisons that stood every third of a mile along its length. There was even a flat-bottomed ditch inside a double berm a short way south of the wall, to protect the garrisons from any southern attack. It was a magnificent piece of engineering, but for all its imposing splendour, the Wall that was also called the Aelian Rampart had seen only a short term of service. It was replaced after just 16 years by the more northerly turf-and-timber wall of Antoninus, which stretched from firth to firth across the waist of Pictland.

I had seen the Antonine Wall before, finding it sadly depleted, a ditch grown so shallow a marching man need hardly break stride to cross it. It was no defensive barrier, but that was immaterial. I intended to march beyond it into the heart of the rebel territory, to take sword and fire to the pesky insurgents. They had slipped away from my forces several years before, and we had wasted much effort for little return. This time, I vowed, would be different. And it was.

Before I crossed the Antonine, though, I had business with natives south of its crumbled barrier, so I quick-marched my legion through the land of the Votadini, surprising them before they could rally enough men to delay us, and we soon came to their craggy fortress south of the great firth. The ancient stronghold called Dun Eidyn was steep-faced volcanic rock on three sides, but the eastern approach was a sloping ramp mostly occupied by houses. We simply fired the town and as the wind was from the east, followed through the smoke and over the rudimentary wooden defences to slaughter the small force of Picts who had taken refuge there.

With their fortress taken, I wanted to wait for my second legion's approach from Chester, and viewed the vast rock as a possible camp. It was unsuitable. After a dry summer, there was no significant water supply on the hilltop. I recalled a natural fortress half a day's march east where an impressive rampart had been built on an old oppidum, or hill fort, and I had sent a small detachment to seize and hold it as an outpost to overlook the firth and the road alongside. There was a brook there, which promised a natural aquifer, and a river was nearby, which would be excellent as both defensive feature and water supply. The hill was the site of a major settlement of the Votadini called Dunpelder, so there would be farmers, traders and others with food and supplies. We moved back there, leaving a holding force in Eidyn's destroyed burh, to wait a month or so for the rest of our forces, and especially of our cavalry, who had to come from the southern downs of Britain.

When the first crisp mornings signalled the beginning of autumn, my two northern legions were finally together. We had a small cavalry force under my longtime tribune Cragus, we had an array of ballistae and a siege train and we even had a small naval force under Grimr the Suehan anchored in the nearby firth. Our scouts had been busy and brought news that the Pict chieftains had established their main force on another volcanic crag, north of the Antonine, where it dominated the lowest crossing of the river that fed the wide firth.

I knew the place. On a previous expedition, we had occupied the crag, which was called Snowdoun or Stirling, and Guinevia had sacrificed a human in the old Mithraic temple there. I remembered the event clearly; a grossly fat mule trader whose guts had been spilled so Guinevia could read them for an augury. The wretch had died whimpering for his mother, but the signs were good, and Druids knew that any offering of a human soul to the gods would be regarded with great favour. Later, I'd credit that sacrifice with saving my life after I escaped execution as a captive. If that summit we'd occupied were defended with any competence, it would be a long and difficult task to take it, siege engines or no. Three centuries before, it had been so established as a strongpoint that even the Romans had bypassed it, leaving it in the hands of the local tribe, and the men from Italia had made their own fortified camp eight miles away.

We marched to Snowdoun, where the Picts cowered behind their vast dolerite walls. We encamped and built a long double palisade atop ramparts and ditches around the base of the towering rock to act both as containment for the besieged and a defensive wall for ourselves if we were attacked. We made a few minor attempts to storm the walls, and then resigned ourselves to a long siege.

In theory, the besiegers should always win, but it would take time, and winter was on its inexorable approach. I did not relish the idea of winter quarters on the river plain under that towering upthrust of rock, but we went through the motions. We pulled down houses on the approach ramp for materials to use for our works and pushed great wicker baskets forward, filling them with dirt and rocks to make a protective wall against the citadel's few archers. We located the two wells just outside the walls and filled them to deny water to the besieged. We began constructing platforms for the siege engines we had brought with us, cutting down an entire copse nearby for the timber we required.

We had needs: we needed siege towers from which we could shoot down onto the defenders' walls, and our engineers were busy constructing the ramps that would let us roll those great towers up close. We needed heavy-roofed galleries that we could wheel close to the walls, to protect our battering ram crews from the rocks that would be rained down at them; we needed to fill the ditch outside the wall so we could wheel our rams up to the stones through which they must smash. And above, all, we needed time, but we would not have enough before the freezing weather came, that I knew.

I was directing the positioning of a battery of wild asses, giant whiplike ballistae that could hurl rocks or pots of blazing pitch over the walls, when Guinevia approached. She looked drawn and weary, for she had been less than her sparkling self for months, since her kidnap and rescue. She wasted no time. "Myrddin is coming," she said quietly. "I sent for him."

I nodded. I knew she had somehow communicated a psychic message to her mentor wizard, just as she could send her mind to view far places. "He will make this fortress fall," she said simply. Mentally, I raised an eyebrow. Myrddin might be a powerful wizard, but he was no military engineer. With our best efforts, fair weather and no interference, it could be weeks or months before we could breach these defences.

Guinevia read my thoughts. "He can do it," she said flatly.

I shrugged. "Any help he can give will be useful," I ventured.

The druidess looked at me coldly, in a way she had never viewed me before. "I told you he will make this fortress fall, and I have seen it happen. It will come before the first snow."

Sometimes, you have to just nod agreement, which is what I did, before turning back to the more earthly considerations of throwing large river stones over the walls of the fortress. A lead missile the size of a hen's egg flattened against the rock near where I stood, and I brought myself quickly back to the present. "Behind here," I said, tugging Guinevia into the shelter of an earth-filled basket.

She nodded indifferently. "Myrddin is close. He will be here in the morning."

And so he was. The familiar long, dark figure strode across the mud to my tent, his crystal-blue eyes sharp under his dark, shaggy brows, a hood concealing the long plait of oiled hair that was his vanity. As always, he carried with him an aura of power and authority, and as always I wondered about this son of no father whose sire was a spirit demon. "Breakfast, Arthur, breakfast," he said by way of greeting. I called for a slave, who soon brought oat cakes, cold mutton and a flask of the thin red wine from Gaul that was the best we had. The wizard ate, then asked to look around our camp.

The place was a maze of muddy earthworks, a jumble of construction timbers. Wooden platforms at the end of the camp closest to the heavy gates of the stronghold supported a battery of big catapults that were firing arrow-headed bolts or rounded river stones at the citadel's iron-strapped entrance. Work parties dragged lumber, stones and parts for siege engines and towers. Archers trotted from place to place to lay down covering fire as the great baskets of soil were moved closer to the walls, and smoke and stinking fumes from the heated pitch that was being used for fire arrows and missiles drifted across the whole scene. It looked like the way the Christians described Hades, I thought gloomily.

Myrddin took it in interestedly. "I'd appreciate a diversion later today, just before sundown, on that side of the walls," he said pointing to the southwestern corner of the ramparts, where a steep slope had been cleared of trees. "Keep it up until the dusk falls, if you would." I nodded. I had expected he'd have a plan, but I was not going to question him. He could probably fly over the walls if he wanted, he was a powerful sorcerer. I touched the iron of my sword hilt for luck. Then I simply gave the orders and waited for sundown. Later, I saw Guinevia speak with the wizard, saw him pat her shoulder and stride off towards the eastern slope. I assumed he had found a way into the fortress, and when I caught a glimpse of a white rat casually slipping under the side of a tent, I knew he probably had…

The siege continued the next morning with plenty of activity from both sides, but by dusk, the defenders were noticeably quieter. I ordered extra guards during the night, suspecting a sally while we slept, but the dawn arrived without any surprise, except that matters were unusually calm. Our ballistae continued to pound the gates, which were showing signs of splintering but little else, but our archers had no targets along the walls, and a puzzled, grizzled centurion came to me. "Summat's up, boss," he said. "There's nobbut one or two on't walls. That's not right." I looked up again. He'd voiced what I had half-noticed, but had been too busy with the artillery to consider. I was puzzling over the possibilities when a shout from the nearest ballista crew caught my attention. Someone had opened the small wicket that was set in the heavy oak gates.

Intuition seized me. "Stop firing, stop!" I yelled in my biggest parade ground voice. I knew who I would see before the tall dark figure stepped out. It was Myrddin. "Go!" I shouted, gesturing 'forward' to the dozen or so soldiers around me. We sprinted across the rubble on the ramp in front of the gates, arriving to find the wizard calm and composed, wiping his hands on a piece of linen.

"Go inside," he gestured in a lordly manner. "It's all yours now. Just don't drink the water."

Within the hour, we had the whole citadel occupied. The streets were littered with dead and dying men, wax-faced and with foam on their startlingly-blue lips. A few wretches were doubled in agony, most were dead, a score or two were still alive but too weakened to fight.

"Poisoned," Guinevia said with a satisfaction I had never seen in her before. "Poisoned, every treacherous, traitorous man." I never questioned Myrddin, never asked how he had done it, but the memory of those gasping, dying men haunted me for years.

Over the next few days, we stacked the dead outside, interlayered with the timbers that had been our siege engine platforms and wooden walls and made them into a number of huge funeral pyres. I didn't think to bury the dead, as they seemed tainted, something the earth itself would reject, so I ordered them burned. Nor did I ever want to know how Myrddin had entered the citadel. He may have spirited himself inside invisible, he may have flown over the walls on a hawk's wings. It was a magician's business, not mine.

Equally, I never asked what he had used to poison the garrison's water supplies, but I have always had my suspicions. Privately I shuddered at the thought of those men, traitors or not, going through such a filthy death. I was not going to berate a powerful sorcerer, not ever, but this was not the way a warrior kills his enemies, I felt.

Today, I am not so sure. In war, things can change. You kill them with a spear, a sword, an arrow, and some may perhaps use a poison. I knew my own choice and what I would use, but I did not question that killing them had saved many of the lives under my command. Once again, I hardened my heart. Anyway, at that time I had no use for philosophy. I had to consider my next moves in the campaign. The snow would be coming, but I still had enough time to roll up the insurgents and bring those rebel chieftains to heel. And I did. I led my legions northeast, along the cordon of the old Roman forts that had been the exact line of march followed on our last punitive expedition years before.

Once again, we took hundreds of prisoners as slaves, and we liberated several hundred unfortunates who had been taken as captives by the Picts in their raids into Britain. These I sent back with a token guard, also herding back to the border country the sheep and cattle that had been stolen over the years. We devastated the Picts' settlements, burned their crops and left dozens of them on crucifixes at the wayside. It was my reminder to the miscreants when they emerged from their hiding places in the heather that the law of Arthur, their emperor, was to be obeyed.

XXX Skegga

Allectus slipped into Saxon-held Colchester disguised as a food pedlar. He was leading two pack mules loaded with wheels of cheese and strings of smoked sausage, portions of which provided the bribes to get him past the gate guards and to the commandeered library that served as accommodation for their warlord, Skegga, who was seated, prising with his seax knife at the semi-precious stones that adorned the cover of an ecclesiastical book.

"I have come to speak of matters more important than sausage and cheese," Allectus said directly, causing the Saxon to look up in surprise. "I bring this for you, lord, with knowledge of where there is much, much more." Allectus placed a soft leather pouch on the table and tipped out an assortment of gold coins and small ingots, scattering them across the surface where some rolled against a painted iron-and-leather helmet.

"You have my attention." The voice was a rumble in keeping with Skegga's appearance. He was a broad-chested, bearded man dressed in trews and a fur tunic, his arms bare, tattooed, and sporting a dozen circlets of gilt and bronze. His fingers were thick with battle rings made from the weapons of defeated enemies, and Allectus noted that two digits on the man's left hand were missing.

"I am Allectus, and I was Arthur's tribune and treasurer until he tried to cheat his people," he said. "I operated the mint in this town and another in Londinium and I can lead you to hidden riches."

Skegga stirred and slid his seax into its white sheath on his hip. Allectus understood the gesture, and bowed. "What is your price for these revelations?" the big Saxon asked.

"I have more than just gold to offer you, lord," said Allectus smoothly. "I have knowledge of Arthur, his dispositions, his weaknesses, his battle tactics. I can help you trap and defeat him."

Skegga stared at the traitor, assessing his smooth sleekness, his serpent-like head and the oiled hair with its long ponytail. The Saxon recognized the man's innate confidence and electric energy even as he felt contempt for his treachery. A devious one, and dangerous, he decided. But, if the gods choose to send him gold and information of his enemies, so be it. "Tell me," he commanded. And Allectus did.

He started by explaining about money. He told the Saxon how his workers were skilled at blending silver or gold with bronze or brass into an alloy that looked like pure gold. This they beat into the correct thickness, cut into square blanks and stamped them with hammer and die to impress each side of the coin before trimming the edges into a round. "The point of having your image on the coin, lord," he said in a direct appeal to the Saxon's vanity, "is to validate your rule to the people who handle the coins and to claim your place in history."

"Yes," said Skegga impatiently. "Where is the gold?"

Allectus nodded, and took him to the mint where he had secretly walled in three iron-bound leather and elm wood chests of coin. "Two for you lord, one for me, and I can lead you to more, in Londinium."

Skegga debated taking it all, but then thought he'd hear what the tribune had to say about Arthur's battle plans. He could always kill Allectus later and take the bullion. Allectus knew what the Saxon was thinking and was unworried. He settled down to talk about Arthur. Retrieving the hoard in Londinium would have to wait until the city was taken.

Two days later, unnoticed, Allectus slipped aboard a trading ship and sailed for Gaul. With him were two hired guards and several heavy leather bags of gold. The traitor was heading for Maximian's camp in Belgica, and would make a similar offer to him regarding the treasure he had hidden in the walls of the mint in Rouen. Then he would accompany the Roman on his invasion of Britain and become a vassal king, once Arthur was dead. It was a pity to give up a couple of chests of bullion, he thought, but he could hardly have knocked down a building wall without being noticed, and anyway, he might well get his loot back in the future.

The Romans were powerful enough, he knew to defeat both Arthur and the Saxons. He would be Britain's next Imperator. He grimaced to himself. The Saxons could have their consolation prize of cheese and sausage.

XXXI Hibernia

Maximian regarded Allectus with distaste. This oily fellow thought he could bribe an emperor with a few stolen coins? His other offer, to reveal Arthur's battle plans, was childish. Maximian's own legions would crush the Britons without outside help from a traitor. He was debating whether to have Allectus flogged for insolence, or merely have him ejected when the tribune, floundering for an advantage, hit a nerve. "I can also tell you, Imperator, where the sacred Eagle has been hidden," he blustered. "Arthur dare not display it publicly, so he has hidden it against it being stolen and used by his enemies."

The statement was a lie, but Maximian was not to know that. "Indeed?" he drawled, "and where is that bird hidden?"

"It is cemented behind a wall in his fortress at Chester, lord," lied Allectus. "I can lead you to the exact spot."

The claim was enough to give Maximian pause. Reclaiming the lost Eagle would be a fine feather in his cap and by itself would almost justify an expedition against the rebel emperor. "We'll see," he said abruptly. "Take this man and keep him safe. He is not to leave the camp."

With the tribune departed, Maximian ran over his own plans again. His shipyards on the Scheldt and Meuse were producing well, building a fleet of invasion barges that could be towed behind a flotilla of galleys. He probably would not have everything in place for an invasion before winter arrived, but he would certainly be set for a springtime campaign.

He would launch the troop barges from the same port on the north coast of Gaul that old Gaius Julius had used, for the shortest, quickest crossing, and aim for Dover and its harbour. At the same time, while Arthur was distracted by that invasion fleet, he would dispatch a stronger force across the German Sea from the Rhine directly into the Thames estuary, arrow-straight for Londinium. With Arthur's forces engaged at the coast, Maximian could count on seizing the capital before heading south to trap Arthur between his two invasion forces. Then, with Arthur out of the picture, he could regroup and settle the barbarian Saxons' nonsense.

They could cooperate and agree to become his vassals, in which case he would cede some of eastern Britain to them, to be held against other incomers, or they could be enslaved and work the land for the conquerors. It looked very positive, and he smiled grimly as he thought of Arthur, that bastard Carausius as was, hanging off a crucifix in Londinium.

The thought of a crucifix was in the mind of the Hibernian sea raider Muirch. He was in a desperate situation, trapped away from his longship with just three companions and faced with several dozen well-armed British horse soldiers. He should never have gone back, he was thinking bitterly. Now he was a dead man, and these Roman-equipped cavalrymen would likely nail him up for the damage he'd done.

It had been a successful expedition, especially if you counted losing two of those irritating women, who'd been taken prisoner after splitting off from the main group. He'd seen his chance and sailed away early, to help the Britons catch them and that bishop Candless fellow from Pictland. After all, it would be fewer people to share the plunder.

But Muirch had not been satisfied with the take so far, and seeing two women working a hillside garden, had hissed a command, slipped his ship ashore behind a sheltering headland and taken three men with him to capture them. Slaves or rape victims, it was all the same. And matters had gone well at first. The women were hunted down and made fast, Muirch approvingly looked them over, young and attractive enough. Might as well do them now, away from the envious eyes of the rest of the crew. The four men took turns on the turf, ignoring the screams that turned to wracking sobs, but a cavalry troop alerted by the raiders' burning of a village two days before were patrolling, and heard screaming they at first thought was the noise of gulls. On a hunch, they checked further and the Hibernians were trapped.

"Put down those spears," the centurion ordered the two raiders who carried the long weapons. "And throw down your knives." Muirch cursed. He had not brought a sword, just a knife, because he had not come ashore to fight. He looked past the soldiers at the sparkle of the sea, green-blue under the sun. That way was Hibernia, his peat-smoke village, his dogs and his several wives. He would not be seeing any of that again. But he knew life went on after this body died. He would go to the feasting halls and join his dead friends. Better that than life as a shackled slave, digging fields and hewing wood through a life of misery. Now for the bridge of swords.

He drew his knife and ran hard at the cavalrymen. It was a suicide, but it was brief, and mercifully quick. The centurion was seated on his horse a length ahead of the line of his men. Muirch ran at him, the soldier raised his heavy spatha and kicked his horse's sides. The animal reared forward, the spear struck violently upwards and Muirch's ribcage shattered open like a splay of white fingers that suddenly blossomed red. The raider's vision dimmed, and far to the west, across the water, a dog raised his muzzle to the sky and howled in misery.

XXXII Concrete

Since learning that concrete will set under water, I had been spending time sloshing about in the River Ouse that ran by our fortress in Eboracum. Several of my engineer officers were as intrigued as I, especially since I had outlined my plan to them, and we had consulted what Roman writings we could find to determine the best mix.

The technique was simple enough: mix the ingredients and pour them into a wooden form. For my plan, to make pilings that stopped just inches below the surface of a river, the form had to be adjustable, but it was possible. The concrete set in two days in fresh water, faster in salt, but even in fresh water it was ready for load bearing in five or six days. When we believed we had the technique perfected, we loaded a baggage train with what we needed, formed a small column of engineers and infantrymen and set off south. We were going to trap a tribe of Parisi who were especially lawless and who lived close to the wide River Humber. When threatened, they would scatter into the marshes. Our troops could view them from the opposite bank, but if we attempted a crossing, the Parisi fled. An approach from the southern side of the river was difficult, and nearly impossible to attain surprise, as they maintained sentries miles to the west.

The only other approach, from the south, was over open marshy terrain that made it difficult to stay concealed, and the tribe would flee into sheltering fens and marshes to the east.

Once, the Romans had used a ferry between their own two settlements, which commanded the river crossing of the Ermine Street high road. These camps were offset to allow for the flow of the tide, which drove the ferry up or downstream depending on its ebb or flow. Now, a ferry would not suffice for us because we could not move enough troops over at one time. Nor did I have enough small ships at my disposal to launch a miniature invasion. It would have to be ground troops, and I wanted to try my concreting idea, which was simple, and might work. If it did, I could see military applications in its future.

We deliberately arrived after dusk, and I ordered that no cooking fires be lit in sight of the opposite bank, which was a mile and a half away. At the lowest tide, the water was no more than chest deep, but that and thick mud was still enough to delay our troops, wreck the surprise and to be dangerous for men in armour. My plan was to secretly construct underwater pilings to support wooden bridgeworks that we would lay immediately before marching over our hidden new bridge.

A local fisherman who had a line of fish traps at the river's second big bend gave us valuable advice. The river, he said, emptied slowly but returned four times faster, getting deeper by the height of a man every hour. A few men could wade across in the half hour when the sandbanks were fully exposed, but there would not be time enough for any sizeable force to cross before the incoming flood made it impossible. The engineers took timings and depths, and opted to shorten the distance we needed to bridge by dumping tons of rubble in the yard-deep mud to form an underwater causeway that would give us footing from the north bank to a big sandbank island in mid-river. From it, we faced the deepest part of the flow, which even at low tide was roughly as deep as a man is tall. That was where the engineers would set the forms and pour the underwater concrete piers, working by night so the Parisi would not observe our actions.

The work took just three nights. We took care to avoid observation and even put the settlement on the north bank under guard so word could not be carried out. When we finished the work, we had an underwater causeway to the water-covered shaped pilings that would accept and hold a wooden roadway. I had the engineers cover the tracks made on the bank by the rubble waggons, and to the casual observer nothing was different, but we still kept curfew on the settlement, and camped our troops out of sight to the north.

We returned to the river four days later, when the concrete had cured. The tide was lowest just after dawn, so our pioneers, roped together against the outflow, established themselves on the big sandbank and floated out the wooden roadbed. The operation went perfectly. Working in the dark, the engineers placed the roadway onto the pilings, and when the first wolf light dawned in the east, our punitive force waded across, scrambled up the steep riverbank and formed up. The attack on the Parisi village was a total surprise. The tribe's outlier sentries miles away in their tower to the west had not raised any alarm, expecting our troops to cross far upstream.

We took several dozen captives for the slave market, collected a number of silver torcs of twisted gold and silver that their headmen wore on arms and necks, and burned their settlement of feral-stinking thatched huts that were so primitive they used thin animal skins as window coverings. A soldier brought me an item he'd found by digging in the disturbed dirt by the fireplace of one hut, a beautiful green glass orb, as round and perfect as an apple, probably Grecian work. It weighed heavily in my hand. It would be perfect for Guinevia and her viewing meditations, I thought.

We made camp a few hundred yards upwind of the settlement to regroup and ready for our long march back to Eboracum, as I planned to mop up any tribesmen on the south bank of the river. That night, we celebrated.

"Gentlemen, the bridge work was highly satisfactory, and a technique we can use in the future when we need a surprise flanking attack, or a secret means of escape," I told my officers. "Well done. I think we have an amphora or two of excellent Rhenish wine somewhere in the impedimenta that we can share with our wet troopers. They need to be warmed up and this thin Parisi beer is not going to do the job."

All went well as we returned to Eboracum, but Guinevia was waiting in our quarters with a concerned look on her face. She had evidently been viewing something distant, she had her obsidian block and water bowl on her work mensa, and I noticed with a shiver that the remains of a vapour cloud, signs of her working magic, was dissipating in the air above it.

She wasted no time. "I have seen Maximian in Gaul," she said urgently. "He was studying charts with two officers. Then, without my volition, I was viewing busy shipyards on two wide rivers, the harbour at Bononia where once I made sacrifice, and the traitor Allectus in a stone town on a broad river." I questioned her carefully, but she had no interpretation of her visions, which did not surprise me as she never wanted to understand what her mind's eye was viewing, only to report it. Translating what she was seeing, she had asserted often enough, could muddy the vision. She wanted merely to see what she saw and let others decide what it meant.

I had enough faith in my sorceress to know that each part of what she saw in a single session was usually related, and it seemed obvious enough: Maximian was building an invasion fleet, he was probably gathering land forces into winter quarters in Bononia, the coastal stronghold that once was mine, and Allectus was almost certainly in Rouen, from the description of the bridge and tall buildings Guinevia gave. This last made me pause. Allectus had operated a mint there on the Seine riverfront, and that would be a likely reason to return to the town. He was creating coinage, or maybe retrieving what he had hidden when the Romans swept across Gaul and drove us out. I recalled that he had escaped the town by water, bringing ingots and coin to me in a couple of cargo vessels, but there was no guarantee he had emptied the whole mint, and might well have hidden some bullion to be retrieved later.

Guinevia was watching me, studying my face as my thoughts flew across it. "All will be well, we're too far into winter for Maximian to mount a campaign just yet," I reassured her. "He'll have to wait for several months, and that will give me time to prepare for him, as best we can." Secretly, I feared the worst. We were too weak even to drive off the Saxons. If the legions of Rome came at us, we would surely go under. Maximian need hardly rely on guile. He could land even against the bulwark of the Saxon Shore fortifications, although that would cost him some lives.

I tried to put myself into his military cloak and assess what he would do. He could come ashore in the southeast, as Constantius Chlorus had tried, but my fleet had been too good for him in the Narrow Sea, and a disastrous turn of the weather had wrecked his bid to sail into the Thames estuary.

He might attempt a landing in the west, after going the long way around, but I doubted that. It was too long an overland march, through hostile territory, to seize Londinium. More probable was a landing in the eastern seaboard, but the Saxons held Colchester and their reaction to a rival invader was unknown. On balance, it was not Maximian's best option.

I thought again about the man, a stubborn soldier whose previous plan had been wrecked by weather and naval forces. He would likely use a similar strategy again: a diversionary raid in the west or south to draw us off and then a direct thrust at the capital, either up the Thames or across the southeast coast after making the shortest crossing of the Narrow Sea.

The Thames river was my first concern. Maximian's fleet could sail into the estuary and straight up the river to the heart of Londinium. Our fortress was on the rising north bank, with one Thames bridge across which Watling Street ran. The city was a century past its pinnacle of prosperity and the waterfront was silting up, but it was still a walled stronghold with forum, several public baths, basilica, Mithraeum and my palace inside the riverfront citadel that defended the north end of the bridge. An invader would choose to land on that north bank, as much of the south side was marsh. On balance, I knew I had to make my defences downriver, before Maximian's fleet could come close to the city. So I went to Londinium and I sent a courier to Grimr and his squadron to meet me there.

Even in the chill of winter, the city was stinkingly noisome. Sewage ran in the streets, the populace, despite the public baths, was an unwashed and lawless mob, so that people locked their doors at night for fear of robbers. Fires were a constant hazard, and the place was just recovering from yet another plague that had filled the cemeteries in the east and northwest. We did not maintain a large garrison in the city, it was a place of craftsmen, merchants, slaves, officials and sailors, for the pool of London was a long-established harbour for traders from far places.

I took a barge trip along the river, and decided I must meet any invader 20 or more miles east of the city. We would get warning, because my defences of the Saxon Shore included beacons and signal towers to alert our forces. If the enemy did manage to put troops ashore on the north bank, I could meet them with cavalry. If they tried to sail right to the capital, I had a plan, and I explained it to my cavalry commander Cragus.

The wide river estuary narrowed dramatically at a point about 25 miles from the city, and swept around a four-mile, U-shaped bend that would force an invader to slow at the first, southerly turn as he came into the long reach of the base of the U. Midway along that reach, I planned to position a floating boom of heavy logs, chained together. I would not, however, order it deployed until the invaders had sailed past, then I would close the door behind them.

The logs would be towed out by Grimr's galleys, and would use the force of the tide to swing across the river. If it were ebbing, the end of the boom would be secured more to the east. If the tide were flowing in towards the city, I would have men stationed further west to secure the loose end. Grimr's galleys would provide protection as the boom was emplaced.

With the boom cutting off any retreat, the invaders would be sailing into a second obstacle I would have fixed across the narrowest part of the U-bend, where the river turned north. This would be a double barrier, prepared ahead of time and reinforced with a pontoon bridge on which I would station artillery and fire archers. I would also deploy ballistae on each bank, where the river narrowed, to plunge flaming pitch and large rocks into the invading fleet.

As a further measure, I would have fire ships stationed at each end of the trap. Whichever way the wind was blowing that day, I could send in blazing vessels to entangle themselves with the invading armada. With luck, we should sink or burn most of the enemy before they could come to land. For those that did get ashore, I would have cavalry and infantry waiting. I only hoped I had sufficient forces for the task, for our regular cavalry had been sadly depleted by the Saxons, and our heavy cavalry was not numerous. As my barge pulled steadily back through the biting wind to Londinium, I pulled my cloak tighter around me, and shivered. If my naval trap failed, the chances were that I would lose Britain to Maximian. I was unconcerned about dying in battle, but quailed at the thought of my Guinevia enslaved, of my son Milo likely executed, of wasting what my soldiers and I had fought for to bring Britain from under the Roman heel. All of that made a shudder run through my bones. The Romans were coming, and I was gambling again that I could somehow stop them. I needed the gods to send me an ally.

XXXIII Frozen

February was the darkest, coldest month and all of Britain shivered in its icy grip. The land was frozen hard, little moved on its icy, rutted surface except the occasional hare or fox, which would limp, trembling through the frozen grass. The few cattle that had not been slaughtered and salted before the worst onset of winter were kept inside the cottagers' homes, sharing the shelter and providing a farmyard warmth of their own. I was concerned about our cavalry horses, which we had again moved north from Aquae Sulis and a growing Saxon threat, to the safety of the great castrum at Caerleon. They and our fleet, which was safely wintering at Portus Chester, were my two greatest military assets. The fleet was stronger than the less-experienced Roman fleet, and the big horses of the heavy cavalry were our unsuspected weapon that should break any Saxon shield wall. I had ordered them housed in good stabling, and an ingenious engineer officer had not only commandeered a small dome-roofed temple, appropriately enough of Epona the horse goddess, that adjoined a public bath, but had piped in steam heat from the bath's own system to keep our precious steeds in winter comfort.

Our soldiers were less well served and less impressive than the horses. They were reasonably trained and equipped, but sadly outnumbered by the two Saxon hordes that had seized swathes of territory in the east and south. If ever those half-rival groups of invaders linked forces, we would be crushed.

Looming ominously on the horizon was the menace of a Roman invasion, which made the Saxon threat pallid and feeble by comparison. I truly did not know what to do, and called on Guinevia's magical viewing to help me. I needed that, and I could well use her tutor and mentor's advice, so she had successfully persuaded Myrddin to come to Chester from his freezing stone home in the Welsh mountains, tempting him with talk of warm rooms, a soft bed, good food and talk of mysticism.

On this day when the wind blasted in from the Hibernian Sea and even the sheltered harbour beneath Chester's fortress walls was choppy with wavelets, I asked the two sorcerers to join me and my senior officers to discuss a campaign. I explained my problem succinctly. "I cannot wait for the spring, when two Saxon armies and a Roman one will come for me," I said. "With miracles, we might defeat one of them, but we could not take on three armies, even one after the other. What I propose instead is to begin a winter campaign and catch the Saxons off their guard."

The idea was outlandish, but it had merit while it also came with great danger. Men did not want to fight in winter, it was a time when they stayed by the fireside. Winter was not a campaigning season, not a time for slogging through snowdrifts, for sleeping outdoors in constantly-wet clothing, shivering under scraps of canvas. There was no food to be had in the countryside, the heavy equipment and impedimenta carts were more difficult to move through slush, or ice and frozen ruts, and breakdowns were much more frequent.

If we could even raise an army, the men would need more sustenance to keep their bodies active in the cold, which meant supply problems, clothing and equipment difficulties. There would be hardships in even simple things like gathering fuel for the vital warming and cooking fires, in communicating with remote detachments, with secrecy of movements that could in winter be tracked by smoke from the vital fires we would need. There would be a host more problems, too.

But we could surprise the Saxons if we went now, unexpected in a difficult time, and surprise was a vital element of military success. It was incumbent on me to plot how to do it. The question was could we campaign across the frozen land? I fell back on my usual military dicta - start with the basics: define the objective, gather intelligence, assign personnel, establish communications, source supplies and arrange transport. The well-used military machinery fell into place for most of these categories, but this time, I had a secret weapon: gathering information. My unusually-compliant seers were skilled at sending out their minds to view remote places and people, they had agreed to help, I explained what I wanted, and hoped for results.

Guinevia and Myrddin both nodded, exchanged glances and went to their chambers with scribes who recorded their visions to read to me later. The seers sent out their mystic inner eyes and described a sprawling Saxon tent camp around Colchester, its herd of stolen cattle and sheep penned in a loop of the river there, rows of beached longships and a very large area of destruction where fire had burned the town and taken away much of the very winter quarters' habitation that the Saxons had sought in the place.

Across the southern stretch of Britain, the sorcerers also viewed the other Saxon force's encampment. They had chosen a sheltered spot in a steep-sided valley and were camped alongside a small stream that meandered towards Aquae Sulis. Their war band was less numerous than the Saxons' force camped by Colchester, and seemed more passive, for neither seer reported much movement. Those invaders, it seemed were content to wait out the winter in their tents and rough shelters.

Guinevia planted the seed of the idea in my mind, Myrddin confirmed what she and he both had seen.

"Can I do this and live?" I asked Myrddin. Then I told him my half-formed plan. He and Guinevia exchanged that glance I had seen before, and they nodded in unison. I noticed without surprise that a white Rat was preening its whiskers in a dark corner of the room. I glanced up over Guinevia's head but there was no vapour cloud, and Myrddin was his usual saturnine and unreadable self. Positive. I saluted them both, kissed Guinevia in gratitude and left, to outline the plan to our war council.

It was dissected, discussed and agreed. The tribunes Cragus and Androcles would accompany me, and we would take a picked force including the elite Chevron warriors who proudly sported badges from the cloak of the officer who had saved our iconic Eagle standard. Three days later, my dragoons mounted on our heavy horses and with my fine black Frisian steed Corvus under me, our war band of six dozen men set out for Colchester, across quiet, frozen Britain. We carried the Eagle that had helped us recapture Britain, and now it also displayed a dragon symbol to show its freedom from Rome.

I wore my cavalryman's helmet with the eagle crest, my purple cloak of Imperator, pinned at the shoulder with the silver and amber badge of a British jarl, and I wore my great sword Exalter at my hip, to show those we might see that this was no raiding party, but their lord riding out. It was a heartening message that would resonate through the markets, hamlets and towns to say that, even in the depths of winter, Britannicus is striking at our enemies. The people will know: he will rid us of the Saxon menace, he will keep the Romans at bay.

We rode across the snow-quiet limestone peaks of central Britain, through a stark, vast oak forest and into the lonely fenlands, which crackled frosty and white under our horses' hooves. Our helmet plumes were matched by the plumes of the breath of horses and men; we travelled light, we made good time and we rode unchallenged across the land of the Catuvellauni. At the north-south metalled high road of Ermine Street, we turned south, to collect certain supplies from the British garrison that still held snowy Verulamium. I was interested to note there that the Christians, who were now unmolested, were building a temple to one of their holy men, Alban, a rebel who had been beheaded at Severus' orders. A criminal to some, I mused, and a saint to others.

After a day to regroup and resupply, we moved on, and it was after dusk on the moonless night we wanted when we came near the Saxon encampment outside Colchester. We ourselves were no fragrant flowers, but from several miles' distance we first scented the smoke, and then their gagging stench of human grease, ripe-sweated, rank wool and dung. We approached the camp as we had planned, in darkness and from the side where the animals were herded in a loop of the Colne river. As I had hoped and prayed to Mithras, the water's surface was thick, hard-frozen ice.

We did not pause. A dozen of our soldiers slipped across undetected and cut the throats of the few sentries, who were all dozing or huddled unmoving in their cloaks. Cragus showed a light, hidden behind his cloak from the enemy, to report the sentries silenced, and I brought our column over the river, our horses' hooves wrapped in sacking to muffle them and to give them purchase on the rutted ice. At my orders, the cavalrymen had smothered their beasts' nostrils and whispered comfortingly to quiet them. It worked. Animals and riders moved stealthily, straight into the undisturbed herd, and one detail of six bold soldiers crept through the shadows to a warehouse where grain was stored, and fired it. That was our signal to start.

It was easy work to move the drowsy cattle, but edging out the flock of sheep proved more difficult, and we had only about half of them across the river when a Saxon who'd stepped out for a midnight piss saw the movement. He ran to the pen, and was ridden down by one of our cavalrymen. From then on, it was a rearguard action. We rode our big horses at the sleepy, alarmed Saxons, many of whom were drunk and stumbling, anyway. We threw flasks of oil into their watch fires to make them explode and flare alarmingly, and we scattered burning brands among the tents. My raiders created a noisy chaos of steel, smoke and blood that panicked the lean cattle to a loping stampede and confused the Saxons into shouting disarray.

We lost some cows who fell through weak spots in the river ice, which at least had the benefit of creating open water to delay any would-be pursuers, and many of the sheep and goats scattered nimbly into the forests along the river, but the damage was done to the Saxons and we had no use for the animals ourselves. The locals would catch and hide away the beasts, and that was good. The Saxons had scoured the region, scraping it clear of food and brought their loot to their camp. Our raiders had destroyed their store, and there was no more. Now, in the depths of winter, they were not only sleeping roofless outside the destroyed houses of Colchester, but they were virtually out of supplies.

Our task accomplished, we slid away into the night like goblins, but we laughed a lot more than those night-walkers do.

Within two weeks, the Saxon longships began leaving, their crews starving and desperate. Some went to Gaul, some scattered around the coast of Britain, but their gathered force was dispersed and no longer a threat. It would be months before the Saxon warlord Skegga could again pull together a force to match ours. They were not defeated, but they had been driven off, for now.

We stayed for a few nights in Verulamium, tending our horses and ourselves, and we feasted on the quarters of sheep that Androcles had somehow butchered and brought back across his saddle bow. Then we set off for Aquae Sulis and the camp the sorcerers had described. This would be a different form of attack and we made it with the utmost caution. We found the encampment, and traced back upstream the brook that ran through it. I had no intention of facing those Saxons with my puny force, but I intended to discomfit them, at least.

Several miles upstream, we found a smallholding that had been gutted, but it had what I needed, an old byre and pigsty, and some timbers. We made several sleds that our horses could drag, and we loaded them with reeking dung from the byre. This we pulled to within a half mile of the Saxon camp, and dumped the lot into the brook. For good measure, we dropped our breeches and added some human waste to the foul mix. The Saxons, ever careless of hygiene, were drinking from that convenient stream next to their tents, and we gave them some additional nutrition.

My spies reported a few days later that there were many raiders vomiting and sick in their camp, and later, we learned that scores had died. By then, we were back in Chester, by our firesides and taking the chill out of our bones. For now at least, the Saxon threat had been nullified.

XXXIV Prepare

Maximian was ready. Frozen February had given way to blustering March and his winter of preparations was ending. He wished to take his invasion force to Britain as soon as possible, he told his officers, because you could not trust the Alemanni to stay quiet for long. There were signs of more unrest, and King Gennobaudes, he had found, was liaising with the Britons. Maximian had brought the Belge before him, tortured him into confession and confiscated the royal treasury.

Then, to entertain his troops, he had the battered monarch sewn into the bloodied hide of a mule and turned loose in the arena at Rouen with a couple of starving wolves. The spectacle had delighted the troops, who were bored after months in winter quarters. Maximian drawled to his officers that watching a tenant king torn to pieces by a couple of his fellow dogs had inspired considerable loyalty among the other vassals. Amazing, he said, what a turn of speed that fellow had shown, despite being wrapped so tightly. At first, that was.

The Augustus Emperor of the West turned his mind from the bloody spectacle in the arena, straightened his purple-trimmed tunic and considered his preparations to retake the mutinous colony. He would divide his forces into three parts, like Gaius Caesar's Gaul. The main thrust would be over the shortest crossing of the Narrow Sea, from Itius, the temporary departure port east of Bononia. From its beaches, he'd launch his invasion barges. About the same time, he would send a diversionary attack from the Scheldt, directly west into the Thames estuary and straight for the heart of Londinium. Those squadrons should draw off the British fleet to allow the main thrust an unopposed crossing of the strait. Once the Romans were ashore near Dover, they could march overland and join the attack on Londinium in a couple of days.

But the attack that would crush the Britons would come from an unexpected direction. Maximian had secretly been gathering a second fleet, further west along the coast of Gaul. This troop-carrying armada would sail at the same time as the Scheldt flotilla, round the western peninsula that formed the land's end of Britain and follow along the north coast of the Dumnonian peninsula and into the estuary of the Severn river. This tidal inlet could be followed all the way to the old legionary garrison at Gloucester, bypassing the Caerleon strongpoint along the way. From Gloucester, the disembarked troops would march overland along the valley of the Thames. They would strike unexpected from the west and join the other two invasion groups near Londinium, to trap and crush the usurper Arthur once and for all.

With the Britons defeated and in chains, the Romans could then turn their attention to the squatter Saxons in eastern Britain. They could, Maximian mused, be left in place as a buffer against further barbarian incomers. Much would depend on their willingness to pay tribute and become vassals, he thought. If not, he would simply put them to the sword as well, or there was always Rome's ever-growing appetite for slaves. But, there would be time enough for those terms to be hammered out when he had Arthur's head on a spear point over a city gateway.

He sent out his orders by courier. The twin flotillas from the Belgic Scheldt and from western Gaul's rocky harbours were to begin their voyages in 12 days' time. Two days later, the invasion barges would leave for their shorter journey from the coast near Bononia. Both should arrive on Britain's shores at the same time.

The activity in the shipyards along the Meuse and Scheldt was observed by Arthur's spies, and several boats slipped hurriedly out of their ports on unscheduled fishing trips that would bring them spy payments of gold. Word reached Arthur before the first invaders had boarded their vessels. He did not receive any notice of the Gallic fleet's preparations.

When the Gauls came to tell me, I rewarded them well, and thanked Mithras that I had begun my preparations. The giant log booms that would close the Thames were already prepared, stoutly chained together and fastened to the northern shore, where we had also built low-lying strongpoints to defend them. I went to Londinium once again, to supervise and to rally my soldiers, and once again, I began moving the pieces around the chessboard. I left orders for the legion in Eboracum to move south to Verulamium, to be ready as a swift response force for any threat to the east coast, or as support for our operations along the Thames.

Equally, I shunted the legion at Chester down the length of Watling Street to Londinium, and brought a sizeable force from Caerleon in the far west to the southern coast in case of an attack on our naval facilities at Portus Chester, where Grimr had his fleet on high alert. He also sent scouts to patrol the Narrow Sea from Dorchester to the deadly sandbanks east of Dover.

Guinevia followed me to Londinium because I needed her psychic spying eyes, but she could not have stayed with me on that wild ride that caused two horses to founder under me, so hard ridden were they. My guards and I clattered into Londinium through the New Gate, and I went at once to the riverfront command post by the Sher Bourne. What my officers told me caused me to change horses again and wearily carry on 25 or so miles east to the first of the log boom emplacements.

It was well-sited, on a vital narrows where the river turned north after making a giant 'U.' The pioneers had done a fine job, and we had sufficient vessels fastened end to end to make a pontoon bridge behind the defensive boom. This bridge would have archers and slingshot men along its length, and they would fire at the enemy from behind a wooden rampart.

The boom itself was made of huge logs, chained and stapled end to end, that floated, barely showing above the surface, and I ordered the pontoon barrier to be placed a short distance further back from it, in case the Roman galleys attempted to ram their way across. I knew they would sink in the attempt, and I wanted a field of fire for my archers to butcher them, clear of any sinking ships.

At the south end, where the log boom was fastened to the land, our engineers had constructed another strong point so we could repel any attempt to unfasten the barrier. On a thought, I ordered the pontoon bridge to be given an extra surface of planking, to create a rough roadway. If needed, we could move troops swiftly across the river to the south bank. If it were not needed, we would use the floating platform as a rampart for the archers. It all seemed satisfactory, so I moved a few miles downstream, to view the first boom the enemy would encounter, the one that would close the trap behind them.

The giant logs floated near-invisible, so low were they in the water and again I satisfied myself that the massive chains which held them in line could not easily be hacked free by some daring axemen. Such heroes would have to swim to them, straddle the slippery logs and wield an axe at the linkages, all while coming under fire from the banks. The archers got instructions should that happen, and I turned to the boom. One end of the chained logs was secured to the north bank, again guarded by a discreet blockhouse, against any effort to loose the boom, the other floated free and would be floated across the river after the enemy had passed by.

An engineer officer respectfully required my attention. He suggested fastening a long hawser to the loose end of the boom, a hawser that would be attached to a windlass or winding gear on the south bank. It would be a quicker and more positive way to move the loose end to its fastenings, he felt, than by towing the heavy logs across the river by galley, even if we did have the ebb or flow of the tide to assist. It would also assist in landing the end to be fastened at the exact place we had readied for it, where we could build a strongpoint. His idea was better than mine, and I nodded agreement, so he set about creating and installing the machinery we needed, and building a fort to protect it.

Next, I inspected the artillery. Most of it was concentrated at the western end of our trap. There were sling catapults called 'wild asses' because they made such a powerful kick, and these could be used to thrown burning pitch or other inflammables at the invaders' ships. I ordered dozens of ballistae to be placed in support of them. These were crossbow-style weapons that could fire big iron bolts with considerable precision, or could also hurl rounded river stones that would stave in the ribs of a lap-straked ship with ease.

Lastly, I viewed the nimble little rowboats that could dash among the invaders. I did not want them to hook onto the enemy ships, I wanted them to perform a specific duty, and I instructed their crews in it and ordered small fighting towers installed fore and aft on these speedy river craft.

All that was left to do was to ensure our watchtowers along the estuary were manned, that the signal fires were laid and that our men and materials were in place along the killing ground we had established. My officers and I went over every detail, from the braziers that would supply burning coals to how we would provide sheaves of arrows for the archers on the pontoon roadway. Finally, I was satisfied we had omitted nothing. Then I went back to the palace in Londinium where Guinevia had arrived and discussed what she could view for me. And I sent couriers to Cragus and Grimr to return and attend a council of war. We had several more days before we could expect Maximian's attack. I wanted everything to be ready for him.

XXXV Thames

Guinevia helped the imperator to prepare, and she managed some of it right, but she also got something very badly wrong and it put Britain in mortal danger. Arthur asked her as a matter of great importance to see what his enemies were doing, and she made an honest attempt. Her technique for remote viewing called for her to specify where she wanted to send her mind, or on whom she wanted to concentrate. She naturally opted to view the doings of Maximian and Allectus. She looked at the Meuse and Scheldt rivers' shipyards and at the harbour of Bononia. She strained to view the places she knew: the Seine at Rouen, the ruined remains of her father's compound on the Tay; the castra at Chester, Dover and Eboracum, the Saxon encampments at Colchester and Aquae Sulis. One by one, she sent out her mental eye and reported her impressions.

Two scribes diligently scribbled down what she saw, and also what she did not see: if the once-bustling shipyards were now empty, that was as significant as seeing a legion encamped outside Bononia. If the vessels in the shipyard had sails hoisted, that was significant. If their masts were not yet stepped, that too could tell secrets. It was a masterful display of magic, but the Druid did not know she should send her mind to examine the rocky coast of northwest Gaul, where Maximian's secret fleet was readying to sail. So, unobserved, the Roman force would arrive in a part of Britain that was unprepared for it, and soon.

Arthur read her reports and was pleased. He thought he had a comprehensive picture of the doings of his enemies, but the portrait was flawed and he did not suspect it.

On their ordered days, the two blue-sheeted Roman fleets sailed their separate ways, from their different harbours. One went west from the Scheldt, another went west from Armorica, the rugged rocky peninsula of northwestern Gaul. The first fleet aimed its menace at the Thames, the second sailed a course around the land of the Dumnonii, who hold the south western arm of Britain, to deliver its threat up the Severn estuary.

Arthur was only ready for the first flotilla. The imperator knew that when lit, the line of beacons that ringed the southeast coastal ramparts of his island were employed as navigation aids by mariners, and he had conceived an idea to use that knowledge. He created a new, false line of beacons inland, to mislead Maximian's fleet as it crept towards Britain in the pre-dawn dark. The British imperator had once been admiral of the Roman fleet that policed the Narrow Sea, and he knew that an undersea ridge of chalk covered with deadly sandbanks lay a half dozen miles off the coast, just east of the narrowest neck of the straits, at Britain's forefoot.

When he was a sailor patrolling those waters, he had often enough taken soundings in fog or dark to determine his exact position, and had tested between his fingers and tasted on his tongue the grit and clay that a grease-covered weight brought up from the sand below. The old sailor's trick to analyze the seabed under his hull was an accurate gauge for the experienced, but was no help to novices in those treacherous waters.

Maximian's new sailors had been made strangers to those seas, because Arthur's own admiral Grimr and his fleet ruthlessly ruled them. The Romans, leaving Gaul by dark to cloak their invasion, innocently trusted the wreckers' false guidelights and sailed unsuspecting to their doom. The first they knew were the juddering crashes as their pinewood hulls ran into the undersea obstructions that make the area a ships' graveyard.

All the Romans had for visibility were guttering oil lamps, carefully guarded and shielded on their wooden ships. They could not see the sandbanks, they could not see their sister ships except for a small flicker of flame, so they wrecked in darkness. Even the calls of alarm and shouts of distress could not save the following ships as they ran into the undersea teeth. More than a third of the fleet that set out for the Thames went ashore on those deadly shoals. The loss of life was horrendous, as ship after ship was misled into a maze of sand, rocks and killing waters.

Dawn broke over the heaving grey seas to reveal the survivors of the fleet anchored or hauled to in disarray among the treacherous shoals. All they could do was drag aboard the corpses floating overside, and edge cautiously out to open water, nervous leadsmen chanting the depths they plumbed as they corrected their course to the north and around the headlands of the territory of the Cantii. Finally, in daylight, they gained the broad mouth of the estuary of the Thames, and began sailing into an even worse nightmare.

When the grey light of dawn revealed the fleet to the watchers on the cliffs, the fire beacons' signals ran ahead to raise the alarm. In full daylight, smoke from the wet hay and oily waste thrown on the blazes confirmed the Romans' arrival and groups of horsemen were summoned to gather along the low bluffs and high hills that rimmed the estuary. They cantered alongside as the invasion fleet sailed for Londinium, and destruction, the warships' beaked rams throwing up a fine spray, their crews pulling in time to the inexorable hammer taps of the coxswain beating out the stroke.

Arthur's ambush worked even better than he had dared to hope. The depleted Roman fleet sailed down the narrowing funnel of the Thames estuary and slowed to a crawl as they rounded the sweep of the bend where the Celtish King Till's burh began. The ships were carried forward, the incoming tide flowing fast and pushing them westerly towards Londinium. Soon, they were struggling along the river's reach where Arthur had created his killing ground. A blustery March wind battered in from the north, raising a chop that made steering difficult, and the push of the incoming tide largely took control from the steersmen's hands. Anxious and struggling with their vessels, the Romans paid small attention to the nimble galleys that pulled out into the river behind them, nor did they notice the long hawser that was being dragged from the water by men and oxen working a windlass on the southern bank.

In a half hour, that windlass and its panting human and animal crews had hauled a heavy log boom from shore to shore and had it fast, and guarded. The door had been closed on the invaders' retreat.

The river funnelled tighter and tighter, and another right-angled bend, this time trending to the north, was approaching. The Romans were uncomfortably aware that both banks were crowded with warriors keeping pace with their vessels, but the ships' commanders confidently waved the fleet onwards. They reasoned that when the banks grew marshy, they would lose their hostile companions. Then they saw the line of the pontoon bridge, a floating span across the river that held clusters of men, and the commanders gestured their archers forward to the bows.

Too late, they saw the slop of waves that betrayed the near-submerged line of the log boom, and the first half dozen longships crunched against the huge timbers, stove in their hulls and began to founder. The waiting archers on the pontoon bridge released the first of a steady barrage of deadly missiles, their first target an unfortunate galley that had struck the underwater boom exactly between two chained log ends. The impact had holed the iron-reinforced bow and the projecting ram was inextricably stuck. The crew of the pinioned ship was forced either to stand and receive a deadly arrow storm at close range, or to leap overboard and face almost-certain drowning.

Because the oncoming fleet was pointing directly at the pontoon rampart, few Roman archers could bear on it to return fire, but the line of British bowmen, standing safely behind a breastworks on the pontoon roadway, had the entire fleet as their targets. The flotilla halted, milling in confusion, and the ballistae hidden in the scrubby undergrowth on both banks began firing.

The big iron arrows shattered gunwales and pierced hulls; volleys of rounded river rocks arced down steeply to plunge clean through the pinewood bottoms of the ships. Smoking containers of burning pitch began to crash down on the huddled fleet, spreading a fog of choking fumes before the taut blue canvas sails flamed, flared, then vanished in gouts of smoke and ash. Then a new horror emerged.

Small, swift galleys rowed by eager Britons brought deadly slingers close, slingers who fired from fighting towers that loomed above the open ships into which they were sending their rain of death and injury. These men, many of them shepherds who used the weapons to keep their flocks safe from predators, hurled with astonishing accuracy lead weights the size of a hen's egg. They had a range of up to a hundred paces, and were deadly at about half that, a distance at which they could kill a horse with a single weighty missile.

The slingers' orders were to assassinate the steersmen and officers, and when they hurled their missiles in volleys from 20 or 30 paces' range, the result was murderous. The mere sight of a scarlet-cloaked officer dropping to the deck, his head crushed by one of the unusual missiles was enough to make the sailors fearful, and the fact that the officers and steersmen were obviously targeted made those individuals more conscious of taking shelter than of operating their vessels.

The steersmen cowered away from the rain of arrows and died under the brutal blows of the slung lead missiles. Dying or panicked, they rammed and crashed their vessels into each other in the struggle to turn in the narrow river, a desperate but vain attempt to escape a maelstrom of burning ships, panicked men and dense smoke. On the pontoon roadway, firing from ultra-short range, the archers poured their goose-feathered missiles blindly into the smoke, knowing that a yard-long, bodkin-pointed arrow would transfix any Roman mail or Celtic leather breastplate when fired from such a close distance. As fast as they fired, they were resupplied by boys who ran crouching behind them with linen-and-willow-wand quivers of arrows designed to prevent the feather flights being crushed.

The British archers' long hunting bows twanged and hummed a dozen times to the minute, delivering a storm of iron death into the hapless throngs in the Roman ships. No man could stand in that storm and live. It was hardly a skirmish, it was more of a butcher's shambles, a slaughter yard on the water, and the Romans who went over the side in hopes of escaping the missiles or the flames or their own sinking ships mostly drowned under the weight of their armour.

The few who struggled ashore were hacked down, and the longships that did manage to turn back were trapped at the eastern boom, and destroyed by two fireships that the Britons pushed among them. The quickest-thinking steersmen ran their ships ashore, where some few score of the invaders escaped their hunters and fled into the countryside.

A rainstorm began pounding the region as Arthur's men took the surrender of hundreds, chained them and marched them to the slave pens. Arthur himself, smoke-grimed, bloodied and soaked, rode to his riverfront palace by the bridge at Londinium, and there, during the victory celebration, heard the news: the real invasion would be coming at Dover. The news from spies in Gaul was that the attack had been a feint to feel out the defences, and it would be a week before Maximian would launch at Britain's south coast. Time to rest. The rain would bog them down on any march to the coast. Give the men a day or two to rest, Arthur thought. What he did not know was that the spies had been turned after the death of King Gennobaudes. Maximian was already on his way.

XXXVI Severn

At Arthur's insistence, Guinevia had taken her son Milo and left Londinium for the safety of Chester before the Romans attacked southern Britain. She opted first to travel west to Caerleon for an important druidical conclave at the edifice built by King Ebranck, which since the Roman invasion had been a temple of Diana. It was still an important religious site and especially important to the Druids, who had been largely underground during the occupation of the Caesars, who regarded them more as a political force than a religious one. Then, the Romans had not allowed druidical beliefs with their usual tolerant indifference. Now that the Romans had gone, the druids were gathering strength again, and Guinevia found herself in a position of considerable influence and power, from both her training and for her closeness to the imperator.

The sorceress took in her entourage the three female Hibernian slaves Jesla, Karay and Caria who had been captured after sailing with their menfolk marauders. Guinevia enjoyed the women's native music and crak, a term they used for lively conversation, and they in turn enjoyed their good treatment as slaves in a wealthy household. It was a life much more comfortable than the one they had left in the boggy green island west of Britain.

Guinevia had taken fondly to the smallest of the women, blonde Caria, whose fake sorcery had bemused and frightened male warriors, and who had the trick, worked best in dim light, of exhaling a luminous glow from crushed shellfish secretly held in her mouth. It looked convincingly like actual fire-breathing. The Druid priestess had retrieved the decrepit skull and handful of vertebrae the girl used for her show of casting auspices, equipment the jailers regarded with superstition and had swiftly confiscated. "How do you use these, dear?" she asked gently. Caria, well aware that she was dealing with a real and powerful sorceress whose goddess was the dreadful Nicevenn, huntress and tormentor of the souls of the dead, shook her head.

"It's for show," she whispered. Guinevia nodded, she'd known that. Neither was the girl was a haruspex, as she claimed. She couldn't divine the future from the entrails of a sacrifice, but she was courageous and intelligent.

"I could teach you a little about divination," Guinevia offered. Caria nodded silently. "The old Babylonians were the experts, and I have had counsel with some of their wise men," Guinevia explained. "They knew that the liver is the source of the blood, so examining it could tell you much about the will of the gods. Animal livers will do, but human sacrifice is very powerful, and you can learn the future from seeing where a dying human moves, and what his intestines tell you."

She paused as the raeda carriages in which the women were riding lurched and splashed through a ford. Something about the water disturbed her, some hidden whisper of faraway threat came to her, flowing with the power of the river. Guinevia scented the air like a dog. Nothing, but an unease prickled the nape of her neck. She leaned from the window to summon the guard captain, who rode close behind. "Stop the column under those trees," she said. "And, where are we on the iterum?"

The soldier knew the list of waystations by heart. "We could be in Glevum, called Gloucester, by nightfall."

"Stop here, I need an hour," Guinevia ordered.

The next minutes were bustling ones as the soldiers set up a security cordon, sent scouts out to survey the distance and picketed the horses. Guinevia took a pouch of soft leather and walked away from the carriages and the stamping horses. The guard captain gestured eight of his men to form a discreet inner ring around her as she chose a large beech tree and sat in its shade. From the leather pouch, she drew out her looking-block of obsidian and rested it in her lap, closing her eyes to meditate before she looked into the gleaming dark glass. It took nearly two difficult hours, but the sorceress sent out her mind to trace the course of the water whose essence had somehow signalled to her. She traced it upstream into a ridge of hills that rose abruptly from a wide plain, but saw nothing except the shadows of water sprites and a wispy hint of the source spring's fern-green goddess, an ancient from before the time of the builders of the stone dances of the west.

She turned her mind downstream, flickering fast as the flight of a kingfisher along the water, seeing the little rill grow and join with larger streams, to add itself into rippling brooks and become an exuberant, tumbling young river. She saw it slow and ease into a wide, willow-lined reach bridged with Roman stone, where homes stood on either bank. Then it widened more, to flow powerful and brown with silt towards the welcoming salt sea that led still further to the immensity of the ocean called Atlanticus.

But she saw no threat, and shook her head in puzzlement. Her inner core knew there was one. Guinevia screwed up her eyes and rubbed them, then pored again into the dark depths of the volcanic glass. At her volition, she seemed to soar away from her view of the green Atlantic rollers that approached the land in serried, smooth-crested ranks, to see from the height of an eagle or hawk, a view opened to her mind by the wonderful charts of Myrddin. Below her, the southwestern peninsula of Britain jutted its claw into the ocean, seeming to grasp at the steep rollers, now curling white at their crests and blowing spume as they moved at the rocky teeth of the land.

And she saw the threat. A Roman fleet was moving around that land's end, and was heading in a long, straggling line just off the cliffs and sea islands of Dumnonia. They were sailing towards the wide mouth of the estuary that gradually narrowed to a river, a brook, a stream and finally right to the rill at her feet. The shock of knowing hit her with a jolt, a hurt and burn in her soul. She wanted to tear her mind away, but rode the hurt, and forced her reluctant mind's eye downwards, closer to the blue sails and banners, rigid in the wind, of the Roman flotilla.

They were pitching, rolling hard, she saw. Men were vomiting over the sides, the hoisted sails were so minimal as to be almost bare poles, but those small triangles of canvas held taut by what obviously were gale-strong winds were driving the fleet rapidly along the coast, with the winds dead astern. An invasion force was headed for the estuary of the Severn, and Britain was asleep to its threat. Guinevia was the only person on the whole island who knew of it, and she must communicate her knowledge to Arthur, or he would be caught between two Roman armies and crushed.

Her first thought was to send a telepathic message to Myrddin, and she tried desperately hard to do that, but could not break through the curtain wall of protection the sorcerer had created while he worked on his own business.

She rose and ran back to the guard captain. She gave him scribbled messages for Arthur. He assigned four young horse soldiers to deliver one to Londinium, and three more to ride to the coast near Dover, where she expected the other Roman attack. Either course was futile, she knew. Two, maybe three days to reach Arthur, plus several days to scrape together enough forces, and that only if he could spare them from the other threat. Then there would be several more days to march them to the west, where they would be already exhausted, to confront an enemy long established ashore… She thought of the garrison at Caerleon, but knew Arthur had already moved its legion to the southern coast. The western gate of Britain was open and undefended.

"We must go to Gloucester," she commanded the guard captain. "Now, quickly."

XXXVII Caria

Far out in the Atlanticus, storm winds were brewing howling fury and thundering waves which they threw against the high grey battlement cliffs of Moher in western Hibernia. The gale shrieked across the arrays of vast green rollers that pounded the sea rocks of the peninsula of the Dumnonii and drove those walls of water, foam-flecked and awesome in their battering power, towards the Severn Sea.

The same blasting storm that was racing the Roman fleet along the rocky north coast of the peninsula and into the mouth of the Severn was also piling up tall, pyramid-shaped mountains of saltwater behind the fleet, where terrified, vomiting soldiers who were so much helpless cargo could only watch as the cursing sailors fought to keep clear of the destructive claws of the shore. A few of the fleet did fall away and were smashed into flotsam and bloodless corpses on that shore, but most passed between the breakwater islands of Steep Holm and Flat Holm in safety. Even in those more sheltered waters, the pitching from the vicious seas was so fierce, and the fleet scudded along at such breakneck pace from the powerful following gale that no commander, determined as he might be, could even consider turning for the shore.

Guinevia knew it. She was standing on a stone bridge over the Severn that ran from a gravel terrace on one side of the river to the fortress on the other that stood above the flood plain at Gloucester. Above her bowed head was a small vapour cloud. Behind her closed lids she was fiercely focused, viewing the onrushing fleet whose energies were coming to her through the water. She knew she had to do something, and she did what she knew best. She called on her goddess, on Myrddin's help and on Myrddin's gods.

The Druid was an adept of the sea god Manannan mac Lir, an elemental and powerful Celtic deity who was familiar to the sorceress. In her mentor Myrddin's name, she implored Manannan's help. Almost at once, the wind rose and began to whip her hair and cloak, streaming them behind her like banners.

Without conscious knowledge, she dimly understood what was being placed in her mind. She grasped that the estuary of the river is so shaped that it funnels the tide into an increasingly narrow channel, one that begins five miles wide, but narrows to less than one hundred paces. Even as the inflowing tide is squeezed by the compressing banks, the river bed also rises, creating a tidal range that is the second highest anywhere in the world.

This March day saw a thousand-year confluence of events that spelled utter disaster for any craft caught in the estuary. It was the time of the vernal equinox, the year's highest tide. It was also the day of a new moon, which threw its extra gravitational pull into the equation and tilted an ocean to slop against Britain. Then there was the vast storm pounding in from the Atlanticus, which came from the exact southwest direction that could cause most damage. It provided a gale-driven blast to push up huge slabs of water into some of the world's biggest ocean waves. The perfect storm of highest tide, gravitational pull, huge winds, and a great mass of racing waters all combined, then was forced into a funnel-shaped channel. In minutes, it jetted a towering surge wave inland at incredible speed. Caught in that torrent was a flimsy Roman fleet manned by seasick, terrified sailors.

The Romans were being carried like flotsam on the surge of the tide, racing past the low shoreline, afraid or unable to turn for the pitiful shelter of the land by the force of the gale-driven saltwater torrent. The tide which 260 times a year runs at the speed of a cantering horse, was now pouring in faster than any horse could ever attain and the steersmen were no more able to control their vessels than a child could control a paper boat on a raging mountain stream.

Guinevia had no knowledge of that, but she did know that Manannan would want a price for his help. She stumbled from the bridge, holding onto the parapet against the blast. Her soldiers were circled around uneasily, well aware of the meaning of the uncanny vapour cloud that had not been whipped away by the wind, and shuffling to avoid catching the eye of the sorceress. Guinevia caught at her flying cloak and wrapped it around her slender self. She scanned the area and found a strangely exhilarated Caria watching from the shelter of the trunk of a big elm.

"Did you call this in by magic?" the Hibernian asked, eyes sparkling.

"I did," said Guinevia shortly, adding: "but it might not be enough."

Caria eyed her speculatively. "Can I help in your magic?" she said.

"Possibly," Guinevia said slowly, "possibly, you could be the most important element of it."

It took several minutes for the Druid sorceress to explain matters, but Caria was calm. "We Celts do not die," she said with dignity. "We go on to the feasting halls of Tir na Nog, and maybe one day we come back for a short time, but to cross the bridge of swords in honour would be a splendid thing. I am not so attached to this existence anyway."

Guinevia looked at her thoughtfully. "If I sacrifice you to Manannan, who is the gatekeeper to the next world, you will feel just a little pain and you will go in glory. However, there are very few sacrifices who immolate themselves willingly. If you chose to go to Manannan by your own hand, he would take you as his honoured bride and as one of his queens, for you would be a rare and wonderful creature in his Tir na Nog, the place beyond the setting sun."

Caria drew herself up to her own small height, a proud and courageous figure. "If I do this, will the bards sing of me?" she said simply. Guinevia nodded. Caria looked at her again and said with the faintest quaver in her voice. "Would you hold my hand while I do it?"

At that moment, the howl of the wind halted abruptly and the silence was so complete that the two women heard twigs fall to the ground from the winter-bare trees. "That is Manannan's answer," said Guinevia gently. "I will hold your hand on the knife, and he will wait for you with his arms wide."

The girl bowed her head, and her response came in a whisper. "Then we should do it."

The blast began again as the women stepped from the shelter of the trees and struggled against the wind to the centre of the bridge arch. Even as they watched it, the water level was rising fast, pushing against the piers, threatening to swamp the banks. "It will not be long now," Guinevia whispered into Caria's ear. "Stand here, put your hands on the parapet and lean forward a little." The girl obeyed, her lips white and moving soundlessly. "Don't be afraid, it will be like a nettle sting, no more," said the Druid.

She reached under her cloak and extracted a bone-handled knife with a slender, leaf-shaped blade, and positioned herself behind the Hibernian.

"They won't be angry with me for pretending to be a sorceress, will they?" Caria asked anxiously.

"They'll be amused that you fooled those stupid men, my darling," said Guinevia, putting the bone of the knife handle into the girl's hand and wrapping her own hand over it. "Her fingers are small, like a child's," she thought sadly. She raised the blade to the girl's neck. "Are you ready?" Caria nodded, wordless.

"Look down the river, see how fast the tide is…" and Guinevia abruptly drew both the knife and the girl's unresisting hand sharply across her throat, pulling towards herself hard and deep. She felt the scrape as the slender, sharp blade touched the spine, the suck and cling as the muscles held the blade for a moment. The girl's head lolled alarmingly and a gush of blood jetted out over the stonework and into the turbulent, foaming river, a momentary blur of pink, then once more sliding green and white.

Guinevia, her hand, wrist and forearm bright crimson with the oxygen-rich arterial blood, unwrapped her arms from their affectionate embrace of the body and gently tilted the girl forward. She slid over the parapet headfirst and fell the few short feet to the water that was rising greedily to take her.

Guinevia nodded. A tear glistened at her eye and her arms slumped by her sides, the knife dangling. "Go," she said, "Go to Manannan mac Lir, gatekeeper between worlds. The feasting at Tir na Nog waits for you. Be at peace, lovely Caria. You are no more a slave, you are a queen now, and the bards will sing of you often."

Far down the surging, boiling tideway, a luminous green shape stirred under the distorting mantle of the ocean. A giant man shape, it seemed possessed of long hair that waved like seaweed, ridged rocky arms and rounded shoulders like barnacle-crusted coastal boulders, and a torso rippled like the hard sand on a wide northern beach. The shape seemed to push at the waves above it, and a boiling, surging wall of water that was crested with a thick cap of white foam rose up.

The tidal bore raced into the Severn estuary at better than the speed of a galloping horse. As it went east, it speed never lessened, but its height increasingly towered over the land. The backwash from the confining banks surged behind the first torrent to form five or six stacked waves and soon the last rollers were four or five times the height of a man. And, the tumbling, roaring green and white wall thundered down on the Roman fleet.

An archer saw it first. He raised his head from retching helplessly over the stern and saw the ranked, stacked waves hurling themselves towards his ship. His shouts did little good. The wall towered over the galley, crashed it end over end, and drove it, ram first, into the sea bed. One after the other, the Roman flotilla was swamped, crushed and battered under in the grinding, pounding churn of those huge waves. Some went to the river bed, some were hurled ashore in splinters, and the tidal wave swept through the snaking bends of the river, carrying everything before it.

Most of the men who died never knew how it happened. In one moment, they were racing upriver, the next, their ship was upended, toppled, speared into the sea bed, into a riverbank, into another ship. Soldiers armed and armoured for battle had no hope of surviving in that chaotic maelstrom of churning green water, but some few did, and were washed ashore pounded and weak, either to be killed or to be enslaved.

Guinevia still stood on the bridge arch. She reached under her cloak to the leather bag she had slung over her shoulder. From it she took a rounded, linen-wrapped bundle and unfolded the cloth. Inside was the girl's sad collection of divining tools: a few neck bones and an old skull. The sorceress cupped it in her hands, kissed it gently and extended her arms out above the racing water. The skull made hardly a splash, and the Druid walked away. She was a hundred paces from the bridge, on the gravel ledge high above the river when the racing tidal wave thrashed against the bridge, washed over the parapet, and greedily took with it the last traces of the blood of the girl who had sacrificed herself.

Something resounded in Guinevia's soul, a sense of great peace, and far to the west, under a heaving green mantle of salt water, a luminous figure welcomed a small, pale blonde girl to joyous life in a world beyond this one.

XXXIII Invasion

Maximian never knew it, but he landed his expedition on the exact beach near Deal that Gaius Julius Caesar had used three and a half centuries before. Unlike Julius, the current Emperor of the West arrived unopposed. No howling, blue-painted Britons, no spear-throwing cavalry charges, no struggling ashore encumbered, against nimble foes.

Maximian's ships deployed neatly, ground ashore gently on the flat, open strand and had a beach head established and military screen thrown out wide within an hour or two, all without sight of opposition other than a handful of pony soldiers viewing from a distance. They would, he knew, take word to Arthur, but the landing, the critical part of an invasion, was going smoothly, and the Serb was unflustered. He began moving centuries of men off the beach and onto the hinterland downs, sent out horse-mounted scouts and watched approvingly as his beachmasters efficiently supervised the offloading of the supplies and impedimenta.

The first British cavalry arrived on the downs at dawn the next day. They were too late. The Romans were already well established, and quickly drove them off before they began a disciplined advance on Dover, an easy two hour march away. There, Arthur's admiral Grimr had just returned from a patrol to the west, and was hastily moving elements of his fleet out of the harbour. He knew the fort could not resist the landed legions and he had no intention of allowing his precious ships to be captured, but he did have a plan.

As the Romans moved west, Grimr's squadron bypassed them on the strait and sailed east to the landing ground. The Suehan found a collection of British troops gathered in a standoff with the small force that was guarding the beached barges and galleys and in a quickly-arranged joint operation, swooped in to burn the grounded fleet while the foot soldiers fought the ship guards. By the afternoon, the Romans, for better or worse, could no longer retreat and sail away, at least until a new fleet arrived from Gaul.

Meanwhile, the Romans took Dover.

Like the admiral Grimr, the small garrison inside the old fort realized that the legions would quickly overpower them, and most simply melted away from the walls and fled west, heading for the fleet's main base at Port Chester. Dover's commander, a silver-haired old soldier wounded at Dungeness, stayed with his post, watched the legionaries march in and was crucified on the lighthouse that overlooked the straits. He was relatively fortunate. Other defenders were skinned alive and salted, several were roasted above a pit fire. It was notice that the invaders would tolerate no resistance and wanted full cooperation with their demands for tribute and supplies. The farm folk hastened in with their waggons loaded.

Maximian spent several days regrouping and listening to the news of his scouts and spies. He had lost his fleet, but he had a harbour, he had an undamaged force on shore and he had an open road to Londinium.

I woke in my palace in the capital with a sore head and bleary eyes. We had celebrated our ambush of the enemy fleet too well and thoughtlessly. I should have been readying for the attack that would come in six days' time, not drinking wine with the troops. I was dunking my head under the water spigot in the courtyard when the first courier arrived, spattered with horse spume and mud. The worst news. The Romans were ashore in force at Deal.

It was the beginning of weeks of a long nightmare. I raced my cavalry towards Dover and lost a tenth of them in a single ambush. Our infantry fared no better against the armoured legions and we fought a bitter rearguard action for days and days as we retreated step by bloodied step down the stones of Watling Street to Londinium. We conceded Richborough and Canterbury and the forefoot of Britain, fought off frenzied flanking attacks through the hills of the North Downs, and we lost a bloody night skirmish at the Medway River but were not yet overrun. Time and again, as we fell back on Londinium we were forced to leave our dead and wounded behind us to the Romans' limited mercy. That more than anything destroyed my men's morale and caused our already-depleted army to shrink even more as soldiers abandoned their weapons and their comrades and ran for their homes.

Finally, we retreated across the bridge to the city at the Walbrook and burned it behind us. A courageous cavalry decurion called Celvinius and a squad of the Chevron elite stayed at the south end of the span and held off the Romans' furious attacks until we had burned it beyond repair. We knew we could not hold out indefinitely, but I resolved to make the best fist of it until we could raise reinforcements from the British tribes.

We tried to reinforce the city walls. They might have been good enough to hold off a Saxon horde, but they would be insufficient against a disciplined Roman siege. We made the two public baths along the riverfront into strongpoints and turned the Mithraeum into a hospital. We tore down buildings for fabric to reinforce the Ludgate and its bridge over the Fleet, just below Holborn hill. We added to the defences at the Newgate and its nearby temple, closed down the Cripplegate, the Moorgate, Ealdgate and the Billingsgate and we blocked the Dowgate on the river front.

Soon, the only entrance to the city was by the stout Aldersgate and Bishopsgate portals on the east hill, which we left open to traffic to encourage the civilian populace to leave. Those gates could be sealed at short notice, and we also needed them to bring in cattle and supplies from the country against the inevitable siege. The prisoners we had taken in the action on the Thames, some hundreds of them, we penned near the cemetery northeast of the city wall. I mentally shrugged. If they escaped, they would be in poor shape anyway, of little use as soldiers. I was not going to risk having them inside the city walls in case of an escape and uprising.

I ordered the Langbourne and Sherbourne streams dammed to provide us with water to fight fires but left the Walbrook alone, as its flow was sufficient for an emergency water supply and many of the townsfolk relied on it for their own needs. I also ordered all shipping away from the Pool. The smaller craft I sent upstream, the larger had orders to try to escape the estuary and turn south into the Narrow Sea. They would sail west for Portus Chester, where Grimr's fleet was stationed, along with the depleted legion brought down from Caerleon. I held little hope that they could pass the Romans at the Medway, but it was a chance and I did not want them where they could be used as convenient pontoons to throw an army across the Thames at Londinium. That jogged my memory, and I ordered burned our own makeshift pontoon bridge at Till's burh.

In due course, Maximian and his army arrived on the south bank, though the numbers made me suspect he had split his forces and some were attempting to cross the river elsewhere. They camped directly across the Thames, just outside the South Wark and established an advance guard in public buildings along Watling Street and Eormen Way, in full sight of our city wall across the river. And they began to build a bridge.

Their engineers chose a spot upstream of the old bridge, and began by protecting it from anything we could send downriver by setting pilings into the riverbed and floating a log boom across much of the flow to catch anything destructive. Then, instead of driving the bridge pilings straight down, they rammed their great baulks of timber at an angle against the current, employing it to give the structure more strength, fastened the whole thing together and finally laid a wooden roadbed across its top.

The project was almost finished in two weeks, a tribute to their engineers and industry, as we bombarded them where we could with missiles. We built outworks where they had to come ashore, full knowing that once they did, we would be overwhelmed in a matter of hours. I spent those two sleepless weeks limping from place to place, for I had been wounded again during our retreat from Dover, encouraging, ordering, chivvying and praising our troops, who were exhausted. It was all wasted effort.

Maximian coordinated his attacks. The first came from the east, down the Viginal Way and through the burial grounds, where they instantly released the prisoners and attacked our wall. Later I learned that the traitor Allectus had crossed the Thames near its mouth and sailed into Colchester, where he made a pact with the Saxon warlord Skegga, who was still encamped there, waiting for reinforcements from the Rhine.

In return for assurances that they would be left in peace when the Romans had reconquered Britain, Skegga's men used their longships to ferry a considerable Roman force across the Thames. That force then marched on Londinium. As they approached the capital, Maximian ordered the new bridge to be finished, and hurled suicide squads across it. In an hour's fighting, they cleared away our emplacements and were under Londinium's western walls, too. Then, with both banks of the Thames secured and bridged, they set about reducing our defences.

The Emperor of the West was an experienced and skilled soldier, and he knew about siege tactics, but he was eager to see my head on a pole, so he risked a frontal assault behind a firestorm. His ballistae threw blazing material over the western walls that were furthest from our water supplies, and his troops controlled the Fleet River access that was so vital against a fire. In a day, we were in desperate condition. More of my men were pulling down buildings to make firebreaks than were manning the walls, and we were hugely outnumbered in any case.

The Romans rolled a heavy-timbered roof forward against the Ludgate as protection against the rocks we dropped from above, and began swinging an iron-headed ram at the small wicket set into the city gate. No wood could resist that for long, and as the postern cracked and fell, their ballistae fired heavy iron bolts through the creaking gap, smashing aside the brave soldiers who filled it. I ran clumsily to rally troops to the breach, but already their axe men were hacking at the rest of the splintered gate. A dozen Romans died in the breach, but twice as many Britons pooled their blood on the stones with that of their dead enemies.

The gate fell inwards with a shattering crash and an armoured wall was through in testudo formation, shields held above and around to protect the soldiers like a tortoise shell. Then the street fighting began and flowed west to east. It trapped most of our garrison where they would die, in the forum by the basilica on the east hill. I hacked my way with Exalter northwest, grimly amused to find myself in a moment of quiet leaning panting on my sword by the Cripplegate. My mutilated foot hurt like hell, the arrow that had caught my left armpit in the fighting at the Medway had left that side of my body feeling crippled, too.

Five of my house guards, Chevrons all of them, were with me and the phalanx of legionaries we had been battling as we retreated were halted warily 30 yards distant, possibly hoping for archers to take on the unenviable task of finishing us. Somebody whistled, and I peered through the smoke at that unlikely sound in a battle. It was the familiar figure of Cragus Grabelius, one of my tribunes, and commander of the cavalry. He looked battered and smoke-blackened but seemed in control. He was standing just inside the big gate, which was still fast and undamaged, but whose small wicket gaped open. Cragus was gesturing urgently. I realized he was not in sight of the legionaries, growled a command at my Chevrons to hold them, and limped to him.

"Outside," he said. "Outside, lord. I have horses." I stooped and peered through the small gate. A miracle. A troop of British heavy cavalry was there, dragoons who fought on foot or on horse, the soldiers quieting their mounts, which were shying at the smoke and sounds of crashing conflict. There, saddled and bridled, stamped Corvus my war horse, and Nonios his stablemate, a horse named for Pluto, two black Frisian stallions held at their heads by a trooper. Never have I seen such a welcome sight. I stepped back inside the wicket and gestured to the Chevrons.

"Back here, slowly, then run!" I shouted in the British language to confound the Romans. "Don't let the bastards see you hurry." Cragus assessed the retreating line of men.

"I have four spare remounts," he said coolly. "One of them will have to double up."

We slipped through the wicket, barred it with a baulk of timber and bought time enough to ride away towards the shelter of the cloaking forest. The only incident was encountering two legionaries who may have defected to find loot, but we killed them and rode on. I was surprised to see the decurion Celvinius in that skirmish. I later found that he had survived his heroic defence of the bridge to swim back across the Thames and rejoin the garrison, and I resolved to promote him for gallantry. We crossed the Ty burn and joined the Praetorian Way, headed for Silchester and the safety of its oppidum's walls. The legionary foot soldiers we sighted as we rode wanted nothing to do with heavy cavalry, nor did we especially wish to join in more combat. I was a fugitive now, not a triumphant lord of war and Imperator. My empire was slipping away.

XXXIX Hilltop

Our big horses ate up the miles at a canter and the occasional small town, farms and hamlets went by in a blur of halts and fodder, of watering the horses and snatching food for the men. People were there, too, incredulous at our news of invasion and war; folk who hurried away to bury their valuables and move their beasts to safety. Everywhere we stopped, I ordered able-bodied men to muster with their weapons in the west, at Caros' Camp, the earthwork fort of the ancients that some premonition years before had caused me to reinforce. Then, I had seen the place as a strongpoint to withstand invasion from the west. Now, it would be a rallying point against the iron Roman tide from the east.

We diverted to the coast at Portus Chester, to see what news there was of the fleet, and what infantry reserves we had there. With a bitter heart, I decided to leave the port to its fate and to move the foot soldiers back to my western hillfort of Caros' Camp. I would need all my force in one place to hold the Roman threat and that would be a good place to meet it. I also had half a legion at Caerleon, directly across the Severn Sea from the hillfort, which was once called Cado's Fort, or Cadbury. It had been renamed for me, as I was called Caros or Carausius when I rebuilt it.

We burned the port facilities to deny them to the Romans, and I ordered the fleet to the safety of the Severn. They would be based at Abonae, a harbour on the Avon just west of Aquae Sulis. There, if needed, they could shuttle my force across from Caerleon, and importantly would have control over the Severn Sea. The irony was not lost on me when I learned that a second Roman fleet had just been destroyed in those waters, the very place where I was now gathering my forces. It had to be an augury from the gods, and a good one at last.

So, within the week and on a beautiful spring day, I arrived to inspect the limestone hilltop fortress of Caros' Camp. I was happy to see that the place was bustling with men and construction. It had been several years since I had ordered it reinforced with stone from Roman fortifications at their nearby lead mines. I thought then that the Camp would be a keystone to the western defences as well as a place of mystical power.

Now, it looked like a bastion from which I could either begin the recapture of my kingdom or face my own death.

The Camp is an ancient earthwork that rises to a commanding height above the rolling countryside around it, and is stepped upwards in four concentric rings of steep-sided ramparts and ditches. Each ring is topped with stout wooden palisades and fighting platforms, and has blind entrances that double back to trap an enemy in blank killing rooms. At the summit of this formidable series of obstacles is a large, smooth plateau that sits behind the rampart of the high stone wall fully 16 feet thick that I had ordered rebuilt. Ironically, we used their Roman-cut stone to make our last defences against them. An attacker who could somehow scramble through four sets of double-gated, defended earth-and-log ramparts would find himself gazing up at that blank stone wall he could not climb, and all the while would be under the deadly lash of missiles directed from the watchtowers and fighting platforms built at close intervals inside it.

I entered that high ring of limestone through a double gate across a cobbled road twice as wide as a man is tall. It opened onto an enclosed, 18-acre expanse of turf, with stabling for beasts, a small stone palace, temple, military barracks, hall, shielded wells, granary, store houses, smithy and an armoury. The hilltop offers long views of beautiful countryside clear to the Severn Sea 30 miles away, or to the nearer Tor at Glastonbury. On the crest of the hill, a towering structure houses the iron cage, fuel and tinder that can send a blazing message across the land to warn in minutes of invaders and to call the region to arms.

At the moment, refugees and troops could already be seen streaming in, black lines of folk moving along the Fosse Way seven miles to the west, trekking across the fields, small coppices and larger woodlands that spread like a carpet around the hillfort's foot. Some folk were dragging carts, some droving their cattle or sheep. The warnings had spread, and the people were seeking refuge. They had been warned to bring as much as they could of their beasts and crops because we were going to denude the area of supplies, to deny them to the enemy. They knew, too, that Caros' Camp was big enough to accommodate them, and was impregnable against even long siege. One especially large, solid-looking group caught my eye as it moved in a military-style phalanx from the north. I squinted and sighted glints of metal. Helmets, breastplates, weapons. It was a contingent that had made the long march from Chester, had halted in Caerleon and Aquae Sulis and would continue to the old stone fort at Ilchester, just nine short miles from Caros' Camp.

In Caerleon, the military group had collected my Guinevia, and with her came news of the tidal wave she had called up the Severn Sea to destroy the Romans. I sent word to the Chester troops to establish themselves at Ilchester, to make the place secure, to fill the granaries and secure the stabling. I ordered our heavy cavalry to Ilchester and gave their commander Cragus some specific orders about the horse herds south of us on the plains where the stone circles stood. Matters are looking better by the day, I thought. Truly the gods are with this place, and I glanced around to see if I could spot a white Rat...

Guinevia arrived with her new female slaves Jesla and Karay, and with a large coffle of captives I needed for labour on the ramparts. Among them was the Pict bishop who had been captured with the women who now served Guinevia. One of my officers alerted me to the man, whom he said had certain qualities I might find useful, so I sent for him.

Candless still wore the remnants of a monk's cowled habit and the broad leather belt from which he had sported a serious-looking sword when he was taken. He was a fair-haired man of middle height, ruddy-complected where he had been working in the fields. He was strongly built and had a piercing, shrewd gaze that met mine in a way that few slaves dared employ. I questioned him, and he told me he was from the Pictish coast, quite near the ancient hillfort of Dunpelder that we had occupied before taking Eidyn's burh. No, he was not an ordained bishop, despite his claims and the tau-rho cross he wore around his neck. He had been given the robes as a gift by a grateful admirer, he said, and people had chosen to accord him the role, so he had not demurred. He wriggled a little under my questions and admitted he was not actually much of a Christian, but he knew about them and had spoken with some of their churchmen.

An idea was playing in my mind, and I asked this Candless what he knew about the things that motivated Christians. "They have a powerful weapon, lord," he said. "They help those less fortunate. They routinely take in orphans, they ignore their own health to treat the sick in times of plague, they treat women as equals and even sometimes elect them as leaders.

"Pagans want the Christians as their friends because they help others, and offer succour even to strangers. They make you part of their family and community, and that makes them popular with the common people who have no rights." I thought about this, and asked Candless what moved the Christians most. "Their Jesus god," he said at once. "He told them to do good to others, and they think he is a loving and merciful god. Anything about him is good."

This Jesus god, I asked him, isn't he the one the Romans crucified for insurgency? "He was flogged and nailed up like a slave," said Candless. "His death is so painful to his followers that they do not use the Roman crucifix as a symbol, but have another version." He showed me the cross around his neck. It was a curious crucifix with an oval shape above the crosspiece, a sort of long-stemmed letter P crossed at about half height. "This is their lord's sign," he explained. "It is two Greek letters and it means 'The Cross Saves.' They believe that if you follow the Jesus teachings, you will go to the Christian feasting halls and will have a good life after death, a life much better than this one."

This gave me a flood of ideas. If I had managed to rally Britain's tribes behind the symbol of a lost Eagle, maybe I could rally Britain's Christians, and there were plenty of them, to fight behind a Jesus symbol. I would need something like the crucifix, or Jesus' possessions, or something important. "What do the Jesus followers prize?" I asked this rogue bishop.

Candless sighed. "Pedlars travel the world selling feathers from the wings of angels, churchmen claim that only they have pieces of the one true cross, or the original holy bush from which the Romans made the crown of thorns. I have been offered the fingernail clippings of saints, wax from the ears of Jesus' mother, a piece of the linen with which the whore Magdalene wiped Jesus' face and a miraculous, still-fresh fish that was one of those that fed the 5,000. It's a whole industry, and the fish went bad, too."

Nails, I thought. The nails that held Jesus on the crucifix. My executioner Davius had a stock of them, he sold used nails from executions as amulets, and made huge profits he thought I did not know about. All I'd need was a few bloodied nails, a rogue bishop and a convincing tale. I could recruit some new forces, if I had the right story, and they'd be eager to fight Romans who persecute them... I told

Candless he was not to leave the confines of Caros' Camp, but he was relieved from fieldwork duties. And, he was to find some better clerical clothes than the rags he was presently wearing. I gave him a piece of silver, told him to keep quiet about our conversation and went to find Guinevia for a talk.

"You can't become a Christian!" she was shouting at me. "You're the emperor of Britain! Who would stand for it?"

I was conciliatory. "I know it's a shock," I said, "but what if a miracle struck me and I saw my way clearly? What if the Jesus god wanted me to drive out the Romans, to make this place a haven for Christians? Let's face it, the chieftains wouldn't care. They regard the Jesus as just another god, and they have plenty of those already. The ordinary people wouldn't care either," I said. "They aren't concerned with those things. You care because you're a Druid and it might be difficult for you to have to deal with me having a different religion, in public at least." Guinevia pouted a little, and turned away, but I caught the scent of the crocus oil she dabbed on herself, and, inspired, I began a more persuasive argument to placate her.

XL Convert

My enemy Maximian held Londinium and the south, and among his first acts he committed his greatest mistake. He too-quickly followed the dictates of his co-emperor and Serbian countryman, Diocletian and ordered the British Christians to be persecuted and their churches destroyed. The news went across the country like wildfire. After a period of relative calm, the Romans were back, rampant and brutal again. Maximian had even cruelly executed the few of my valiant Chevrons that he had captured. These were the elite guards who had been with me when we found the lost Eagle and the only reason he had for torturing and murdering those soldiers was to send a message to me of my fate should he ever capture me.

I grieved for the men, but had no time for much else. I was busy readying for the invaders' assaults on our strongholds, but the opportunity Maximian offered by persecuting Christians was so good and so obvious, I seized it. I called in as many of the Christian leaders as I could find at short notice and introduced them to 'Bishop' Candless, a Pict I told them who held high office in the one true church north of the Wall.

We were in the hall of the stone-walled fort at Ilchester on an achingly beautiful summer's day. Outside, the jingle of harness, stamp of nailed boots and shouted commands of the officers reminded us that this was an armed cavalry camp, and that war was coming even to this lovely part of our island. I looked around the sunlit hall at the ragged assembly of shabby, suspicious bishops, fat priors and anxious-looking canons, and thanked them politely for their attendance, noting privately that many had brought their drabs of wives, probably in hope of receiving gold from their emperor. I made a note to do just that. I needed them.

I had dressed impressively for the day, a warlord and Imperator in white tunic with purple trim, silver and amber badge of British office, imperial circlet, segmentata armour and the huge sword Exalter at my hip. I explained to the clerics that we were meeting in the cavalry fort as a more convenient place for them, because of the difficulties and dangers of ascending the earthwork of Caros' Camp through the defensive construction that was ongoing. In fact, I wanted none of that untrustworthy motley viewing the preparations I was readying for the Romans, and I certainly did not want them anywhere near Guinevia, who might turn them all into toads, or worse.

An intelligent prefect had decorated the hall with Christian symbolism, including a red cross on a white banner which hung suspended below the tile roof. It served at least to keep the falling dust and insects off us. 'Bishop' Candless was enthroned next to me, wearing over his cowled habit a fine green and gold surplice looted from some northern abbey. Guinevia had insisted on a full report of the proceedings, so had sent her female slaves Jesla and Karay to monitor the meet. She had cleverly dressed them in flowing white linen to suggest angels and they formed an impressive presence, towering over the superstitious canons and shooing their wives like chickens out of the chamber.

Recounting the meeting is tedious, as the wrangling and counter-offers went on all day, but eventually, the bishops accepted matters, as they must. They knew that the Romans would crucify them, and had already begun their oppression; we needed the clerics to rouse the Jesus followers to our cause. In return, we would guarantee their safety and uphold their right to practise their faith. I did not foresee that one day they would deny us good pagans the right to practise ours, but that was in the future.

I would publicly become a Christian because we needed the new Christian army to be led by one of their own, so I agreed to be baptized and was duly dunked in the willow-lined River Cam, which runs just outside the fort, while Candless droned some nonsense pig Latin over me. At least, standing waist-deep, he got his fine surplice wet. I also saw to it that my chief officers got a dunking, to share the grace, though I noticed that the Suehan sailor Grimr covered up the amulet of Thor he had around his neck before he went under, so I didn't consider him as enthusiastic a convert as we all pretended to be.

Back inside, with meat and mead filling and warming their bellies and softening their resistance, the bishops were given the knockout blow. Candless was superb. He stood, his tau-rho cross glinting in the firelight, and delivered a sermon of hope.

"Now that we have a Christian king," he intoned, "I can reveal the secret that will carry us to success over these invaders. I can show you the Precious Artefacts that guarantee the Hand of God is with us." I could almost see the capital letters emerging from his mouth. At a signal, my tribune Cragus, still steaming damply from his immersion in the Cam, entered carrying a linen-wrapped silver casket.

Candless opened it reverently, with a fair display of showmanship. Inside, carefully wrapped in embroidered linen, were four bloodstained, nine-inch iron nails that he'd obtained from my executioner Davius. "These are the very nails with which our Lord Jesus was fastened to the Holy Cross," he declared. "His Holy Blood is on them, the blood He shed for us and all mankind." My fake bishop was so impressive that even I gaped in awe, and most of those in the room fell to their knees, praising and praying aloud and calling out churchly phrases. Candless next spun an involved story of how the nails had been saved by a member of the Jewish Sanhedrin religious court who had taken down Jesus' body from the Cross.

He told at length a story involving the burial sheet, a palace called Britio Edessa and wise men from Mesopotamia who had brought the relics to Wales. An angel, and he glanced meaningfully at the two tall Celt women, an angel had come to him in a dream to tell him where to find the nails in their casket, safe in the fastness of Yr Wyddfa, Britain's sacred mountain. I was stifling my yawns but the audience was rapt, and I noticed that one of Candless' angels was blushing, which intrigued me. Then Candless reverently held up the nails. "Four," he was saying, "four, like the gospel writers." The assembly of churchmen nodded and muttered to each other.

Of course, there's a doubter in every group, and Cragus had seen to it that one of his officers was it. He called out: "Four nails? Four?"

Candless was expecting the interruption and silenced those who hissed at the officer. "One through each forearm, one through each heel. Our Blessed Lord was nailed with his holy feet fastened to the sides of the upright, in the Roman manner," he intoned. "The angel showed me, in the dream."

I thought it was time to get away from nebulous dreams and on to military matters, so I coughed meaningfully, silenced Candless with a look, and announced my plan. The four sacred nails would go out to be shown to the faithful in Britain's north, south, east and west. They would be used to raise a Christian army, and I would supply spears and equipment from the armories in Eboracum, Caerleon, and Chester, where captured Pictish weapons were stored. The bishops, who received gifts of gold from the Ilchester mint, were to persuade their followers to gather at those three centres for training, and soon, under the holy banner of the cross of Christ, we would defeat the pagan Romans.

Then we all knelt while Candless mumbled prayers and blessed us. Somewhere, Guinevia was spitting in fury, I knew, but now I had the promise of an army and a chance to save Britain. I'd done it once with an Eagle, now I had to do it again, with four bits of old iron. I glanced around the chamber and sure enough, a white Rat was sitting upright in the corner, cleaning its whiskers. Mithras didn't, then, take my 'conversion' too seriously.

XLI Siege

Maximian was in full vengeful mode, and he was impatient to take Arthur and aware that the winter was approaching. In his haste, he did not first establish supply dumps or short, defendable supply lines, and that later told heavily against him.

The Romans arrived in force at the foot of Caros' Camp, made a series of unsuccessful attempts to storm it, then settled in for a siege. They threw up a double palisade to trap the besieged and to protect their rear, and began the slow process of building a ramp of rocks and packed dirt, planning to drag a tower up it as an archers' platform to fire down into the fortress.

At the same time, Maximian's engineers began mining through the earthwork walls to breach them from the opposite side of the hill. Arthur, however, had anticipated his rival's moves, and fought off the engineers and miners. He also had expected a long siege and had scorched the earth for miles around, destroying crops and driving off beasts so the Romans could not live off the land, and the loss of the cargo fleet Grimr had burned meant he could not supply from Gaul.

Additionally, the British cavalry forces in nearby Ilchester raided widely, cutting Roman communications, intercepting their supply trains and keeping the Romans largely confined to their own siege camp. On occasion, a British infantry force supported by the heavy cavalry would sally out to disrupt the siege, damage artillery and engines and undermine the semi-starved Romans' morale. Even when it was not a military skirmish or other action, the constant knifing of sentries and deadly arrows from the dark kept the invaders on edge, and it all had a cumulative effect.

Maximian was also unable to prevent the British from restoring their light cavalry from the horse herds of their southern plains, and as the autumn days shortened into winter, found himself increasingly in the role of being the besieged, subject to harassing cavalry raids, while he was himself sitting frustratedly waiting for Arthur to descend from his impregnable hilltop. Maximian made several attempts to reduce the fort at Ilchester whose cavalry was such a thorn in his side, but there was little possibility of a surprise attack, overlooked as they were from the hillfort, and the approaches to Ilchester were over ground ideal for cavalry, so the British horsemen were able to ensure that each incursion resulted in heavy losses on the Roman foot soldiers.

By Michaelmas, in mid-October, the first frosts were biting, the auxiliaries were slipping away to ready their homesteads for winter and Maximian was being forced to bow to the inevitable. He withdrew his hungry legions to winter quarters and returned himself to Londinium in frustrated fury. Arthur's head would not be adorning any pike shaft before the spring. Maximian sent Allectus to parlay again with the Saxons, who were settling into their winter camp outside ruined Colchester and prepared for another campaign when the snow and ice was ended.

Meanwhile, Bishop Candless' crusade was having an effect. In town, church and village, hedge priests and consecrated canons eager to enhance their spiritual standing by displaying the True Nails of the Cross to their congregations were recruiting for Christ's army. Through the autumn and early days of winter, a steady trickle of men were arriving at the old legionary fortresses in the north and west, some drawn by faith, some by the promise of loot, others from simple allegiance to their Imperator, who was now a Christian with the cross of Christ on his shield.

Candless was thriving. He enjoyed the prestige of being guardian of the Holy Nails, he had quietly salted away considerable coin given as offertories, he offered discreet confessions and absolution to the prettiest wives and to the angel in white who occasionally slipped into his quarters, and, as God's Gatekeeper, he was eating and drinking like a lord at the tables of the faithful who wanted access to heaven.

Arthur had no qualms about him. The cheerful rogue bishop knew which side of the trencher held the gravy and the trickle of recruits was increasing to a stream, so he was doing his job. The only constraint Arthur put on his military missionary was to keep him on the south side of the Wall.

"If you go back to Dunpelder or wherever and are recognised as no bishop at all, you could undermine the credibility of the whole miracle.

I've already told Davius about keeping his mouth closed, you know how critical this is, too," he said.

Candless nodded. "Aye," he said, chewing thoughtfully on a hazelnut, "aye, it would be a pity to disillusion those poor wee souls." And he took another draught of wine.

We spent that long hard winter in preparations. I calculated that Maximian would be reluctant to repeat his fruitless siege of Caros' Camp, so would try to tempt us out with an attack elsewhere, an assault maybe on a garrison town. He likely would not want to bring us to battle in a place favourable to our cavalry, as his own mounted troops were few, and he had seen the killing efficiency of our heavy horsemen. He had a new fleet stationed at Dover and Port Chester, making my title of Lord of the Narrow Sea a hollow one, as my best admiral, Grimr could no longer match the new Roman war galleys who guarded the seaway between Bononia and Dover, so it was they who controlled the straits, although they did not yet venture west.

Spies had brought me news of Allectus, who had been negotiating with the Saxons and, word had it, with the Catuvellauni whose lands in eastern Britain were most under Saxon threat. If the Romans, through my treacherous former lieutenant made agreements with the Saxon invaders and the Britons who felt most likely to be enslaved by them, I would face a doubled threat. I knew that any pledge Maximian made with the Saxons would be broken in time, but that would come long after my defeat and the enslavement of my troops and my country. Perhaps, just perhaps, I should do again what we had done last year, and make a winter sortie.

The Christians had been alternately praying and doing arms drills all winter and Candless, fierce in breastplate and helmet over his cowled habit, seemed to be everywhere. He had marched most of the recruits from Eboracum over the snowy backbone of England, through Mancunium whose name I recalled from a long-ago treasure map that had started me on this journey to be imperator. The shivering raw soldiers found themselves in the vast citadel of Chester, with new drillmasters, new quarters and a new mission.

They would train with the elements of the 2nd and 3rd Parthian legion, the 2nd and 8th Augusta and the 1st Minerva who were the professional backbone of my legions. And, before the frosts of February had properly ended, they would move south to join my heavy cavalry and the rest of the Christian recruits at Caerleon, where they had been wintering.

My plans were not fully formed, but I expected Maximian to bring enough of his forces to Caros' Camp to push me back up to my hilltop while he sent the main body elsewhere to do damage. So, I intended to create the impression I was in the ancient camp, but I would not be on that hilltop. I would hold my forces in Caerleon, then move them as Maximian left his winter quarters.

If I could conceal my legions and cavalry in a place some discreet distance along the Fosse Way, we could use that ancient road to could strike fast and hard at his marching columns. If I could reduce his numbers by crushing his expeditionary force, I could then deploy my new Christian legions to seek the rest of the Romans.

We prepared our weapons, we readied our horses and our marching supplies. The troops were drilled, we had a strong contingent of archers and we had during the winter developed some lighter weight ballistae that we could move quickly on paved roads. We were as ready as we could be with a mobile force capable of a hard strike, although I knew we could not take on a prolonged ground campaign. It would only be a matter of a few weeks before Maximian would be moving and that was when we would try to surprise him. What I did not know was where he would march, and when I discovered his destination, I was in shock.

The Romans were pulling their troops out of Britain. Diocletian in his palace in Split had called his fellow emperor back to the Danube, where the barbarians were seriously threatening the empire. Britain was no longer important. The safety of Rome was at stake, and the legions sailed away from our northern island in their blue-sailed galleys with their frustrated emperor.

We got roaring drunk that night, and even the Christians joined in. We had created an army and to the ignorant foot soldiers, the Romans' retreat meant we had defeated them. I knew better. Marcus Aurelius Valerius Maximianus would not be deflected from his purpose. He had attained his high rank through menaces both personal and political. He was energetic, ruthless, aggressive and coarse.

It was a mark of the man that, when he was charged with violating an elderly Vestal virgin, his accuser was found strangled on the steps of the Temple of Mithras. As for the Vestal herself, who faced being buried alive outside Rome's Collina Gate, she had somehow obtained and evidently taken poison despite being under close guard to ensure she didn't do just that. Maximian had escaped unpunished because lawmakers nervous of his powers had agreed the Vestal must have imagined it all.

With Maximian's single-mindedness, his wish to regain his military reputation would be eating at him like acid. He had lost an empire and a fleet to me, I had executed his junior emperor Constantius Chlorus and, despite a successful invasion, he had not been able to pry me out of my stronghold. Now, he had been forced to leave, business unfinished. I knew how that would rankle him. He would be back, and he would not rest until he saw me dead.

The reports I received from Londinium brought bad news. When the city fell, Maximian had found among his prisoners four soldiers of my personal guard, the Chevron elite veterans who had been my war companions and who had gallantly earned their proud distinction. At the urging of Allectus, a man who had never put on armour in anger, a snake who whispered and manipulated his way to power, Maximian did not just execute my men, he had stripped and whipped them, paraded them naked and bleeding, put out their eyes, then had personally gutted and beheaded two of them on a scaffold so that his cowed, assembled troops could witness it all.

That done, he had addressed the mob of citizenry to castigate my men as responsible for the destruction of Londinium. Two of my good soldiers of the Chevron still stood, naked, blinded, bleeding and torn from this Roman's cruelty, but the bastard was not done. He incited the mob again, and they behaved as he knew any mob would, and led by a few planted ringleaders, stoned those two brave men to death. I have seen stonings, and thank Mithras I did not see this one, because it is a brutal way to die and there is nothing very much left of the body when it is done.

I would have wept in rage had I been there, but I do not cry. No tears came from my eyes when I heard of the crime, but my heart ached and I vowed that those responsible, chiefly Maximian and Allectus, would be punished, and in their own coin. Blood trickled between my fingers from the split flesh where I had squeezed my fist too hard around the hilt of my dagger.

Maximian's brutal demonstration had two purposes: he was showing his own soldiers what punishment might await them for wrongdoing and he was telling me how he would treat me should I ever become his prisoner. I spat at the floor. I'd eat his heart for what he had done to my companions. He and Allectus would both die for their deeds, and I would see to it that they died at my hand, knowing who was administering justice. I'd done it to one emperor, I'd do it to another. And, doubly to the traitor who had betrayed his own Imperator.

XLII Raid

Allectus had never forgotten viewing the map Guinevia had composed, a view from the skies of the land beneath, and he had set his spies to work to discover who made it, and how. A girl slave who talked too much and who listened too hard outside doors had learned Guinevia's psychic spying secret, and soon, Allectus had it, too. The worm promptly had the slave girl strangled. He was building bridges with the Saxons who had promised him a kingdom of his own and a secret like that was worth a great deal. It must be his alone.

The traitor confided to the Saxon warlord Skegga that Myrddin and Guinevia had a magic that he must unravel and he needed the use of a war band of warriors for a few weeks. He would take one or both of the wizards and torture them into giving up their secrets, which he, Skegga, could use for himself.

"You will be able to see your enemies, you will be enabled to view the world, lord," he urged. The Saxon was reluctant. He had doubts about interfering with sorcerers.

"They have nothing to protect them, lord, but a few incantations," Allectus dismissed his fears. "They are women's weapons, things only to scare naughty children." Skegga was hesitant, unwilling at first, but Allectus assured him that any evil could not come to a great king, and the manipulator got his way. Soon, he set off with a war band to cross the country to misty Wales, where Myrddin had returned to oversee the springtime lambing of his flock.

Guinevia was in her chamber with Milo, a sturdy seven year old by now, watching the boy as he played on the floor with toy wooden horses, galloping them up the flanks and back of Arthur's big hound Axis, who was lolling, grinning alongside. Since the big dog had almost died defending the boy from a wolf, he had been Milo's constant companion, tolerant of anything the boy did, but alert to any potential danger. He offered a threatening growl to any stranger who approached too carelessly or too closely and was perfectly capable of guarding his small human. Arthur, who had seen his hound kill an armed man to save his own life, pretended to complain that Axis was no longer his dog. Secretly, he was pleased that the big hound had adopted the role and still grieved inwardly over the tragic mistake he had made in killing the dog's litter mate.

Guinevia smiled at the peaceful scene in the chamber and turned to the table where she had been writing. She glanced down into the obsidian block that was her viewing stone and her trained eye discerned a movement. On the instant, the dog came alert and growled, looking at her with chin lifted and intelligent brown eyes staring. The growl started something in the seer's mind and she seemed to click into another level of consciousness that was ancient, deep, and primitive. Her eyes turned back to the glossy black volcanic glass.

As if she were viewing it from the distance of just a few hundred paces, she saw an image. Allectus, his cloak streaming behind him, was cantering his horse at the head of a column of armed men along a hawthorn-hedged road. The vision faded swiftly, the dog was still growling, still fixing her with his intent gaze. The Druid looked again, deeply into the obsidian's smooth blankness. Another view waited her. Here was the familiar image of tall, dark Myrddin, his rangy figure in its scholar's grey gown striding across a sheep-dotted field. Axis growled again and in a single heartbeat, Guinevia understood.

She stood quickly, sweeping her skirt around her legs, and gave her son a perfunctory smile. "Stay with Axis, little one," she said. "I'll be back in a moment." The dog thumped his tail on the floor, the boy nodded, unconcerned. She left swiftly, heart pounding hard. She had to find Arthur and tell him of the dangerous and imminent threat she had just viewed.

They were saddling Corvus and detailing off troopers while I threw a few necessities into my saddlebag. A handful of gold in small ingots, some dried mutton, a flask of wine. My red wool military cloak rolled and tied behind the twin rear saddle horns. Exalter on the hip. Stuffed forage net slung behind the saddle, too. Forget the shields, this was swords, bows, lances only. Check that the horn-handled, narrow knife was at my waist. Climb grunting into the saddle. We were to travel fast and light and our corn-fed, Frisian horses were up to the task. I did not know where Allectus had been when Guinevia viewed him. He was probably still on the long Watling Street that sliced diagonally northwest across Britain, if he had come from Colchester. Or maybe he was ahead of us already.

At Chester, we were only two hard days' ride from Myrddin's Welsh eyrie under Yr Wyddfa, but I did not know when the traitor Allectus had left on his mission to harm the wizard, so I commanded extreme haste. It would take at least five days for the murderers, for so I assumed them to be, to cross the country. I had already dispatched four couriers to ride to Myrddin at top speed, to go ahead of our armed group and whisk him away to safety, but I had no way of knowing when Allectus had started his journey, and even a half hour could be vital.

I had ordered extra guards on Guinevia's quarters and sent riders to monitor the Roman roads west, both the coastal route and the inland high road we would join. Now we were cantering our big war steeds out of the gates and westwards, up over the moors. We would head for the long lake and the bleak rockfast mountains before we could turn again to the wind-blasted crest of the high pass where Myrddin chose to live and commune with both his gods and his demons.

Our route took us close to the village I had burned down, one that had been the lair of brigands who had kidnapped and abused Guinevia, and who had killed two of my soldiers. They had paid their grim price, and Allectus would pay another. But first, I had to intercept him, or else Myrddin and perhaps through him, Guinevia, would be paying another. I kicked my heels into Corvus' sides to urge him on. We did not rest that night, we halted only to water our steeds and to give them a handful of oats, but otherwise, we walked them on all night. We had to push forward, and anyway, they were war horses and we were hurrying to a private war.

We saw the horse when we were still several miles from Myrddin's house, and a jumble of thoughts poured through my mind. The sorcerer's retreat, I knew from previous visits, was a square edifice built from cut Roman stone taken from the old marching fort nearby. The Romans had chosen the spot strategically, at a place where three passes came together high under the north eastern flank of the sacred mountain Yr Wyddfa. Partly because the region was a wind-blasted one, Myrddin had enclosed his precious gardens inside a high-walled courtyard. Partly because of its remote location and the threat of strangers, he had equipped the wall with two iron-bound oak gates. He could lock those gates at night and enjoy fair security as he slept, I knew, and this gave me some hope that even if we were late arriving, he might have been able to hold off Allectus and his men.

When we saw the horse and realized it was the mount of one of my couriers, whom I had sent ahead, my chest tightened. A loose horse usually meant a dead rider. Had my couriers been intercepted? We kicked hard at our big horses' ribs and galloped the last distance over a spur of the mountain until the house came into view, down-slope a quarter mile or so distant. Allectus' band was there, between us and the building, but they were dismounted, crouching in the hummocky grass. Two of his riders were about 200 paces, a full stade, away from their comrades and holding the horses.

At once, I signalled a stop. The house was upwind, noise of our arrival had not reached Allectus and his men. I called out my instructions urgently. Four of my men rode off at once, full tilt, spears levelled, at the two horse holders. Their job was to drive the beasts away. If they killed the two raiders, so be it. I wanted the raiders and their mounts separated. Then we could kill them more easily.

The rest of us kicked our gallant Frisians forward, holding them to a canter. I wanted to arrive in a line, I wanted to arrive with thunder and terror and death-dealing steel, a sight of irresistible power that would freeze our victims. The raiders felt the thudding of our horses through the ground, turned, gaped and we were upon them. Foot soldiers caught in the open by dragoons are destined to be raw red meat for a butcher's shambles and this was the case.

Two of the raiders fired arrows but had no time to nock another. Most ran, and were cut down from behind, great gashes opened in their undefended heads and shoulders. Several fought and died under my troops' heavy spatha swords, but the rest, including Allectus, knelt in submission, hands on their heads, weapons laid down. It was done in just minutes and my weary troopers were binding wrists, removing personal weapons, herding the cowed, sullen captives. A few were out on the moor, finishing off the badly wounded with that short upward thrust of the knife under the ribs, then the twist that is such a merciful release.

For the first time, I examined the house. The gates were bolted, there were scorch marks on the stone of the walls. A face peered warily out of the barred Judas hole in the gate. I called out that it was Arthur and heard the bolts slide and the door creak, then a sword point came around the slowly-opening barrier.

"Is that you, Arthur?" I heard Myrddin's voice, querulous.

"It is I, Lord Myrddin," I said.

"Well," he answered.

"Where have you been until now?"

The story came out swiftly, and left me agape at Myrddin's magic once again. At dusk the previous evening, the gardener Pattia had run in from the pheasantry outside the walled garden, breathless with the news that three horsemen were approaching, and fast. She and the house slaves had secured the gates before the men arrived. They gasped out their story: they were Arthur's couriers, sent to warn the Druid, and just a few miles back they had crossed paths with a raiding party that Arthur believed was coming to kill Myrddin. The raiders had missed the road and were coming back to it, guided by a shepherd they had caught. When the two groups clashed, one of the couriers was killed, the others had sped away, and now the raiders were only a short distance behind in the gathering dark.

The Druid assessed the men, told them to turn their horses loose on the moor and brought the riders into the walled compound. "Be ready to defend this place," he told them. "I am going to get something to eat." One of my couriers later told me what happened next.

Allectus rode up at the head of 20 or so raiders and demanded that the gates be opened and Myrddin handed over, or he would slaughter all within. Myrddin had reappeared from inside the house, where he had ordered all the oil lamps extinguished.

"It was getting dark, lord," my courier told me, "and the wizard had a glowing evil face. It looked like moonlight, but there was no moon. It was real magic. He went to the gate in his big cloak and he had his left hand under it, I thought he was armed and ready to strike. He was holding his big black staff in his right hand. He ordered us to open the gate for him, and he stepped outside."

The man did not see clearly what happened, but he heard the parley between the sorcerer and Allectus, who was still mounted on his horse. The traitor was demanding Myrddin come forward to be bound, the Druid was making an incantation. The courier glimpsed through the hinge gap that Myrddin had levelled his lignum vitae staff at the mounted man and his horse shied away.

"The wizard ducked his head into his cloak and I thought he took a swig of something, lord," said the courier. I nodded. I had an idea what that might be. Myrddin said no more, but took a couple of paces back, retreating into the gateway. Allectus must have nudged his horse forward, because, the courier said, still shocked at what he had seen: "The wizard, Lord Myrddin I mean, stretched his neck forward and bellowed at Allectus, and, lord, fire came out of his mouth!"

His conjuring trick accomplished, Myrddin stepped smartly inside, and the gate was bolted against the raiders. What Allectus thought of it, I never knew, but his men were certainly awestruck. I did not tell my courier the truth, either. I knew, because Guinevia had showed me the trick, that a mouthful of a certain shellfish, crushed, gives off a luminescence. In the dark, it looks exactly like fire. A quick mouthful of piddock, crushed then exhaled hard makes you look like a dragon. Cunning Myrddin had also daubed his face with the stuff, evidently. It had bought time: the raiders would not attack the wizard's lair in the dark, and that night the house was undisturbed.

It was full daylight, and mid-morning at that before Allectus could convince his troops to attack, and Myrddin had another trick up his sleeve. He had spent the night hours preparing a number of leather tubes that he packed with a mix he concocted in his workshop. He also instructed the slaves and my couriers to make some crude ladders to place against the interior of the garden's high walls so they could view the enemy outside.

As the Druid expected, Allectus attacked from two sides simultaneously. His men ran at the walls and attempted to hoist each other over. Myrddin had handed out a number of the leather tubes to his defenders, with careful instructions and two slaves stood by with burning tapers. As the first attackers arrived, yelling, the defenders lit the leather tubes and dropped them over the wall. For the first time, those attackers met what the Qinese had used for centuries: flame-spitting, crackling, noise-making, smoking fire dragons that can terrify evil spirits, and that sent those raiders running, howling in terror.

That was why they had been still crouched at a distance from the house, with their spooked horses even further away from the Druid's awful presence when we arrived and captured them. So that, I thought, explains the scorch marks on the stonework.

XLIII Heart

Myrddin refused to return with us to Chester. "I am perfectly safe here," he insisted. I glanced around. A couple of Parisi gardener slaves who were about to be pensioned off, several household cooks and bedmakers, and a wizard with burned-off eyebrows. Quite a military force. Myrddin skewered me with his piercing eyes. "I am perfectly safe," he repeated. I sighed. I might be imperator of all Britain, Lord of the Narrow Sea, a native-born jarl in his own right and commander of legions but this dusty Druid in his scorched scholar's gown with the sheep dung around the bottom hem had no intention of being obedient to me.

"Very well, you do seem able to look after yourself," I conceded. "Just stay in touch with Guinevia. I'll be needing you very soon to help deal with those damned Saxons." And we left him in his gateway with a satisfied smirk on his lean face, but only after he had given me the secrets of making leather tubes that exploded and frightened demons. Bat guano, wood ash, charcoal and yellow brimstone, eh? Who would have found that out? I resolved to put someone to work on it, soon.

Back in Chester, I ordered Allectus' surviving raiders merely to be sold as slaves. They had obeyed military orders, theirs was not the crime, but I had little hope of converting them to my army and wanted rid of them. They could go and till the earth or build roads and bridges for some ruler around the Inland Sea. But for Allectus, I had other plans.

This man had betrayed me to the Picts, to the Romans and finally to the Saxons. He had stolen from my treasury, and he had cruelly boiled Guinevia's father to death. I also held him responsible with Maximian for the brutal deaths of my Chevron elite soldiers, captured at the fall of Londinium, who had been tortured, blinded and gutted or stoned to death simply because of their connection to me.

I looked at the smooth-faced, wolfish traitor as he knelt, chained before me in my audience chamber. I had recounted his deeds to the crowd, now I turned to him.

"Your actions divided my kingdom and drove my queen almost to madness," I told him. "You deserve the sort of death I gave Chlorus. Do you remember I once told you: 'You only have to behead a few, but the right ones?' You, traitor, do not deserve to be beheaded. That is a death for a Roman citizen, a clean death. You took a blood oath of treachery to divide our kingdom. You deserve a traitor's death, to be sewn in a sack with vipers and thrown into a river, but I would not pollute a British river with your filth."

Guinevia came into the hall, saw Allectus and went pale. She looked at the man who had tortured her father to death, and hissed at him: "I have vowed to Nicevenn, witch goddess of the Wild Hunt, that I will take your foul heart." I stepped forward and took her elbow, but she shook me loose. "I want his heart," she said quietly, in a tone that chilled me. I began to protest but she must have sent the thought into my brain, because suddenly my calm vanished like smoke and all I could think was of my brave Chevrons who died so shamefully at this man's bidding.

The blood madness swept over me. My ears roared in my head, I felt the fighting mist rising, that tidal wave of thundering rage when nothing matters except to hack and hew, to overwhelm by sheer power and force of will. In that time nothing, not breath nor life nor hurt, matters. All that is important is to wreak violence on whatever, whoever, stands in your way. No price is too much, nothing stands against that berserk insanity.

My forearm was impacting something, hard. My hand had acted of its own volition, and my leaf-shaped puglio, my punching knife, had gone from its hidden sheath and into my hand, involuntarily. It was tearing up under Allectus' rib cage, lifting him with the power of my arm from his knees and to his feet and off the ground. A gush of his blood, oxygen-bright, spattered down his chin, his eyes were wide in shock, dazed, just inches from mine.

"You had it all, but you betrayed us all, you slime," I breathed into his blanching, dying face. "At least I'm letting you die quickly." I released my grip and he slumped sideways to the floor, but even before I could step back, Guinevia was kneeling, grasping at the knife I had left protruding from Allectus' chest.

The man must technically still have been alive. Maybe there was enough oxygen still in his ebbing brain for him to know, as Guinevia thrust her hand into the opened torso, under the breast bone. She pushed into his vitals, seized and yanked the heart downwards, slashing at the aorta and releasing the organ in a flush of blood.

She knelt over Allectus, cupping the severed heart in her two hands. His eyes fluttered and he may have seen his own heart pulse several times before his vision blurred forever. He made no sound. Guinevia stood, walked in a matter of fact manner across the chamber, the crowd parting hurriedly, and approached the big fireplace.

I could not hear and never asked what she said, I merely assumed she was speaking to her goddess, or perhaps to her dead father. After a moment's muttered incantation, she lowered her cupped hands right into the flames and gently released the bloodied lump that once was a human heart.

I looked for magical drama, but there was none, no wispy cloud, no thunder or lightning, just the burning smell of bloodied meat and some choking smoke. One part of justice had been done, and Guinevia began properly to heal from that moment. On my way out of the hall, I spoke to the major domo.

"That," I gestured at the leaking body, "should be displayed. Put the head over the north gate. Send the hands to his Saxon friends. Give the rest to the beast-masters. The arena bears can eat him."

XLIV Defected

Skegga was readying to move. Spring had arrived a month ago, and the longships of the Saxons were landing daily, so many that the riverbanks at Colchester were crowded with the beached vessels for a half mile downstream. The big Saxon had considered his options and made show of consulting the handful of lesser lords who were his allies and even his relatives and who commanded smaller forces of their own. The coalition members were sworn to follow him, but he knew from bitter experience that they would often obey their own whims and wishes instead, arguing that this or that alternative was better.

His skill was in persuading these contentious underlings that what he proposed was best for them. This time, his arguments carried the day. Londinium was ruined after the Romans left, Arthur looked impregnable in the west and his strength had grown with the addition of some Christian warriors. So, one place offered no rewards, the other option offered only some bitter fighting. The Saxons' best chance of land and loot seemed to be in moving north. They could traverse the fenlands, some, whom he knew had secret hopes of extra plunder could even sail north, and join the land forces to take Lincoln and then Eboracum.

They might even carry out a river assault on Eboracum, sailing up the Humber and Ouse to rejoin the footslogging army. Then with a proper base established at Eboracum, they could welcome more of their countrymen and re-form. Next year the whole army could move west across the spine of Britain, or across the limestone peaks of its midlands to drive Arthur out of fortress Chester and into the Welsh mountains. First, though, to move north.

Skegga sent for a Catuvellauni underlord to learn the best routes across the marshlands. He did not yet wish to risk using the north road alongside the Car Dyke because, on the march, with their women and baggage to protect, his men were an unstable fighting force. It was better to establish themselves in a camp somewhere, park the women and loot, and then to lead his oath-men forth, drunk and bare-chested, to battle the enemy. The route described, landmarks noted, all was agreed. The

Saxons would move north and would leave in three days' time. They began stripping bare their winter quarters.

Guinevia told me they were moving. She had viewed their camp at regular intervals, and she saw the men loading carts, the women wrapping precious cooking pots, and she broke her habit of no interpretation to describe what she saw. I was grimly delighted. For once, I had a sizeable force, comprising my professional soldiers, some promises of aid from the Brigantes, the Welsh, the Coriani and the Cornovii, all tribes from the north and west. I'd lost the support of the Cantii, Belgae and Trinovantes tribes of the south east, where the Saxons had already conquered and enslaved the population, and the invaders' new subjects around Colchester, the Iceni of Boadicea and the Trinovantes were all crushed under their Saxon heel.

But I had the deciding factor: a sizeable Christian army raised for me by the bishop Candless and his clerics to carry the banner of Jesus against the Christian-persecuting Romans. Those troops, whom I had trained and armed, would bring my strength up to just over half of that of the Saxons. It would be enough, I felt, when allied to the discipline and organization we possessed and which the Saxons did not. If we brought the invaders to battle at a suitable place and could withstand their initial few crazed charges, we would grind them down with our better-armoured soldiers.

I sent for Candless, who had taken up residence in a churchman's luxurious quarters just outside the city walls, and asked him to call in his outlying Christian troops. We had a week to gather and move them. In less than two weeks, I expected to intercept the Saxons, who would move slowly with their huge train, and would probably bring them to battle near Lincoln.

Candless did his work, and within two days, the Christians who had established their Deeside camp outside Chester so as not to be polluted by our pagan selves were gathered on the vast parade square under the fortress walls. I gave them the news of the Saxons, told them how we would meet and destroy them, instructed them to ensure their weapons were in good order, or to draw fresh from the quartermasters, and went to meet my officers for a final briefing.

The next day, the Christian troops gathered their possessions and simply went home. The army of the red cross of Jesus melted away like frost under spring sunshine, and just as quickly. The men quietly folded their tents and left to return to their villages and farms.

Candless explained it to me, patiently and gently, out of consideration for my boiling temper.

"We only raised a Christian army to fight the anti-Christs, the Romans who would persecute us. Now the Romans are gone, we have decided that we are going back to our homesteads and towns. It's not personal. We don't have anything against you."

My head was aching as if I had received an axe blow on it. "But what," I spluttered, "about the Saxons? They are still here!"

Candless nodded. "Aye, they are, but they are not burning our churches. You and your tribal chieftains will have to deal with them. The bishops do not think the Saxons are their problem."

Just like that, my army was halved. Worse, I was committed to marching against the Saxons. To delay would be fatal because they would only grow stronger, and they would also take our fortress at Eboracum. To fail to march would be just as bad. Word would go to the Saxons that we considered ourselves weak, and they would come for us, before the Christians could be recruited again, if ever they could be, I thought bitterly.

We had to march, we had to fight. We were outnumbered about five to one, but at least I could fight under the banner of Mithras, not of some rabble-rousing carpenter. I tore off the leather with its red cross that covered my shield. I was a warrior emperor and I was going to war without the blessings of some snivelling priests. It did not surprise me that the Pict Candless showed up at my chamber door, shuffling his feet and requesting to come along. He was, he said, somewhat trained in military matters and would like to… I told him happily that he should shut up, put on his sword again and draw some equipment.

Back at my mensa, I looked over the army list and checked off my assets: Parthians and First Mithras, some Sarmatian horse archers, two detachments of Augusta; Cragus' heavy cavalry, some good squadrons of light cavalry under the decurion Celvinius, and Grimr's depleted but effective fleet.

I had other assets in reserve, too. I had money for mercenaries if I could find some, and I had sent riders out to do just that, I had two sorcerers who were worth a legion and I had some smoke-and-looking-glass ideas. I gave the orders, sent a polite request asking Myrddin if he would care to follow us as soon as was convenient for him, and assigned a bodyguard to Guinevia and her two Celtic warrior women. These had attracted considerable interest among our archers after they had demonstrated some prowess with the hunting bow. I wondered sourly how Candless' white-clad angel fitted with some lethal Diana, then shrugged.

The next morning we left Chester along Trajan's road through Northwich and Mancunium to the big legionary fort at Castleshaw. From there, the Nont Sarah road across the Pennine chain went along ridgelines and high places where the chill winds whistled in our ears and the vistas were treeless moorland and wide skies of high, scudding cloudscapes populated only by the occasional curlew. We felt we were on the roof of Britain, and the wild country exhilarated us and showed us what we were fighting to keep.

We tramped east and north along a line of ruined Roman way forts, through Slack to Tadcaster where a small garrison was stationed, and we encamped. That night, we had local beer, roast pig and a warm, unexpected celebration with the bored local troops, who welcomed the prospect of action. From there it was a short morning's travel on to Eboracum.

We had made excellent time, quick-marching right across Britain, a testimony to the good roads those old engineers had built. Just four days after leaving Chester, we marched north over the Ouse bridge, through the Praetorian Gate with its inscriptions to Trajan and the Ninth Legion and into the fortress where I had been acclaimed emperor. That day, I recalled, a hawk had dropped a white Rat of fortune at my feet. I had not understood the augury until later.

Now I eagerly looked for that Rat at important, decisive moments of my life, to see if the gods were guiding me still. This day, I looked carefully, but in vain. Perhaps, I thought as I rolled into my red woollen officer's cloak to sleep, this time the gods have forsaken me, perhaps because I had pledged to the Christian Jesus. Before I slept, I humbly told Mithras: "Please stay with me. I never truly left you." I even sent a prayer to thunderbolt-stupid, mighty Thor, but there was no response, no sign. My last thought before sleep was that I should find and sacrifice a bull. After all, Eboracum boasted a fine Mithreum and I had a week or so left before I would be killed. I may as well offer a small bribe before I joined the others in Valhalla.

XLV March

Like a huge migrating herd of beasts, the Saxons covered the land as they moved north. Their swarming mass of humanity had abandoned the flea-infested, wattle-and-mud halls where they had wintered, outside the conflagrated ruins of Colchester, and King Skegga himself threw a burning brand onto the thatch of his own mead-hall. This was a narrow, rectangular, moss-insulated building that stank of smoke, human grease, wet wool and animal dung.

"Someone else wants to live here, they can build their own. I'll have a stone palace soon enough," he said cheerfully as the flames leaped high and a handful of field mice scampered for safety. It had not been a lucky place, he felt, with the disease that had followed them from their previous camp, and with the desertion of so many troops the previous winter. Let the fire have it.

The trek north had begun hours before the king burned down his hall. First, even before wolf light had edged the darkness, the mostly Jutish scouts had trotted their ponies out of the palisaded settlement. Behind them, once full dawn had brightened the sky, spear-carrying pickets had marched out, shields slung over their backs, leading and guarding the pioneers whose task it would be to clear the muddy tracks and good, paved roads of obstacles. They would prepare the way, cut gradients into stream banks for the following waggons and ensure the solidity of any bridges their army must cross.

The pioneers' horse-drawn carts were piled high with tools and axes, with coils of braided rope, sawn timbers, blocks of tar pitch, even some flagstones; all the paraphernalia needed to build, reinforce or repair the route the heavy waggons must take.

Behind the pioneers marched the vanguard, roughly-formed phalanxes of spearmen flanked by a few archers, all mustered by tribal affiliations. Minor warlords in heavy furs led their own small war bands, but a handful of the greater thegns formed a mounted group around their king, Skegga. He rode proud at the head of the next contingent, which was the main body of his army, and his under-chiefs vied to imitate his bearing.

They were bearded and long-moustached men, shaggy as Bactrian camels, with scarred faces and bodies. They showed bare arms heavy with bronze and silver rings, blue with tattoos, hands that were thick with rings made from the weapons of defeated enemies. All wore the big seax daggers that marked them as Saxons, the leather-wrapped hilts glinting with wrapped gold wire.

Beside them trotted their personal house carls, one carrying his lord's elm-and-leather shield, another hefting his heavy, ash-shafted spear. Trailing them was the main army, bearded, long-haired spearmen in conical leather and horn helmets who carried small round shields. They kept together in rough columns and village or tribal groups that spread wide across the fields and fens, and they foraged as they went.

The multitude travelled at different paces and moved not much more than ten miles a day. Some squads marched steadily, some men dawdled and straggled idly. Some spent the day busily elbowing their way forward, hurrying to reach the front, others could be seen simply standing still in the track, letting the onward tide of humanity wash around them. And some had fallen out of the line of march and were sitting, picking at their feet, eating or drinking, or just watching the world walk by.

After the main body of the army came the baggage train, strung in a long column along the roadway. Lines of patiently-plodding packhorses carried bundles and bales in wicker baskets slung over their sides; slow-moving oxen pulled the rumbling wooden-wheeled farm waggons that brought heavier impedimenta, everything from grain and cooking pots to siege ballistae, animal-hide tents, caged chickens and sharpened stakes that would serve as palisade pickets.

Mules stepped daintily under tall loads of forage and firewood, flocks of sheep bleated and skittered under the supervision of shepherds and their crazy-eyed dogs, some scrawny cattle were herded by small boys and even a few goats plodded along in the mud, droppings and farm stench that trailed the host.

Behind all that was the rearguard, who comprised the most disciplined-looking group of all, swinging along in unison, sometimes chanting or singing, their officers riding beside them. These men carried their spears and shields purposefully, well aware that any attack would likely involve their participation, and they were staying alert to the threat. The last couple of ranks of the rearguard were made up of archers who constantly looked around, nervously checking the woods and ditches, conscious that an arm's length of iron-tipped pinewood loosed silent from cover could steal a life in seconds.

    Last of all on the rutted mud trail that spread wide on either side of the roadway came the stragglers, laggards, whores, pedlars, fake doctors, cutpurses, bards, holy men, thieves and beggars, a ragtag horde of camp followers, their curs and their children like those that have trailed every army in history. They and the rest of the motley progress were scattered far across the landscape, but the horde still covered several miles from head to tail. All trudged slowly north, moving at every muddy step or rumbling turn of a cart's wheels inexorably closer to battle, fire and plunder. The wealth of Britain's woodlands, and the lure of its landscapes of fertile farmlands had drawn these Saxons. They had come to seize and settle the land for themselves. The British could concede, or die, and only Arthur could prevent a Saxon conquest.

XLVI Humber

Even by Roman standards, the palace at Eboracum was lavish, but I had no inclination to enjoy its luxuries. The emperor Septimius Severus had used it as his base for an invasion of Pictland, but had died here, the task unfinished. I needed to accomplish my goals, or I'd be like Severus, and dead. I had to turn back the Saxons with a much-outnumbered force, now that the Christians had deserted. I called on Guinevia to send out her mind's eye and tell me what she could, I had a squadron of mounted scouts viewing the Saxon horde as they moved slowly north, and I was forming a plan.

"We just cannot defeat this army head-on," I told my assembled officers. "The odds are too heavy. We must either trap them, surprise them or bluff them, or all three. I'm leaning towards a trap where they will be unable to deploy all their force at one time, and I am thinking about this place here-" I showed them a map.

The Saxons were now close to Lincoln, which should be safe from them, as the invaders had little siege equipment and that well-defended citadel on a hill would not tempt them to linger, for I had ordered the land around laid waste. Starving the Saxons of supplies, our bedrock policy of attrition, called resource tactics, meant cutting their supply lines and stripping the country bare. Scorching the earth might hurt our peasants, but it would make an invader move on. This, I reasoned meant the Saxons would continue north to confront us at Eboracum. I planned to meet them elsewhere, and showed my officers just where. Mentally, I ran through my usual checklist: objective, intelligence, communications, supply, personnel and transport. Then I addressed the tribunes and prefects to explain the strategy.

If we could persuade the Saxons to stay to the east side of the river Trent, we could confine them between it and the Humber's estuary. The Trent ran north and emptied into the Humber 30 or so miles before that wide river met the German Sea. My hope was to tempt the Saxons to the south bank of the Humber, onto a strip of sandy land between its mile-wide flow and a vast marsh to the south. I knew the region. We had surprised the Parisi tribe there by building a hidden crossing from the Humber's opposite bank. With luck and the right incentives, we could meet the main Saxon army in a place where they had no room to fully deploy, and our smaller but more professional force could defeat them. It was a slender chance, but it was the best we had.

What might tempt Skegga's army into that watery trap was bait, and I knew what to use. I gave Grimr some careful instructions for his fleet, and he sailed away that afternoon, down the Ouse and into the Humber, to carry out the preparations. Cragus, the commander of the heavy cavalry, also had his instructions, and my newly-promoted tribune Celvinus, now commander of the light cavalry, trotted his columns out of the Decumana Gate the next morning.

Our pioneer and engineer cohorts followed, taking a long baggage train of equipment, and I ordered several cohorts of archers, the last of my house guard Chevrons and a half-legion of infantry to go with me on our part of the mission. I was disappointed to see that Candless, the Caledonian Pict who had been so enthusiastic about going to war, seemed to have quietly vanished, but there was a great deal else to occupy me, and I soon forgot about him.

Myrddin arrived that day, listened to my proposal with interest and agreed to help. I think he was secretly delighted, and I gave him several assistants so that he could set to work.

My war horse Corvus had gone with Cragus and his heavy cavalry, so I rode out of Eboracum, perhaps for the last time, on a tough little moorland pony. I had just a dozen outriders. We were cloaked and cowled like monks, our swords hidden. We seemed to wish to leave undetected, but we did leave in daylight and as I hoped from what Guinevia's later messages told me, spies in the city were soon on their way to tell Skegga what we had done. We caught glimpses of the scouts who followed us at a discreet distance and we were careful to let them keep us in sight.

Some miles down river, we came to Seletun, a hamlet raided years before by Hibernians, one of whose actions led to me recovering my father's silver and amber badge of British office from the escaped slave Mullinus. I had arranged to meet a sizeable infantry force there and we moved on with them south and east, to cross the Trent and march along the south bank of the Humber, the place where I wished to lure Skegga.

The terrain was perfect for my plan: a river almost a mile and a half wide on one hand, a vast marsh on the other. We moved along the sandy banks for several miles until we came to a place Grimr had scouted and told me about. The Saxon spies who trailed us stayed inconspicuous and we affected not to have seen them as we set up a camp.

It took three more days, but the wolf eventually poked his head into the trap, to take the bait. Our hidden outliers warned me in plenty of time that the Saxons were coming in force, and we lit the signal fires. As the invaders moved up the Humber's bank to trap us like a cork going into a bottle, we moved away, down to the eastern beaches of the estuary, out of the bottle's base and onto Grimr's longships. We left a few ponies behind, but they were the only captives the Saxons took that day. We simply sailed across the river and left our enemies on the wrong side of it.

Skegga had marched his men hard to catch our small force between the river and the coast, so he halted at the old Parisi settlement to rest them for a few days. There were some crops to be had there, since I had ordered the region spared, and the whole Saxon horde seemed to have moved in, soldiers and camp followers alike, to rest and eat.

Once the locust-like multitude had stripped the area clean, the Saxons began their slow move back west, and we met their vanguard at the River Trent with the larger part of our force. Our archers and infantry used the Trent as a bulwark and the slaughter as the invaders struggled out of the water and up the steep banks was fearsome.

"They never got the chance to form their shield walls, lord," one of my centurions boasted later. "They waded what they could, then came out of the water with more arrows sticking out of them than a hedgehog has spines. They couldn't charge at us, they were dead meat."

The Saxons suffered the punishment for two hours, then withdrew while they sought another crossing of the river. As dusk was falling, Celvinius and his light cavalry caught them and cut the unprepared columns of foot soldiers to pieces. Again, the Saxons retreated, retiring to their new camp, where we heard the sounds of their drinking and their fury for the whole night. In the morning, I knew, we would face an organized shield wall with all the devastating power it could bring to a battlefield, but I had no intention of waiting.

Grimr had beached his longships two miles east of the Saxon camp and landed his men after dark. Many of them carried crossbows as well as spears, and they moved quietly along the south bank of the Humber to our rendezvous. I stood on the north bank, waiting for the tide. Under the swirling water in front of me and my elite force of foot soldiers was a hidden causeway and a set of concrete piers. The wooden roadbed that would turn those piers into a bridge across the falling tide was ready to be floated out by a cohort of pioneers. They had done this once before, when we had constructed that same secret crossing to surprise a rebellious tribe. Now we would use it to save Britain.

Myrddin came silently to my elbow and coughed discreetly. "I am quite looking forward to this," he said. "I have never been in an actual battle before."

"You won't be in any battle, my lord Myrddin," I said abruptly. "You will stay back, behind your assistants. I do not want you and your gifts taken away by some scrap of iron."

He snorted huffily. "I am quite capable of looking after myself," he declared. I turned away. The last thing I wanted was to argue with a sorcerer, and I needed his full cooperation in the coming hour. Bite your tongue, I muttered to myself. The tide was dropping, and I signalled to the engineer troop to move. They pushed out the timber roadbed to float and waded along the underwater causeway to the sandbank that was rapidly rising out of the river.

The timing was exact, and daylight began to show as the pioneers made the last of the roadbed fast. We had a small group of infantry already on the far bank, shivering and soaked from their crossing, but the rest would cross in relative comfort. The first of our troops were wading the causeway when the flames erupted in the distance.

XLVII Firedrake

Upriver, on the southern bank, Cragus' heavy cavalry had stormed into the Saxon camp, emerging from the gloom to throw torches of blazing pitch among the sleepers' tents. Drunken, dazed Saxons were staggering out to the confusion of thundering horses, flames and shouting soldiery. As they began to form a ragged shield wall, our own infantry emerged from the dark, in wedge formation and shoulder to shoulder behind their big heavy-bossed shields, to clash against the Saxon line.

First, the rear ranks hurled volleys of heavy iron-bladed javelins over their comrades' heads, then the front wedges crashed into the Saxons' ragged line.

They smashed shield to shield, stabbed and thrust with long spears, pushed the Saxons back and when one fell, stamped him with their nailed boots as they moved forward, leaving him to the next, onward-pressing rank to slaughter. Our determined formations split the Saxons and they fell back. That was when Celvinius' light cavalry charged in, hacking and stabbing, driving the broken line back still further. But there were far too many Saxons to be defeated in minutes, or in a single charge. Even as their fragmented shield wall collapsed, another was forming to the rear, under the bellowed commands of King Skegga himself.

I saw him there, for I was now across the river, on the Saxon's right flank, unnoticed. With me, I had a small force of archers and infantrymen, a group of Suehan sailors armed with crossbows and spears and a tall wizard in a long grey gown, and I hoped it would be enough to defeat a Saxon horde.

The enemy had formed a long and competent-looking shield wall that would surely wrap its ends around our own, surround and hack our warriors to the ground. My small force could only be useful if we had some magic. And that was when Myrddin saved Britain. I nudged him, he gave an impatient wave and the battalion of archers he had drilled for the previous few days, and which surprisingly included the two Celt huntresses who were Guinevia's slaves, raised their bows.

Myrddin caught my glance at the two women and grimaced. "Needed every archer," he said. I looked again. Was that Guinevia and several slaves with lighted oil lamps in their hands? Before I could ask Myrddin, he dropped his upraised arm and with a sound like harps being plucked, the archers released their specially-prepared arrows fizzing into the sky above the enemy.

Explosive fire dragons rained down on the Saxons. The effect was devastating. Our troops had seen a demonstration and had been given instruction, but even for them the sight of the oriental devil-fire was awe-inspiring, and they halted. The effect on the Saxons was stunning. Many dropped their shields and turned to run, and that was the moment when the British centurions began the shouting: "Punor, Woden, Saxnot!" they bellowed. Our ranks took up the war cry they had been taught, beating the enemy ears with the evil names that threatened death.

A second rain of crackling fire dragons exploded overhead, and again the chant of the names of the most dreadful of Norse demons erupted in the dawn gloom. Some Saxons turned to locate our small group of archers, and Myrddin produced more magic. He looked like a ghost. He had smeared his face and hands with the luminescence of the piddock shellfish and he breathed its fake fire at the Saxons who were running at us. It halted them like startled deer.

At that moment, Grimr's crossbowmen fired their bolts, each with its fire drake tip of flaming, crackling salt petre, level into the hostiles' ranks. A few men fell, but the sparking, fiery bolts' real impact was from the comet-like trails they made when they flew directly into the Saxon mob. With the bellowed names of fearful demons in their ears, the ghostly face of the fire-breathing wizard and the meteor trails of fire both smashing into them and dropping on them from the skies, the superstitious Saxon host broke and ran.

Our British cavalry, led by dragoons on the heavy Frisian horses galloped in, each horseman supporting a foot soldier who clung to the man's stirrup leathers. A few yards short of the enemy ranks, the infantry dropped clear. The horses crashed the line, the dragoons stood in their stirrups and slashed the big spatha swords around them, the foot soldiers who seemed to have come from nowhere ran into the gaps and the Saxons broke.

Soon the dragoons were hacking and plunging through the fleeing Saxons like reapers in a wheat field. The lighter cavalry went in as they had trained, in the Parthian way as horse archers, galloping in then turning to fire over their mounts' rumps to deliver volley after volley of arrows at short range, then retreating nimbly if needed.

A bloodied decurion cantered up to me, leading Corvus, and I climbed onto my war mount's back. So, I became a cavalryman again, and Exalter and I went to taste blood. My heart was singing. I knew we had the measure of our enemies, and we did. We sent many to the feasting halls of Asgard that morning.

A good portion of the invaders' horde tried to fight their way across the Trent, hoping to escape south, but our infantry held them, and just at a time when our line was weakening, Candless and a cohort of Picts arrived to reinforce it. I told him later that I thought he had abandoned us, but he simply grinned that no Border reiver would pass up the chance for loot, and the Saxons must have made a fine collection from the soft southern people, must they not?

By the time full daylight broke over the scene, the Trent was pink from the blood of floating corpses, and the Humber was washing bloodless white bodies out to the open sea. Hundreds of refugees had stumbled into the marshlands and a long column of disarmed Saxons was being made to pass under the spear, sign of their new status as slaves. I had the usual decisions to make about executions. Defeated soldiers do not always make good slaves, they are strong men and desperate. The old Romans either killed them or sold them as gladiators, but the latter course was not really viable to me. I ordered most of the big Saxon warriors killed. Regrettable, but necessary.

Some offered gold in return for their lives, but our men took that anyway. The camp followers, wives, children, whores were rounded up and penned. Slave traders would arrive soon enough to fill my coffers, as the southern slave dealers had an unending appetite for fair-skinned females.

I ordered all of the Saxon warlords executed publicly, and set the example by hacking off the head of King Skegga myself. He died bravely, asking to hold his sword as he knelt to Exalter, for dying with sword in hand would admit him with honour into the mead hall of Odin.

Some of Candless' Picts wanted to inflict the 'blood eagle' on Skegga, but I ruled that execution was enough punishment for the Saxon king. The eagle is a brutal torture that involves severing the ribs at the spine, then dragging the victim's lungs out of his opened back to make warm, bloody wings over his shoulders. That death is one of suffocation, if the victim does not die of shock and blood loss.

I declined to use it. Torturing one invader would not deter the next, and might lead to worse atrocities being committed on our people by vengeful raiders.

My decision was simple. I was Imperator and a British jarl. I was not just a lord of war, I had united the tribes of Britain and I had a nation to build and protect. I needed to come to terms with the Christians, who wanted to oust our pagan gods, I had an uneasy peace with the Picts, and had quieted the Hibernian sea raiders. My greatest fear was the return of the Romans. I had defeated them once, and had escaped their wrath another time, but my enemy Maximian would return. I had executed a Caesar and he and his armoured legions would not forgive, or forget.

And, the Saxons would invade again, it was inevitable. British cavalry, ships, magic and spears had saved us once. Could it happen again? I had only a mind-wounded sorceress and an eccentric wizard to help me, our gods were being supplanted and the white Rat of good fortune had vanished. In the reeking smoke of that killing ground, as wounded men were out of their misery or others had their lives ended because they were too dangerous, I decided that I should gamble. I should take my battles to the enemy's territory and force the Romans' hand while they still fought on their eastern borders. Only then could I defeat them convincingly, and settle Britain's peace.

I needed to invade Gaul.

Historical and other notes:

Although this trilogy begins by following the general outline of the life of Carausius, the narrative of the second book necessarily must take liberties with history. In *Arthur Britannicus* we read how a soldier became admiral, and then emperor. This was Carausius, a Menapian from what is now Belgium, whose Roman enemies claimed he was of 'the humblest birth.' Or, he may have been nobly born, perhaps even the son of a Roman administrator.

Carausius' later actions in referencing poetry on his coinage indicates a higher level of education than would be expected from a peasant upbringing. Some sources attribute Roman ancestry to him, which may be supported by his name, a classic Latin one. Some sources say he was a British or Irish prince.

Even by Roman historians' disparaging accounts, he was a skilled river pilot who joined the Roman army and became a successful soldier, then admiral of Rome's British Channel fleet, based in Boulogne/Bononia. The evidence also points to him being a charismatic leader.

Around 284 CE, he was accused of diverting pirate loot to himself and was summoned for court martial and likely execution, which may have been a political move to rid the emperor Maximian of a rival. Carausius' response was to seize power in northern Gaul and Britain, places where he commanded legions as well as a fleet.

His ambition was to extend his military sway beyond Boulogne, even to Rome itself, but he was frustrated by Maximian, who was tasked with bringing the renegade to heel. The Roman's first endeavour, in 289 CE, was a failure. The new fleet he had built was either destroyed by storms or more probably was defeated by the seasoned flotilla Carausius took with him when he defected to Britain.

Carausius reinforced his military position there with the popular support he gained by tapping into the Britons' discontent with their avaricious Roman overlords, and he skilfully used propaganda on his coinage to suggest he was a messiah returned to save the nation.

The self-proclaimed emperor became the first ruler of a unified Britain, and entrenched himself behind the chain of forts he built along the south-eastern coast. These Saxon Shore fortifications were intended to guard against an expected Roman attempt to retake Britain as well as to repel Saxon or Alemanni invaders.

Maximian had to wait four years after that failed invasion before he could drive Carausius out of Gaul. He retook Boulogne, besieging it and sealing the harbour against relief or escape by sea. The city fell in 293 AD, the year of Carausius' demise. The loss of the port and the weakening of Carausius' position probably caused a power struggle with his chief functionary Allectus, and led to the usurper emperor's death that same year.

He had ruled a united Britain for seven years when he was either assassinated by Allectus or, more probably, betrayed by him at a battle near Bicester. Allectus, whose identity is obscure (the word itself simply means 'chosen' or 'elected') took power, and announced himself as 'consul' and 'Augustus arrived' on his coinage. He began work in 294 AD on a great building in London that went unfinished, as his reign lasted for only three years.

A Roman expedition defeated him after a sea battle off Chichester, and a land engagement near Silchester. Constantius Chorus now Caesar, landed in Britain after the fighting was over and signalled his triumph with a famous medal declaring himself 'Restorer of the Eternal Light' ('*Redditor lucis aeternae*') implying 'Restorer of Roman power.'

Imperator Carausius was the first British ruler to unite the kingdom, and deserves his place in history for that, but he actually is best known for his fine coinage. On exhibit in the British Museum are some of the 800 Carausian coins that were among a hoard of 52,500 Romano-British pieces of silver and gold discovered in a Somerset field in the summer of 2010. Such coins, the Penmachno headstone and a single milestone uncovered near Carlisle are the only known memorials of Britain's lost emperor.

Of course, the narrative of this second book is fiction. The real Carausius died by Allectus' actions, but as Caros/Arthur he may indeed have driven out invaders and brought Britain peace. (See '*Legend and links*')

Readers may note that some 'modern' technology was used by Arthur hundreds of years before Europeans adopted it. This is not impossible. Myrddin learned of fireworks from his magi, who had contact with trader Chinese. They in turn had been using 'fire dragons' since the second century before Christ, although it was only much later that gunpowder was developed.

Similarly, Myrddin may have heard of the L-shaped stirrups that appeared in India about that same time 400-plus years earlier, or of the later circular and triangular stirrups that are known to have been in use during the First Jin Dynasty of the third century AD, or 700 years before the Normans' Conquest and their devastating 'first' use of mounted warriors who could stand to fight from horseback.

Also, I should make a small apology for the use of some modernisms in this book. In the interests of clarity and to prevent the need frequently to thumb back to a reference page, I opted not to use many possibly-unfamiliar Latin place names from Britain or France, making just a few exceptions that are intended to retain the flavour of the narrative. Two of those exceptions are Eboracum, which is 21st century York, and Bononia, the French seaport of Boulogne-sur-Mer. Portus Chester is modern Porchester; Colchester or Roman Camulodunum, appears as itself; Chester was once Deva, Snowdoun is modern Stirling and Eidyn's Burh is better known to us as Edinburgh. There is a fine hillfort to the city's east, at Dunpelder, where Arthur waited for his forces. The harbour on the Severn estuary, Abonae is modern Sea Mills; Aquae Sulis is Bath, and Dumnonia is of course Cornwall.

Generally, the Romans did not name their roads, so their great highways were only named by later generations. The famous 'Streets' of Watling, Ermine, Dere, Stane and Akeman are well enough known, as is the ancient Fosse Way, which was once the Romans' frontier rampart of western Britannia. It was not until the first decade of the 21st century that archaeologists traced the Nont Sarah, a trans-Pennine military road that had been forgotten.

Arthur and Carausius: legend and links

There are connections between Carausius and many of the traditional Arthurian sites, and Carausius' triumphs are closely echoed in the legends of Arthur. The monk Gildas (circa 500-570AD) created Britain's earliest written history and described a 'lord of battles' and 'outstanding ruler' whose triumph at Mount Badon was the decisive, culminating victory to rout the Saxon invaders.

The triumph was so celebrated that Gildas did not bother to identify the location of Badon or even to name the victor, noting only that 'Arth' – Celtic for 'The Bear' - was such a great overlord that King Cuneglasus of Powys humbly acted as his master's charioteer.

Gildas was writing a century or two after the events and muddled his calendar. He wrongly dated the construction of the walls of Hadrian and Antoninus by two centuries, but he likely got the sequence right: the walls were built, the invaders came, a leader arose and drove them away. It suggests that Arthur may have lived earlier than believed, at a date that fits with the actual reign of Carausius. Many scholars think that the Badon battlefield may be at the Iron Age hillfort at Cadbury South, ('Caros' Camp,') some think it could be Buxton, in Derbyshire.

There's a great poverty in the era's history and some of it was written 800 years after the event, but folklore often holds remarkably accurate memories. One such tale is that the Pict Ossian's son Oscar was killed when he attacked the emperor 'Caros' as he rebuilt Hadrian's Wall.

Carausius' image on his fine coinage shows him as a thick-necked, bear-like man and the British for 'bear-king' is 'Arto-rig,' and language experts say there are links between 'Caros' and 'Artorius.' Even the hill fort at South Cadbury that tradition says was the castle of King Arthur was once 'Cado's Fort.' Certainly, there was once a mass slaughter there, and there are stone foundations of a palace on the site.

A significant part of Arthur's legend is his Christianity. Welsh tradition holds that Arthur 'carried the cross of Christ on his shield,' and was mortally wounded at Camlann. That conflict site has been placed in Gwynedd, where a very early Welsh 'Stanza of the Graves' says Arthur was buried. In the 19th century an antiquarian described the discovery of a Roman grave there at the head of a pass, a place where a ruler might be buried, overlooking his lands.

The headstone is inscribed 'Carausius lies here in this cairn of stones,' and carries the staurogram, or third century tau-rho cross of a Christian, the earliest found in Wales and one of only a dozen found in Britain.

The man memorialized was so important that the stone and maybe the bones were moved to the nearby church of St Tudclud, in Penmachno, which is an important early Christian site and reputed burial place of Iorweth ab Owain Gwynedd, father of Wales' greatest king. This, then, is a royal graveyard. The fact that Carausius was so famous that he needed no 'Soldier of the XXth' style of identification could therefore be highly significant.

The only other known memorial to the Lost Emperor is in the Tullie House museum in Carlisle, on a milestone that was inverted and reused. The buried portion concealed the honorifics the Romans elsewhere redacted after they re-invaded Britain in 293 AD. That glorious title reads: 'Imperator Caesar Marcus Aurelius Mauseus Carausius, Dutiful, Fortunate, the Unconquered Augustus." It should add: 'The Forgotten.'

Map of Arthur's Britain

Printed in Great Britain
by Amazon